MW00667692

FRAIDY HOLE

STACI ANDREA

Black Rose Writing | Texas

ISBN: 978-1-68513-311-5
PUBLISHED BY BLACK ROSE WRITING
www.blackrosewriting.com

Printed in the United States of America
Suggested Retail Price (SRP) $19.95

Fraidy Hole is printed in Minion Pro

*As a planet-friendly publisher, Black Rose Writing does its best to eliminate unnecessary waste to reduce paper usage and energy costs, while never compromising the reading experience. As a result, the final word count vs. page count may not meet common expectations.

Love Ya Always!

To the little quiet me that sat in the back of the class, too scared to raise her hand. To the little brave me that learned to blend in, becoming invisible, making her way through fourteen different schools. To the young me that was terrified of lunch hour because there was no one to sit by, so I hid in the bathroom more times than I could count. And to my sisters and brothers, Angie and Mikala, Taylor and Chris, who always knew that I had something a little more to give and kept me going along the way. Together, we are never alone.

I humbly thank all of my family who have always stood strongly as one, weathering the darkness together and laughing like nuts along the way. Never have you questioned my craziness, and you have always let me fly. To my husband, Dustin, and my kids, Paige, Skylar and Zach, you know you are my world, and I thank you for being my soft place to land.

To my Gramma Brager, whom I deeply value her opinion and am grateful for her editing services, telling me exactly what she thinks of what I write. (Also, because she's an exceptional Gramma and will get a kick out of seeing her name in here.)

To my mother- and father-in-law, who have never treated me as an "in law" and have always supported me and my wild ideas.

And to my mom and dad, I still feel like the little kid running home from Challenger 7 Elementary School in Cocoa, Florida, excited to show you a poem that I wrote. The feeling just never gets old. Thank you for giving us that world to grow up in.

And to my daughter, Skylar Hayden, a huge thank you for taking author pictures of your mama and for letting me use your gorgeous photography skills for my cover art. This is pretty cool.

"There's an emptiness that both veils your heart and leads your soul when you are put into emotionally damaging situations. When a person is exposed to something so shocking, so profound, it's almost as if the soul leaves your body and assesses the situation from above, trying to make all the broken pieces fit back together and somehow make sense, trying to appease the heart."

Staci Andrea

FRAIDY HOLE

PROLOGUE

THE BRAIN is a curious thing. How does it know when to shut off the pain sensors, leaving a person blissfully unaware of what their heart and body have endured? How is the human psyche able to put to sleep the areas of life that haunt you in the echoes of a still and quiet night, yet humans are able to recall the most insignificant memory when they need to, in order to restore their faith in humanity and to keep mindlessly trudging forward into the unforgiving unknown?

"This little light of mine…" She was calling to me from somewhere in my past, high above where the gritty dust swirled over my head and the salt flats licked at the edges of the quarry mines. I was still conscious, staring up at the glowing mid-afternoon sun, noticing a small flock of geese flying overhead. This was probably the start of their fall journey to get the hell out of Freedom. There was an odd number, seven of them, gliding effortlessly upon the dusty breeze, bonded together with their tribe, making their journey to a safer winter home. One of the last thoughts I had before a blissful, yet forced, unconscious peace weighed down heavily upon my eyelids was thinking about how geese mate for life, and that the odd number must have meant that one had been killed or separated from the group somehow, so now one member of the flying tribe would live the rest of his days alone, still determined to help take care of the flock, but now with no mate to cling to for the rest of his life.

There was no pain, as my body had instantly and blissfully been hurled into a numbed state of shock. After years of working in the quarry and managing these big old rock crushers, I did not need to look down to see what kind of shape I was in. Those giant crushing plates of cold steel cannot decipher between rock and bone. I had figured that if not one, then both of my legs were surely gone, severed just as quickly as I had mistaken that frantic last step while trying to save my son. I knew that in order to save my sanity, in order to keep holding on, I shouldn't look down. Instead, I glanced from the blazing sky and the struggling tribe of geese that were high above, to the right of my field of vision, where I could make out the shocked, pale face of my son. Rhoads, still a teenager himself, who, without knowing, and with a look of utter shock and terror in his dusty blue eyes, had just been forced into an adult world of responsibilities, regrets and pain without even knowing it. I could have prepared none of us that day for the changes that were about to be hurled upon us, or how our worlds would now spin out of each other's orbits because of it.

Her voice, though. Her voice was what had lulled me out deeper into the abyss, first enticing me to relax and let go, and then later, begging me to go back and keep moving on. "Hide it under a bucket? No! I'm gonna let it shine…" V would sing this to our son when he was just a wee tot. Music followed that woman everywhere, and our lives seemed to have adopted her soundtrack. She was full of life and had a quiet grace about her, but don't you mistake her for being anything less than tough. Although she had seemed to have the demeanor of a proper southern gal, my V liked to tussle in the dirt, get mud on the tires, and kick back a shot of honey bourbon every now and then.

In just a few years' time, I would come to see those same qualities in Rhoad's daughter, my only granddaughter. It would be V's courage, love of music, grace, and a ferociously strong will that would keep that girl alive, even when her soul would be edging towards the blurred line of defeat, egged on by depression in an ugly world that had treated her so unfairly.

"This little light…" I could hear her hushed voice slowly lulling me into a warm sleep now, void of fear, too tired to fight. Opening my blood shot and gritty, dirt-filled eyes wide one last time, I stared up at my terrified boy, who had just been forced into adulthood way before his time. He was standing on the edge of the platform a few feet from where I lay trapped and bleeding. I grinned, drew in one more broken breath, kicked my head back and closed my eyes as the little tribe of geese, minus one, continued trudging along on their journey high above me.

CHAPTER 1
SEVENTY-TWO HOURS

HER BLONDE curls lay tousled on the pillow. Only small remnants of the coagulated blood remained matted into the tangled golden ends. Her grandma, Nonna V, would have sat right next to her there in that tiny sterile room, patiently combing the rats' nests out with her little black fine-toothed comb while teasing her about cutting off her snarly hair. "Hold still girl," I could hear her voice caution, chasing us from our past, "Before I cut this mess off to your chin!" and she would let out a wicked giggle. Nonna V always loved Arlo's long hair, and was none too happy whenever that child would get it tussled up or wanted it to be cut off.

Nonna herself had lustrous, thick, long black locks when she was younger, but cancer was a thief, leaving her with little left to work with. Because of this, she took to delicately wrapping the fine graying hair that she had left up into a tidy bun every day, while patiently trying to tame the young girl's mane that was as wild and unruly as the child.

Nonna V was long gone though, and all this girl had left was me, a 68-year-old grandpa who walked with a limp and kept the light on in the trailer just waiting for her to come back home. A grandpa who doesn't always understand where her life is dragging her off to, but who will always be there with a bear hug and a beer, should she make her way back to me. She always did.

I was lost in thought, feeling the weighted loss of my beloved V, missing the faint smell of her cold cream she would rub on her face at night, listening to the soft hum of the machines working to keep our girl on this side of the great unknown, when I heard that little voice finally cut through the chilly air.

"Bobo! Bobo, you here?" the weak little voice pleaded with me. But make no mistake… there isn't a weak bone in her whole little body.

With tears of anger and pain blinding my eyes, I reached one calloused hand to her forehead, patting the top of her head gently, as if she was my old Coonhound, Bus. "I'm here kiddo, I'm here," I croaked out the words, amazed at how frail her 22-year-old body had become. Life is hard, and her life has been one gut punch after another. Don't get me wrong though, she's no princess either. This girl could spit into the wind just as good as anyone could. Her whole little body heaved a sigh of relief when she realized it was her good old grandpa standing there. She went to lift her left arm up to reach for me, and only then did the cheap and scratchy Velcro restraints tug at her dainty wrists. Panic immediately shot across her face, and I could see the wild fury dart across her seemingly otherwise calm green eyes.

"No, no, no! Oh no…." Arlo began to helplessly relent to her current situation. There were no tears. Not immediately, at least. "Bobo, you know I didn't mean to…" her small voice began to trail back off and her gaze went out the window. The effect of tranquilizers and pain medication was overwhelming for such a small body. This isn't the first time that I have traveled this road with my girl. I have had to coax her back from death's edge on more than one occasion.

The sweetest cherub of a nurse walked in just then, all smiles and side glances. She was all of five foot two and a little on the chunky side with wild red hair that Nonna V would have raved about, pulled up loosely onto the top of her head into a messy little bun with little pieces of hair falling down around her face. Sweat was beading up on her forehead and her light blue scrubs with the little dogs on them had become obviously damp in the armpits. She was all smiles as she was absent-mindedly patting all of her pockets, apparently searching for her glasses, then giggled as her chubby little fingers located them on the top of her head.

"Hello, my little lamb," she cooed towards Arlo as she was glancing quickly at her chart. "You gave us all quite a scare, kiddo! Aghhh... your stats are looking so much better! My goodness, are you getting hungry yet?"

"No thank you, Ma'am," was all that came from the little defeated bed that Arlo now lay strapped to. "Can these things come off soon?" she pleaded sheepishly, halfhearted, really, since she already was guessing the answer, while cautiously raising one of the Velcro restrained frail arms.

"Not quite yet, my dove," the chubby little red-headed nurse quickly fired back. "It would really do you some good to eat a little, though. Can I get you anything at all?"

A small giggle erupted from an otherwise sad and defeated face. "And how the hell would I eat anything like this?" Arlo dryly grinned in defeat, only slightly lifting both of her restrained arms towards the air, making sure that the chubby little nurse had understood her meaning.

"Oh, hon... I can feed ya! No problem! Believe me, girl, I have seen people in far worse situations than what you are in now, child. You just let me know when you are ready, and I will run down and fetch ya something, OK?" the chubby little nurse cooed, never dropping the smile that was plastered on her sweet face. Then she turned to face me.

"Now, Dr. Grady would like to meet with you in a few minutes to discuss the case, let you know options and fill you in on how she's......" she began, but I cut her off.

"Yes, Ma'am, I know all about how this is supposed to go. You can tell that Dr. Grady that I am ready to meet with him to see what I need to do to get my girl home," I said kindly, yet matter-of-factually.

The little chubby nurse with the wild red hair kept her composure, but looked stunned as she scurried towards the door. "It may be a little more complicated than that sir...." she began as she was heading out towards the nursing station in the hallway. "The attempt that she took on her own life is cause for her to be evaluated a little more closely and I…"

"I understand all of that, of course, but this is not our first rodeo, Ma'am. She fell off a little, and now she's getting back on up there and has a fighting shot at it again. Please let the good Dr. know that I am ready to talk to him about getting my girl outta here when he has a moment. I thank you kindly," I said with a forced and overly warm smile across my cracked lips, not letting her get a word in edgewise while she was heading out the door. I was giggling a little to myself as I heard her voice echoing from the room behind me…

"Bobo…. Where's Bast?" my sweet Arlo asked in a confused voice. All the air left my lungs in a long, exasperating outward sigh and I hung my head, trying to come up with an answer. Her rock. Her confidant. Her best friend. Alabaster, or "Bast" as she has called him since he came into our lives when they were right around ten years old, was who she had turned to when the rest of the world would get too hard.

In fact, this current situation had been brought about because my sweet 22-year-old Arlo, who is fearless and strong, gave her heart to a foolish mama's boy, Derek. Arlo had thought that he was the man of her dreams, and for a couple of years, they had a great time. He enjoyed hiking and camping, fishing and concerts…. And he liked Arlo's roommate a little too much. So much so, that just a few months ago, Arlo actually had the misfortune of walking in on the asshole in bed with the roommate… who also happened to be one of her best friends.

My girl was shattered, as she had every right to be. So, she headed home. Came back to me at the trailer park just outside of Freedom, Oklahoma, but not before she gave that boy an ass whooping that he deserved and took a hammer to the roommate's newer Mazda. And when she came home, who did she find?

The great and powerful Bast, whom she hadn't seen since right before she graduated high school. Here is the thing with those two kids… they had always been blissfully unaware of just how dangerous they were when they were together. Since they were just knee-high, if one had an idea, the other would follow along. When they were together, they were inseparable and menacing. He was her security blanket, and always had seemed to make things better, until he just made them worse.

Now, I'm not blaming Bast. We are who we are, not forged from other people's ideations, but a product of upbringing. Arlo definitely didn't get a fair shake in that part of her story. Arlo's daddy is my son, Rhoads. He and Arlo's mama had her when they were in high school. I think Tara, her mama, was fifteen when she was born, and Rhoads was seventeen. Just dumb kids in love. They were good kids. They just didn't know that the world was about to kick their asses. That's the way it is when you're young, though—so damn oblivious to the hardships in the world and to life in general that you ignorantly rely on faith and love to get you through it.

Rhoads worked road crew and was away all the time. Hell, out here in the middle of Oklahoma, there aren't a lot of options if you don't plan on going to school. You either work out at the salt flats, the quarry, or you get the hell out. So that's what Rhoads did. I can't fault him for it. He was trying to provide for his daughter and little family. They had dreams of a life far away from the middle of nowhere.

Arlo's mama, Tara, worked for a local mattress company the next town over, doing the accounting. She always was a hard worker. Aside from her accounting gig, she would also work some weekends tending bar at the VFW. That child was always good with math and school, but when she got pregnant with Arlo, her dreams of a different life came to a terrifying halt. Tara's own mama remarried after her daddy died when she was in elementary school. Her daddy was a good enough man. He just couldn't fight the bottle hard enough. He would fight with her mama, and she would threaten to leave him.

Late one evening, after hours of him drinking and her screaming, she threw some things in an overnight bag and got the courage to leave, taking Tara with her. Her daddy's brain was clouded with enough libations that, when he decided to chase after them, he ran his old Chevy Pickup head on into the side of a parked train car. It didn't matter that the train wasn't moving; the damage had been done, and he had laid in that mangled truck, passed out and gasping his few incoherent final breaths as they ran. Tara blamed her mama for that somewhere deep inside, and it had stunted their relationship. They have always remained civil towards each other, but that's about all there was left between them. The tightly woven mother/daughter relationship had begun to unravel the moment that mama tried to save them. After his death, Tara would forever be searching for someone to belong to, while at the same time fighting to remain independent and not really wanting to be restrained or tied down to one place or one person at all. That sweet girl had battle scars on her soul that no amount of time was going to soften.

Tara and Rhoads had started out OK, as far as immature love goes. She knew a little about cars, which was his favorite pastime, and he appreciated her cooking and taste in movies and music. It was just a simpler time, before age complicated it. Tara had a hard pregnancy. That girl was sicker than sick most days. I remember Nonna V stopping by their place on many mornings with sleeves of store-brand saltines for the poor thing to munch on just to get her well enough to make it into work, or head into school.

In fact, when Tara went into labor, it was Nonna V who she called into the hospital, not her own mama. I know that must have been hard for her mama, but by that point, their relationship had been so splintered that there was no hope of repairing it anymore. Plus, she had remarried and moved to Florida, leaving Tara to us to tend to.

They almost died, you know, Tara and the baby. I don't reckon I can remember what that thing was called, but Tara's womanly parts were tipped backwards and Arlo was pushing out feet first. Something tore, and we almost lost the both of them. Rhoads had never been so scared in his whole life. He loved those girls. His entire world existed because of those girls.

That's why it was a bit of a surprise when Tara decided to leave him when Arlo was in sixth grade. In the simplest of terms, and with no apologies, all I can say is that after Tara left, I guess my son got lonely out there on the road and forgot a little more of home every time he left. He kept searching for a life out on the road. He kept thinking that the answers lied with a new girl in every town, but he never found one that made him want to stick around and be a better man. He never found a gal that made him want to stop running from himself.

As years wore on, he came home less and less, until Arlo was about sixteen and he stopped coming home at all. They talk still, every now and then, when the mood strikes either of them to defeat their stubbornness and pick up the damn phone and reach out. But distance is a great divide and time hasn't been gracious to either of them.

I stood there, lost in thought, gazing at this small creature that had become such a steadfast part of my world. Arlo and I were always thick as thieves, but after I lost my V, Arlo took on an even more prominent role in my world. There were many nights that we would be sitting in the kitchen, eating big old stuffed olives out of the jar, just trying to sort out the world together.

The truth was, that for many of those nights, while Arlo thought we were working through her problems, she was actually bringing a clarity and focus into my own life. At twenty-two, the girl's still just a kid, but like the feisty cat she is, she has also outlived her nine lives at this point.

"Hey, Bobo," the small questionable voice shakily hesitated, quickly pulling me back from the warmth of the many broken roads that we have navigated together. "You know I didn't do this, right? You have to know that I would never…," she began until she softly started to cry, her wholehearted and tough girl persona shattering around her, reducing her to the scared and fragile kid that she actually was beneath it all. "Find Bast…. He'll tell you!" she pleaded in a vulnerable voice that I hadn't heard since she was just a grasshopper. I looked at her with eyes filled with astonishment and pain.

Someone had sliced deeply her left wrist, and they had bandaged it pretty good, but I could still see the now dark and crusty remnants of blood that had seeped through the bandage. She wasn't as successful with her right wrist, being right-handed and all. I don't think this was that serious of go at it, but more of a cry for help…. Just another in a string of many cries for help that have echoed their way to me in the darkness on too many nights over her lifetime.

"Bobo, just find Bast! He'll tell you," she pleaded as the fiery plump little red-headed nurse made her way back into the room, this time leading the way for the young doctor that padded along in her wake, looking about as sure of himself as a newly born calf on wobbly legs straight outta its mom's swollen belly.

"This is Dr. Grady. He will be tending to your granddaughter's recovery," the little redhead announced as she plodded over to the window and snapped the curtains wide open, allowing the sun's rays to creep along into an otherwise dark and sterile room. She then turned towards Arlo and, with the same crisp grasp, tugged the sheets up a little more snugly around her, gently smoothing out the wrinkles on the bedspread as she cooed to her, "There now, child, nothing to get yourself all worked up over. You need some rest. Your body will not recover if you keep fighting the effort."

Arlo looked terrified now at the realization that she just may not be coming home as quickly as she had hoped. I saw a flicker in those dark green eyes, and the small light that had been in there was dulled as quickly as it had started. In a stark hushed and flat tone, Arlo now turned her eyes to face the wobbly kneed young doctor. "Then what the fuck do I need to do to get out of here?" she demanded in a loud, harsh and flat tone, more than she asked. Her armor was up. There was my fighter.

Just seconds ago, she appeared as though she was a scared and frightened child, confined to this bed by arm restraints that looked as though they were meant to hold down a serial killer. Now, she had transformed right in front of my eyes and became a pissed off trailer park girl from the Middle of Nowhere, Oklahoma, who had a little fight left in her after all. She would be just fine. I even let out a small chuckle, which threw the new doc off a little. He looked as confused as ever, not knowing if he should be addressing me or his patient.

The deer-in-headlights little doc in his freshly washed white little lab jacket and gym shoes that hadn't even seen blood, sweat, spit or piss yet, picked his jaw up off the floor and decided he may be able to get a little further in conversation with me instead. "Sir, may I speak with you outside please?" he asked with eyes as big as saucers and confusion plastered across his seemingly newborn face.

"Arlo, be good, ya hear? Be back soon sweet girl," I walked over and leaned in to kiss the top of her freshly washed head that still had the bits of congealed blood dried on the ends of the golden ringlets that lay about on the pillow.

"Bobo don't leave. PLEASE DON'T LEAVE ME!" she shouted in my face, the panic setting into her eyes yet again. I looked her dead in those broken green eyes, knowing that she could see the seriousness that took a hard stance in mine. I leaned in closer towards her ear and whispered in almost a stern hiss, "Arlo Marie…. There will NEVER be a fraidy hole that you will barricade yourself into that I won't be able to rescue you from. You stay here and do what they say. I WILL come back for you, ya hear?" I backed up and looked her right in the eyes, which had softened some.

"Love ya Bobo," was the only response that she uttered back in a defiant but broken whisper, her eyes then rolling their gaze back towards the window, just in time to watch a small formation of geese fly towards the horizon.

I followed the new doctor out the door, where he stopped abruptly in the hall, turning an about face towards me that just about knocked me over. The boy looked wet behind the ears and in over his head. "Sir, I was reading through her chart, and I could see that this isn't the first time she's been admitted for trying to take her own life. In fact, over the years, just her emergency room chart alone is rather extensive. Now, what I would like to do is…." I cut him off before he finished his little speech. "In patient therapy. What are you thinking, thirty, sixty days?" I asked casually, grinning.

The good doc stumbled over his words, being caught off guard by my response. "Uh…. well… ya. Yes. I would like a full psychiatric work-up first and then I would recommend, at minimum, a thirty-day course of treatment if you and the patient would be agreeable to that?"

"Agreeable…. Oh, my boy, you obviously haven't spent much time with Arlo," I chuckled, right as I heard arguing coming from behind Arlo's door. I could hear the little chubby red-headed nurse saying something about meds and Arlo was being less than agreeable. Again.

"But sir," the little doc began again, "I am very concerned for her well-being. Although I don't think this was a serious suicide attempt, I am more concerned about finding out a little about this, Bast, as she refers to him. Could it be possible that he did this to her, or tried convincing her to do this?"

My defensive reactions kicked in at the mere uttering of his name. I quieted the laughter that was welling up in my gut and took in a deep breath, choosing my next words very carefully.

"Listen Doc. I have raised that girl. I have seen her go through some things, things so painful and deep wounding that the average human would have given in a long time ago. Hers was never an easy road, and because of the cards that she was dealt, life comes at her a little tough and she reacts a little tougher sometimes. I can guarantee that Alabaster, or "Bast", as she calls him, didn't do this. There is no need to go poking around looking for him," I began rather sternly, looking him straight in the eye.

"But sir, for her own safety…" the nervous doc began again.

I let out a hard exhale, tired of this little man's crap. He was well-meaning, but he wasn't able to understand what we had been through, the years that we had battled together. "Look. She has grown up with him. Yes, they aren't always good for each other and through the years, they have raised some hell. But he didn't do this. Now you know damn well that the little fighter on the other side of that door will never consent to you admitting her inpatient for thirty days, right?" I let out a laugh as I turned to walk away.

"Well, no… I," the new little doc tried to begin again, struggling to string a few thoughts together. Nervously he tried one more attempt to persuade this old man, "I can keep her here on a hold basis if I must. She needs to be evaluated, sir. She may still be a threat to herself," he was now shouting into the air as I was already making my way down the hall.

Without even turning around, I raised a hand to wave goodbye and said, "Here in Oklahoma, son, you can only hold her for seventy-two hours, as long as the threat has passed. Good luck to ya! I'm fixin' to go get something to eat and head on home now. I will be back to get her."

I grinned, limping down that hallway, away from what I am sure was a young doctor falling apart behind me, unsure as to his next move. We'd been through so many doctors, police reports, DHS visits when she was younger, this was old hat. As I reached the elevator, I could now hear a bustling back towards her room, and a 22-year-old grown woman's voice let out a growling, "Fuck you!" where a frightened child's voice had been just moments ago. I stepped into the elevator and leaned against the wall, grinning to myself and closing my eyes. "Give 'em hell, kid," I blurted out to no one, grabbing the keys out of my pocket. "See you in seventy-two hours."

CHAPTER 2
BUILDING ELVIS

WALKING OUT of the hospital that day, the sun caught the side of the car just right, and I could still make out the scrapes where Arlo and I had tried to repair and buff them out a few years ago right before her graduation. Actually, it was right before prom. We had resurrected this old car from a scrap heap and if it could tell stories, it would tell you all about the many hours that me and that kid had put into her.

Not that Arlo was a car nut or anything. I think it was just that there was a time when she was younger that she was going through some shit and needed to connect with something and someone. I had just lost V, so I'd been trying to keep myself busy. I was spending a lot of time piddling in the garage on this old car, just trying to keep my brain busy so that it wouldn't pick up on how broken my heart was at the time.

V and I never had a lot, but this damn car was one thing that she got a kick out of. I'd had an AMC Javelin just like it, but in far better shape, when we first got together. It was a 1969 model, just like this one, but it was a dark menacing blue, same V8 engine. I tell ya, that thing could move, and V would just giggle when we would take it out for a drive. Then life happened, and we had Rhoads.

Those cars were small and weren't made for carting families around, so we sold it. We sold the damn thing to purchase a more family friendly piece of crap; I think it was a 1975 Chevy Vega station wagon in a nice shit brown color. What a step down. But it was by far more practical, and V hauled Rhoads and groceries around in that thing for years. It wasn't until V got sick that I started thinking about the old Jav. We didn't have a lot of money, never really did, but a neighbor had come across this car by way of a cousin of his dying and they were trying to sell it.

I remember taking V to go look at it, even though the chemo had made her so debilitatingly sick. My V was always up for an adventure, no matter what. The day that I had planned to look at it, V had been having one of her better days, so she wrapped her head up in her striped blue scarf, slapped on her huge plastic black framed sunglasses and a big old sunhat and we were off.

The drive was only about forty-five minutes away, but we had to stop a few times along the gravel road so she could get sick along the side of the car, where no passersby could see. She had handled her sickness with such dignity and grace, but this trip had broken my heart because the V that I knew and loved for all those years was feisty and still in that body just trying to escape. But the body that held her had been failing her, leaving her broken physically but not in spirit. V is who I hold fully responsible for Arlo having both grit and grace, even though the grit can be a little overbearing at times, not leaving much room for the grace.

I stood in the parking lot at the hospital after leaving Arlo that day, staring at the Jav, lost in thought, thinking back about the adventure V and I had gone on to pick up that old car. We had made our way out past the salt flats, where we were met by my buddy and his Springer Spaniel, Elvis, on a desolate piece of property that housed a derelict house and an old lean-to building that was barely leaning toward anything anymore. I had helped V out of the car and followed Elvis into the lean-to. I had to let out a laugh and I can remember V asking me what was so damn funny.

It was all I could do to look at my V, in her scarf, dime-store sunglasses, red painted lips and over-sized sunhat, being led around on that sunny day by Elvis. Who would believe us? Then again, my V would have been too good for Elvis anyway.

The minute that my buddy pulled the old drop-cloth off of the old Jav, I knew V was all in. She gasped and started to cry. At first, I thought it was because this old Jav was in such bad shape, but I found out later that the moment she saw that car, her mind reached back to when we were young, and her heart ran screaming back to where we had begun.

It didn't matter that this car wasn't the same color as ours had been, or that this one looked like it had been ridden hard and put away wet, dented all over, paint scratched off, a cracked windshield, or even that Elvis the old Springer Spaniel had commenced to licking his balls in the front seat, which had a torn interior and ripped headliner hanging down, by the way. That damn car represented where we had started, and V wanted it all back. I didn't have to think about it—just made arrangements to tow the damn thing home.

The fun thing about that old car is that before it became Arlo's and my thing, it was mine and V's. For a few treasured months, it gave us something to look forward to and laugh about, a subject lighter than death.

She had picked the new paint color and given her opinion on wheels. She was adamant that I get the old eight-track player working in it so that even when it wasn't running, she could sit out in that damn car at night when it was cool, windows down, listening to some of her old favorites.

Before she left us, I got it running, eight track player and all. She never got to see the fresh paint, though. Never got to hear the new engine roar to life or even see the new interior be put in. Those things would be finished much later and picked out by her granddaughter in her place.

I can remember when Arlo first started hanging out with me in the garage. She was maybe in sixth grade, right around when her folks split. Sometimes she would come alone, and sometimes she would bring Bast, if he was around. It was good for me to have her out there, because in all honesty, I had times where I just wanted to quit. Without V, it hurt sometimes just to look at the old car, just to remember. At first, I think Arlo just needed an outlet, something to take her mind off what was going on in her life. She would come out and kind of lean in under the hood, just looking at what I was doing, even though she didn't know what anything was under that old dented hood.

But it didn't matter. What would start with her asking questions about the car would sometimes lead to just a conversation about her day. Our visits might have begun by her laying under the car in a pair of my old overalls and welder's skull cap, asking about the steps in changing oil, but then they would often either lead to her telling me all about who was pissing her off at school, or what she was scared of, or who she was in a fight with now.

There were also other days when she would just disappear for a while, living her young life and leaving this old fart alone, slumped over a wheel well, trying to get her buffed to a nice shine, clinging to the hope that I could somehow still hear V's voice bellowing out from the speakers as I listened to her beloved eight tracks.

As time went on, we would putz on the Jav bit by bit. I would collect and turn in enough scrap metal to buy parts and Arlo and I would go to town to either order new pieces or crawl over and around the cars in the junkyard to see if we could find something that we could just make work. By the time she was in high school, she would start investing a little money here and there too.

Between her working and me scrapping, we got her seats reupholstered the summer before Arlo's freshman year of high school—a light caramel color, as she calls it, and some new wheels Arlo's junior year, true to the year of the car, not "drug dealer wheels" as she liked to call them. And the summer before Arlo's senior year, she picked out the paint color. I like to call it Kermit green, but really it is a deeper, darker green that has a fleck of spark to it. Arlo says it looks like the paint off a bumper car.

That old car has saved us many times. I like to think that when that girl had nowhere to run and too many bad thoughts rumbling around in that sweet brain, that she would come home and work on it, calming her thoughts and keeping her brain and hands busy for a little while, helping to soothe her angry soul. I can also tell you that there were many a night that missing my sweet V became too much, and to calm myself, I would get lost in the car, either mindlessly buffing along her smooth lines or meticulously cleaning under her hood until either my mind walked itself back from the edge of disparity or I came up with a new plan or idea for the car that just kept my mind busy for a little longer.

Oh. And we named her Elvis.

It was no surprise to me then that Arlo's senior year, she announced she was taking Elvis and Bast to prom. That was the original plan. With all my heart, I wanted that girl to live out loud and have a little fun. It was a difficult time in her life. She wasn't getting along with her daddy and her mama had just gotten remarried and moved to Florida, just like her mama's mama had, and I think it just made Arlo feel abandoned.

She had spent hours by herself getting ready cause there was no mama or Nonna around to help, then she came out of her room to get Elvis and go. She wore a long flowing gold gown that made her look like a movie star, leaning against Elvis' green speckled paint. Her hair hung in curled ringlets past her shoulders, and she was fussing about getting there in time while I was taking a couple of pictures with my old Polaroid. One of my favorite pictures I have ever taken of that girl was of her sitting in the front seat of Elvis in her gold gown, one hand on the wheel and the other waving a goofy goodbye out the window. She was grinning a toothy grin, but there was always a little fire behind her eyes.

The week before prom was a rough one, and she was spending a lot of time in her room. Since Rhoads was gone most of the time and her mama moved to Florida, my trailer was her home now. The spare room with a red carpet that V had lovingly picked out years ago had been transformed to a teenage girl's hangout, complete with posters of boy bands attached to the walls and hidden beer cans (of course I knew…) beneath the bed.

Like any young girl, Arlo struggled with friends and bullies, heartaches and crushes. Many times, I had heard her crying in there, and just as many times, I left her on her own to sort it out.

Handling teenage problems was not my strong suit. I was just trying to survive life myself without V, trying to do the best I could with what I had. I always just figured that when she needed to talk, she would, and other than that, I wouldn't bug her too much. I may never know what really happened the night of prom or what the intentional outcome actually was meant to be. All I know is Arlo's side of the story...

Arlo had left with Elvis that night to head to prom. The kids' prom was to be held in the gymnasium at the school, with a formal dinner before the dance that was put on by the junior class's parents. Afterwards, there was a traditional lock in at the school, where the kids spent the night playing games, listening to comedians, dancing and winning prizes that had been donated by the local businesses or purchased through fundraising events.

It was a warm May evening, so Arlo had rolled the windows down. She said that she picked up Bast, and they were driving along towards the school, but that they started talking and weren't ready to head over to the prom yet, so she put in one of V's old eight-track tapes and they just kept driving and talking, driving and talking. She told me that she was telling him all about the stuff she had been going through with her folks and began to cry. She said that Bast had thought that they shouldn't head over to the Prom yet because she was too worked up, so they kept driving and talking, driving and talking.

They had been talking when V's favorite old song came over the speakers, "Alice's Restaurant" by Arlo Guthrie. Arlo said that the instantly recognizable melody stunned her heart for a second and the tears that welled up blinded her and then trickled down her perfectly made-up face. I was sitting on the couch watching TV later that night when the local sheriff pulled up. I knew before she said anything.

"Bobo, it's Arlo. They have her over at Methodist." Sheriff Lee said as soon as I opened the door.

"Is she…" I began, my breath caught in my chest in a hard lump, too terrified to let the question form words that could have an answer that my heart couldn't handle.

"She's OK, Bobo. She'll be OK."

I rode with Sheriff Lee over to Methodist Hospital. It was a quiet ride for those twenty miles. Sheriff Mindy Lee's brother, Todd, was pretty good friends with Rhoads growing up, meaning she had seen some shit. She had seen a *lot* of our family's shit. Bless her, though. She's a graceful gal who does her job and doesn't pry.

When we finally got to the hospital, an older doc, maybe my age, stopped me before entering Arlo's room. He put a hand on my shoulder and asked if we could speak first. I could hear Arlo's voice behind the door frantically speaking with a nurse, so I at least knew she was OK.

"Are you this child's guardian?" the good old doc questioned.

"I am, sir. What's going on?" I remember calmly asking. Now that I was able to hear Arlo's voice, I had my wits about me once more.

Well sir, that's what we are trying to piece together," the doc began, "She's OK, first of all. She will be just fine, a few stitches. Pretty good gash on her head though, which could be leading to all the confusion," he trailed off. I brushed past him and entered Arlo's room.

And there she lay, gold gown now in tatters, hair matted around her sweaty forehead and stitches under her right eye and across her right temple. She looked exhausted and angry.

"Bobo, I am so sorry about Elvis!" she blurted out and began to cry hysterically. At that point, it hadn't even occurred to me to think about the car. All I had worried about was the girl, that she was OK.

"What happened to the car, Arlo?" I blurted out.

"They don't believe me, Bobo. They think I'm covering for Bast, but I'm not, I swear!" she said as tears were rolling down her swollen and dirty face, her lipstick long gone and her green eyes dancing in confusion.

Before me, I had two versions of events, hers and what the police believe may have happened. Her story was that while they were driving around and talking, she had become upset telling Bast about the stuff that had been going on with her folks and how she wasn't ready to go to the prom, so they kept driving. They were talking about teenage stuff, mostly the fear of the upcoming graduation and the all-too-real prospect of having to figure out what to do with the rest of their lives... how they were going to make it in the unrelenting, all-too-close world of adulthood.

In Arlo's recollection of the night's events, the eight-track player began playing her Nonna V's favorite song, Arlo's namesake, and the player started to eat the tape. Out of panic, Arlo took one hand off the wheel to struggle with the tape player, taking her eyes off the road and putting Elvis in the ditch pretty hard.

What Arlo's version doesn't include is the empty beer cans and the partial can that were rolling around in the car. When the police found her, she had crawled out of the upside down car and was wandering down the center of the dirt road, crying and speaking incoherently, makeup running down her confused face, her golden gown spattered with crimson blood and now badly tattered.

When she had settled down enough to tell the responding officers her version of that night's drama, she was adamant that Bast was the passenger and that she was driving. She wouldn't admit to them who had been drinking, whether it was one of them or both of them, but they figured out pretty easily at the hospital that she, for sure, had been, although not heavily intoxicated. The police figured she was covering for Bast, whom they were unable to find. That was the last time she had seen him. He was out of our lives for a long while after that. Until recently.

She didn't do too much damage to the Jav, for as bad as the wreck had looked. She'd been lucky that she hadn't been going too fast when she hit the ditch, and that the overgrown ditch-weed cushioned the graceful rollover a bit.. The front fender took a hit and scratched the paint up pretty good, all the way down one side, from the dry weeds and bushes that had dug into the paint. There were some dents to pound out, and the frame seemed to be a little off kilter, but all in all, manageable. It would give me something to work on.

The doctors had their theories. While the police worked under their assumption that she was covering for Bast, the doctors and therapists were concerned that she may have been depressed, suicidal even. She was only seventeen at the time, so legally all she got from the judge overseeing her case was a stern lecture about the pitfalls of alcohol, the urging to be a better citizen and a fine of which amounted to be a slap on the wrist. She stood by her story to me, though, so that is the story that I chose to believe.

I stood there in the hospital lot a few more minutes, running my hands over the barely noticeable spot on the Jav now, thinking of how far away that night seemed. She had been doing so well out on her own over the past five years, really finding her place in this world. Sure, I missed her like hell, but I also knew that she needed to get out of this town and live her life. She needed to outrun her past in order to get ahead.

I crawled into the driver's side of Elvis and brought her to life. The engine gently rumbled as I had a death grip on the steering wheel and shouted out, "Damn it!" while wondering what V would do had she been here. Am I a fool to want to believe that Arlo didn't mean to hurt herself this time? Damn Alabaster! His influence on her had never been good. Those two had always been a violent combination of childlike excitement and walking on the edge of insanity.

Together, they pushed limits that shouldn't be pushed, and the waters never stayed calm for very long. She'd had a few good years in his absence, but what the hell was I bracing myself for now?

When I was to go pick her up in 72 hours, I knew damn well this wasn't a kid anymore! She was twenty-two now. There's only so much left that I can do.

Driving out of the hospital parking lot, I glanced into the rearview mirror towards the building and wondered what she was telling them in there, what kind of story she had been concocting this time. Did she really understand that I wasn't abandoning her? That I would be back to save her, like I always had? With an exhausted sigh and a heavy heart, I pulled Elvis out onto the road and headed for home, turning on V's old eight-track player as I drove.

CHAPTER 3
DESTINED TO DIE

AS I drove, my heart found some comfort in the familiarity that my eyes were absorbing, feeling as though my body and mind were on autopilot. I had traveled these miles alone so many times in the past few years. That damn hospital has had it out for me since Arlo was born… well, maybe even before that, I guess.

I felt a sharp throb in my right knee as I let up on the foot pedal to release the gas and it immediately brought me back to that day… one of my first run-ins with the thorn in my side that is Methodist Hospital. Who knows how any of our lives would have turned out if that hadn't happened? Maybe Rhoads wouldn't have felt so pressured, so burdened, for the rest of his time at home. Things may have sorted themselves out differently…. Who knows?

All I knew is on that August day so many years ago, one of the most traumatic and emotionally draining things to ever happen—happened, and everything that I had known before would cease to exist. It was almost as if that day was the abrupt, stunning end of the life I knew, and the staunch and gritty beginning to the next half, the half that was deepseated in darkness and pain, sadness and struggles, and a different man who would eventually emerge.

As I drove along, windows down and warm air licking at my weathered cheeks, the old familiar scent of a dry dirt suddenly hit me. I didn't have to look around to know exactly where I was. Glancing at the plastic blue Casio on my left arm that had been perched on the door, half out the window, I realized I didn't give a shit what time it was. What the hell was I in a hurry to get back to?

The trailer? There was no one there. Everyone who had ever been there had been violently ripped from my grasp. With a somber sigh and a little rage bubbling right underneath my heart and burning a hole in my belly, I thought, "Fuck it," and turned at the quarry entrance.

I pulled up to the mouth of the first gravel pit and parked Elvis. Staring out into that dusty hole, glancing around at the piles of rock and stone, I felt at home. Funny how that worked. The place that had pulled me into the depths of hell for years was now where I ran to settle my soul.

I got out of Elvis and limped my way over to the base of one of the smaller gravel piles. My eyes were scanning, trying to find a little shimmer within that tiny mountain. A younger me would have been able to chase a younger Rhoads right up to the top of that pile. But the new me, the older and broken me, could only manage a slow hobble towards the side, steadying myself down into the shallow portion of the hill. As soon as my butt hit the gravel, I sunk in just a little, and using my arms, scooted up the side of the hill backwards just a short way up.

There is a feeling that engulfs you out there at the quarry, a small yet freeing feeling. The quarry sits on the edge of a chain of underground mines. Not that the little town of Freedom is much to begin with, but out here on her edge, on the outer banks of the Cimmaron River, there is truly nothing but the wind, dirt and rocks. If I had been a younger man, I could have crawled right to the top of the largest gravel pile and would have been able to see the glory of the outlying salt flats and the lush greenery that perches on top of the mining cave systems. Up there, you truly feel free.

Down here, though, on the lower half of the smallest rock pile, you are surrounded by only rock dust and wind. There's still a magic to be found here, though. I sat breathing in the dry dusty air that tasted gritty like home and, while steadying myself with one hand, dug my other hand deep into the cold and dusty pile of grimy rocks. I fumbled my fingers around and felt for a few sharper-edged pieces. As my older, arthritis-afflicted fingers struggled to grasp my perceived prize, I had a quick vision appear in my heart.

When Arlo was just a small bug, I would bring her out here. Sometimes for fun, but most of the time out of necessity, to escape the pain and madness that seemed to hurricane around her, persistently trying to push her back into her very own fraidy hole. We would hang out here when her mama and daddy were fighting, when she was struggling with school, when the pain of losing V would become suffocating.

She instinctively could see the beauty in the dust bowl and felt at home here, too. It became an adventure just to see what grimy and banged up rocks we could collect and then get 'em home, scrub 'em up, and let 'em shine. Sometimes we would even take a few out to the workshop and try busting them open because as that girl knew, even way back then, some of the ugliest stones could be worth a lot if you could identify what was inside. She would giggle if we were lucky enough to crack one open and see that inside, it sparkled like a Geode or was striped and smooth like an agate.

I hadn't realized that thinking about Arlo had calmed me down a bit and time seemed to have escaped me. The sun was now a glowing ember, slowly making her descent beyond the larger gravel pile. I swear to ya that I heard her small voice, the voice from years ago that sounded like Kermit the Frog... "This little light of mine... I'm gonna let it shine."

Now, I'm not too proud to admit that I had to swallow the lump that had formed in the back of my dry throat. I loved that wild child. I loved that I could bring her voice to the front of my mind even when she was away, which had been a lot lately. "Hide it under a bucket... NO!!!" she would sing and giggle when finishing up that little song. It took a lot of coaxing to get her little light to shine in this world, but when it did... man... you better watch out.

Carefully, I grasped the couple of rocks between my gnarled fingers and pulled them back out of the rock pile to see what I had unearthed.

Peering down into my calloused palm, I could see a couple of smaller round and smooth gray stones and a larger dirty piece of a light salmon-colored rock. I figured the pink one must be pink gypsum, which would have tickled that girl to death to have found, When that grimy piece of stone is cleaned up, it turns a soft pink with a little sparkle to it, until it dries out and becomes a grayish tone once again. When Arlo was little, she equated it with magic. I giggled a little and slid that one into my shirt pocket for safekeeping. I sat there watching the sun run away and thinking about how much love and hate I'd had for this place.

When Rhoads was little, we didn't have much money. We worked hard, V and I, but let's face it... in a tiny little town, there ain't too many options. While V was working at the local drive-in when Rhoads was in school during the day, I was a welder and part time mechanic, doing a little engineering work on the side. A buddy of mine had just quit his job out here at the quarry because the son of a bitch was lucky enough to have married into some money and was expected to move out to the help run the family farm which the family then lost years later because of some sideways spending, combined with a wild love affair with alcohol.

Anywho, after hearing about the job opening, I went right on down and got myself hired. At first, I was on a crew that was driving the loaders and dozers, lumping the gravel piles from the mouth of the quarry to the outward banks, and from there to be loaded onto trucks as they came in. It was a decent job, and the people that you spent long hours with were pretty colorful characters who you came to lean on like family. I carried on this way for years, making a pretty good penny off those dirty old rocks, while still taking small engineering assignments here and there on the side.

By the time Rhoads had made it to high school, we were both working out here in the dirt and heat. He cleaned the muck that would build up in the tracks in the machines and shoveled the spillage from the side of the trucks on transfer. By that time, I was dividing my hours between my typical duties and running the old rock crusher as the day allowed.

There was a definite shortage of people wanting to move to this insignificant speck of a town, so more often than not, it left us shorthanded. The August before his sophomore year, Rhoads had found his way into the crew, helping where he was needed and heating up his lunch of Spam and ears of sweetcorn on the truck engine with the rest of the guys. My boy was a hard worker and was willing to learn.

One day, I had grown tired of trying to keep up with loading the swarm of trucks hauling rock and keeping the crusher running, so I took it upon myself to teach Rhoads how to run the crusher. That damn old thing. You have to remember that this was before the sophisticated machines of today and even before OSHA started hanging around job sites, being the pain in the ass that they've turned out to be. We had jobs to do and no time to pussyfoot around.

I had Rhoads follow me up the old, grated ladder that was attached to the side of the crushing platform. I had to shut it off to show him cause that damn thing was so loud and grimacing that you couldn't hear your own thoughts up there, let alone anyone else. This is also why I have lost sixty percent of my hearing in my left ear, the one closest to her engine.

There we were, sweating to death because the dang August sun was relentless. I remember Rhoads was getting irritated because he felt like he knew what he was doing, and being a young kid, he just wanted to get on with it, get the job done so we could finally call it quits and head home for the day. We were all hot, tired, and cranky.

Basically, all he had to do was stand on that rickety metal grate, babysitting the crushing plates. From time to time, as the big rocks were fed into the crusher by trucks, some would get lodged and you'd have to stop the machine and grab a whammy stick—nothing more than an old metal pole that had been retrofitted with a smooth tapered lip on the edge, kind of like a crowbar—wedge that thing down in-between the larger rocks, and loosen up whatever was stuck. Then, you'd have to crawl back down from the platform and restart the crusher because when the rocks would stick, the machine would throw a warning and seize up, not being able to be restarted until it was manually turned off and on again. Not that the process took long. It was just irritating to have to do it over and over again when the workers were trying to load the crusher as fast as possible and be on their way, to get home to their families.

When I thought he had it handled, I crawled on back down from the platform and headed over to where one of the cranes had become stuck because her track had slipped. It was always something... those goddamn machines were older than dirt and always falling apart, needing to be pieced back together again, "Frankensteined" together, I would say. I grabbed my tools and headed out to repair her.

I shit you not. It was no more than a few minutes that I had started working on that damn crane that I noticed the crusher had stopped already. I glanced over that way and saw Rhoads up there with the whammy stick, pushing and pulling with all of his strength. After watching this for a few minutes and noticing that the truck haulers were getting visibly pissed, climbing out of their trucks and flailing their arms around in the air while screaming at my boy, I had figured that I better go see what the boy was having problems with.

"Awe Christ Bobo, what's going on up there?" Mike, one of the haulers shouted, wiping the sweat from his face, standing by his truck.

I raised my hand in a wave of acknowledgment and dropped what I had been working on, making my way back over towards the crusher and her platform. I headed up the narrow steel grated steps, making my way to where Rhoads was struggling.

There was an awful grinding noise that came low from the belly of the crusher, and I can still smell the burning of a belt from somewhere below. That shit smells. It permeates up through your nostrils and you can't get the smell out of your brain. Hell, I can still bring that smell back in my head if I just think hard enough about it. Something so putrid, so volatile leaves its mark, and no amount of time can make your senses forget. Especially when it's 102 degrees out and the wind is down.

While making my way up that platform and smelling that nauseating aroma, I was trying to quickly wrap my brain around the panic that had been unfolding, the situation that I was once again being thrust into and being made accountable for. It was strange that the machine hadn't fully shut off the motor at this point, almost as if it was trying to power through being stuck, grinding the inner wheels and burning up her belts. If that thing didn't get fixed fast, it would be even more expensive and with no back-up crusher, it would hurt a lot of families' paychecks for at least a few weeks until we could ship the parts in and get her operational again.

I made my way towards my boy and slapped him on the back. "What the hell, boy? What's stuck down in there?" I shouted into his ear. Rhoads didn't let up on trying to pry that whammy bar as he screamed back, "Fuck if I know! I've been trying to separate it, but the damn thing won't budge! Why hasn't the motor seized up yet? The more I'm fighting it to try to get her loose, the more the damn belts keep moving, trying to pull the rock through."

"Aw Christ!" I hollered back, flexing my jaw, one step from turning around to make my way back down the grated stairs to the platform to see if I could trip the breaker and halt the son of a bitch.

That was the exact fracture, the mere millisecond in time that the life we had known would be gone, the millisecond that I would lose my steadfast grip on reality, and all the faith that I had left in this world.

There's one thing you have to know about a rock crusher, particularly the old ones, not these high-powered fancy beasts of today that have all the safety guards and are completely mechanically-controlled and managed by computer boards. Strip the crusher down to what she is, beneath the fancy mechanics, beneath her slick design. That majestic bitch's basic function is to pull the rocks through, almost like a conveyor, and then crush the large ones into smaller chunks. This happens by the use of jaw-crusher plates that are made of a medium carbon, low-alloy cast steel, which means they are unforgiving, merciless and good at crushing shit that doesn't want to be crushed.

On that sweltering August day as I watched my boy man-handling the whammy stick on top of the platform of that beast, the sweat trickling down his arms and down towards his blistered and calloused hands, my heart paused in fear for one long second as I saw him falter and begin to lose his balance while working the whammy stick. His body shifted, and while his pissed off mind was only thinking about using that damn whammy stick to dislodge the clogged jaws of hell, he was losing his footing without even knowing it, only seconds away from falling into the grinding pit beneath him. Within seconds, my reaction happened with no coherent thought process. My world went deafeningly silent. I saw my son about to fall, so I simply sprang forward, shoving him back against the guardrail on the platform, and I then slipped on the dusty steel, tripping feet first into the menacing crusher.

I can tell you that blood spilled in the heat smells just as gritty and irony as it tastes. I can tell you that when your body is put through severe pain, you go into shock and only feel a warm glow about you. I can tell you there is a stunned and ghostly look in the eyes of onlookers when they believe you are destined to die. I can tell you about the relief in this old man's heart when I looked up and saw Rhoads standing safely on the platform, a few feet above me, shaking like a leaf and white as a ghost, the splatter of my own blood dancing across his brow.

These are about all the things that I can remember. I know from what my son has told me that somehow, I was lucky, because the whammy stick had gotten jammed beneath me with a couple of enormous boulders, so only one of my legs had become entwined in the crevice. The truth is, it wasn't really the crusher plates that got me, but a couple of large rocks that were being crushed between those plates. It was the quick thinking of Mike, standing below the deck and overriding the switch to shut that damned thing off right away that saved my life. That and Mike helping Rhoads dislodge the rocks and pull me out so I wouldn't bleed to death in minutes.

Rhoads said that when they unwedged the rocks and pulled me out, my lower right leg was hanging and only attached by skin and a tendon on the outer side, right at my knee. He had held himself together until Mike used his own belt to tourniquet that damn leg, and as soon as they had me in the truck, only then did Rhoads hyperventilate and black out.

And that was that. A small fraction of a millisecond in time that would then viciously shake up our lives and turn us all into very different people. That day was the end of my son's childhood. I was laid up completely for six months and on disability most of the time after that. Although I could do side jobs—short-term engineering assignments that only required the use of a computer and my brain to design the needed parts—and scrapping metal for cash, I had become basically unemployable in a matter of seconds.

We had no choice but to depend on Rhoads to fill the income gap. V kept right on working at the drive-in and also took hours as a nursing aide at the local old folk's home. Money had become tighter than it already was, and my spirit had become broken.

To save us, my boy would work at the quarry after school during the year, but the summer he turned sixteen, he took a job a with a local road crew and traveled all summer, living out of the cab of an old pickup, sending his checks home along the way. I didn't enjoy depending on a kid to keep us afloat financially, but hell, what choice did we have?

Saving Rhoads was what actually had put the wedge between us. It's a strange bag of tricks when he could feel so much anger towards me, the man who saved him. In saving him, though, the trade-off had been taking his childhood, stealing any feeling of youthfulness and just being able to be a carefree kid. It was all wiped away that day, in the jaws of that damn crusher.

That boy worked his ass off clear through graduation, and even then, he would send money home to his mama if we were having a tough time. Oh… his mama. V was a saint during that time. Who was I kidding? She was a saint most of the time I was graced to have known her. She never complained and was always so thankful that I had survived at all, even when it meant her having to work two jobs and always trying to make do with what she had, which was never enough. In fact, one of Arlo's most favorite meals was invented long before that girl was around!

V's potato soup came about one night when our boy,Rhoads,was on the road, while I was still bedridden, and V was exhausted from working two jobs. We had no money to shop for groceries, so V looked around and found some potatoes left in the cellar, a couple of hot-dogs in the back of the fridge, half an onion and a few pieces of bacon. She whipped them all together, added a little milk and flour, salt and pepper and …. boom. The best potato soup this side of Oklahoma.

Just sitting out there on that damn rock pile, smelling the dirt and tasting the grime, I was salivating for some of V's potato soup, while reminiscing about the past. My stomach let out a low rumble to agree with me and I decided to head back towards the trailer. I still had a couple days before I was supposed to go pick up Arlo, plenty of time to fill my hours reminiscing about the past, the things that had gotten us to where we were. Right then, though, all I wanted was to go back home.

I stood slowly, balancing myself, and made my way back down the side of the smaller crumbling pile of grimy rocks, the dust billowing in the air with every move that I made. My right leg limped along as I made my way back over to Elvis. As I reached for the door handle, I looked back towards the larger rock pile and the sun that had almost set behind it. It wasn't lost on me that these rocks that had held all of Arlo's dreams and some of her best memories were also the keepers of my own hell, the place where my life changed, and my son was lost.

For years, Rhoads had carried me, even when his pain was too deep to actually return home. I took in a few lungs full of that comforting dust and grime as the wind began to pick up again, kicking the dust airborne and making it hard to see across the mines.

I patted my pocket that held Arlo's rock, trying to remind myself to give it to her. "I've got her from here, Rhoads," I whispered to the rock piles before slowly getting back into the Jav. "He's carried me this far," I thought out loud. "I got it now, my boy. I got her for ya."

CHAPTER 4
AND THEN I LOST HER...

AS I pulled Elvis into the dirt drive that was now visible by my high beams, clouds of dust rose to the dark skies, illuminating the menacing moon with a gritty and blurred glow. As I got out and began to take the labored steps to the front door of my old trailer, the slightest beam of moonlight illuminated something towards the side of the old trailer. I shifted my weight a little onto my good leg, as I felt the full realization of what was pulling my gaze.

I froze there in the gritty moonlight, staring at her. Funny how something so common, so much of a bystander in your ordinary days, can bind such a small chapter of your past into the forefront of your brain. In the summer darkness I stood there alone, waiting to see if the memory would come for me, if she would take over my soul and render me helpless. I have tried to keep so many things blocked out, so many things held in my life at arm's reach, but her. She houses the memory that tipped the scales of faith in my life. The memory of the night that I lost Arlo, or at least the Arlo that I had known.

I stood there staring at that old fraidy hole with just as much pain as fear running through my soul. Shit, this was stupid. It's just a storm shelter. It's built to keep us safe, not drag us into the mouth of hell. I shivered off the chills that had crawled up my spine and turned away from that boarded up cellar. The boards warped with time and needed to be replaced. I didn't need to go in there to know what I would find. Every year, I restocked the fraidy hole with flats of water, replaced the weather radio batteries and took care to kill all the creepy crawlies that I found scurrying around. I know she's just a storm shelter. So why does the sight of her make me want to throw up so badly?

With a turn of my stomach and an uneasiness about my soul, I ignored the haunting fraidy hole and headed into the trailer. It had been such an exhausting day; it was all I could do to grab a can of stew, pop it open, grab a spoon off the counter and collapse on the couch. I had just tipped my head back to rest my eyes when I felt the most unexpected damp sandpaper scrape its way along my right exhausted eyelid.

"Hey kid," I whispered without lifting an eyelid. Poor cat. I had almost forgotten Arlo had brought her here when she came back. Fifi, short for Defiance—and I have taken to calling her "my Feefs"—was a cute enough little thing that Arlo had taken with her when she walked in on that bastard, Derrick, shacking up with her best friend. She'd walked right out of her new life, falling right back into the old life she had fought for so long to escape. Arlo had found the defeated little cat one night on her way home from work, limping down the sidewalk. She looked like she'd been in a pretty good fight with something that was much bigger than her tired little body had been. She ended up losing a rear right leg, and going blind in one eye, but it ain't slowed her down none.

I patted the scruff on the top of her head, scratching that jet black fur while she settled down to feast on my half-eaten jar of stew. With my eyes still pinched tight, I once again tipped my head back against the old floral faded couch that V had hand picked out all those years ago. A smile crawled across my face at the thought of V.

V had never complained when we had to make do or go without. She was an honest, hard worker, and she made our doublewide trailer a true home. Our home may have always been small, but that woman loved it no differently than if I had bought her a mansion. She had a passion for all things pink or covered in frilly roses. She loved nicely carved pieces of wood furniture, and her eyes would dance if she could make anything sparkle.

The couch that I had collapsed onto was one of those pieces of furniture that was a slight blip in my history of life with V, and I just couldn't let it go. What was once a pretty sharp looking three seated couch and loveseat set with an upholstered footstool had been worn away to only the lonely foot stool and larger couch surviving. They didn't look good; I'll give you that. What had once been a cream fabric with a fine blue pinstripe with salmon-colored roses (I can still hear V hollering at me that the right term for that color was blush), was now tattered and worn, and half covered with a cheap blue stretchy couch cover that I had picked up. It looked pretty bad. It should be thrown out, but sometimes all a person has left are worn-out memories like that old couch to keep them warm on lonely nights. I just couldn't let it go.

As my body finally relaxed and gave in to peace on V's beloved couch that evening, a world from somewhere not long ago visited me while my eyes were closed. As I lay there, patting Fifi on the head, both of us content with a full belly and napping peacefully on the old couch, my ears began to pick up on the faint sound of my eleven-year-old Arlo.

"Bobo!" I could hear a panicked voice travel across the yard, teasing me as the wind picked up. "Help, Bobo please!" I could hear the pleading before the faint scent of smoke had hit me. I had been down the hill working in my little shop earlier when she buzzed by me, chattering about her plans with Bast and looking for the small first-aid kit that I keep in there, usually tucked behind the "Classy Crap This Way" old garage sale sign of V's that was still proudly displayed over my cluttered workbench.

"Whatcha want that for, kid?" I remember asking while only half paying attention. I'd been buried contently under the Jav's hood.

"Me and Bast are just playing lost kids, Bobo. We're gonna pretend to get hurt. It'll be fun!" she had excitedly said as she ran quickly back out the door, first aid kit tucked neatly under her armpit. We had already lost V and by then, Arlo's mama and daddy weren't getting along, so she was spending a lot of time with me. It was such a welcome distraction from the void of not living that I had been forced into after I lost V.

It wasn't until I heard that scream that I even gave the whole situation another thought. Arlo and Bast were always running off somewhere, burying or finding treasures, pretending to be pirates, animals, racecar drivers, explorers. They were constantly either dreaming up worlds where they could be other people and live different lives, or pretending to be on the run from something like a life they didn't want and couldn't make sense of.

As soon as I heard that scream from the distance, instinct carried me to her. I'd dropped a wrench that had landed on my damn foot as I hobbled off towards the sound of the commotion and the faint smell of smoke. As the fraidy hole came into view... I immediately knew something was very wrong.

First, I noticed that there was a faint, yet billowing plume of smoke now rising from the hole, and second, the scream that had initially sent me into a frenzied panic had now turned into coughs, intermittently placed between stressful gasps for air that was being smothered by smoke.

"What in tarnation?" I shouted out loud as I hurried towards the fraidy hole. As I made my way to the doorway, I could still hear her coughing in there.

"Arlo Marie, get your ass outta there!" I shouted into the gritty darkness. There was no response uttering its way back to me. I quickly ripped off my old tee-shirt (the one that V had given me a few birthdays before with the cartoon stick people around a campfire on the front that was captioned, "It's all fun and games until someone loses a wiener,") and tied it around my mouth and nose.

With a shaky gate, I gripped the handrail and descended into the hazy darkness, unsure of what would be waiting for me in there. The smoke was lightly pluming towards the door, but there were no large flames lashing out at me as I made my way down the few steps into the earth. By the glow of the lonely light bulb, I could make out her tiny figure towards the right corner of the hole, crouched over and coughing, as a dark pool of blood had begun to form around where she was sitting.

It was only then that I could see from where the smoke was building. Close to where she was crouched over, I saw a small pile of rags balled up into a mound and somehow lit on fire, which was now beginning to smolder. Right next to them, on the floor, I faintly saw a tiny sparkle of rhinestones glistening off of V's old Elvis lighter that had been haphazardly tossed aside or dropped. The smoldering pile of rags had been greased rags, from my shop no doubt, which was why they must have ignited so easily.

For the next few seconds, I moved with a speed that only the good Lord must have blessed me with, because I was able to scoop those old rags into an empty metal pail and run them outside. It was just a blessing that the flames hadn't leapt over towards where the pile of extra blankets had been, or I may not have been able to save my girl at all.

After I had the rags out of there, I flew back down those couple of stairs back to grab Arlo. She was a sad sight, hunched over on the floor, gasping for air. Her hair was a wild mess, as always, and her peach-colored tee-shirt had been smeared with blood. I grabbed her left hand to see where the blood had been pooling from, only to see that she had somehow cut open the palm of her little hand, and it was a rough and angry looking gash. I grabbed her outta that fraidy hole and ran her over to the hospital, grabbing a washrag from the trailer first to wrap that hand in.

To hear Arlo tell it, she and Bast had been playing lost kids, just like she had planned on. They had decided to pretend to light a campfire in the fraidy hole with V's old Elvis lighter, but Bast had held the lighter a little too close and one of the rags had begun to burn. And what about that nasty gash on her hand?

Apparently, they had tried to become "blood brothers", something they had seen while watching a movie. She said it had been Bast's idea, and that he had cut her palm first before starting the fire, maybe a little deeper than he had meant to. Once the fire started, she said he got scared and took off. The imagination of that girl was something that I'd always equally envied and feared. It seemed that for so much of her life, you couldn't tell where reality stopped and her dreams and nightmares began.

The hospital wasn't fully convinced of her story, so they made her talk to the child psychiatrist on staff, and she went through a very invasive line of questioning. They were determined to rule out that she wasn't a threat to herself, even at only eleven years old. The explanation of a child's very vivid imagination simply wasn't enough to quell their fears at the time, so, with my consent, they held her for seventy-two hours.

That poor kid did not know why she was being kept there, and it still hurts my heart to think of what that little face looked like when I had to walk away and leave her behind. Her pleading eyes followed me as she watched me walk to my car through the window in her little room. I didn't want to look at her. I didn't want her to see the look of regret and failure that I was wearing as a cloak around my soul.

I had fully believed that her being in there directly resulted from me not taking care of her the way that I should have been, me not being there enough for her and me not knowing just what the hell I was trying to do raising that girl on my own. But I was all she had.

After those seventy-two hours, the Methodist Hospital released her back to me, and we went home. We never talked about that day again, as I had always found it easier to bury things that were in the past and find ways to just pick up and move on.

Memories are all I've had to cuddle up with in the nights anymore, no matter if they're good or bad. My trailer was now a haven for echoes from my past, and it comforted me that I was still able to remember. I had fallen into such a deep sleep on that old couch that I didn't hear him come into the trailer. It wasn't until he was shaking me awake that I jumped and almost pissed myself.

"Dad, it's OK, it's just me!" I heard his voice say before my eyes even opened and my brain could fully understand what was going on. I sat straight up on the old couch, almost launching poor Feef into the air.

Unless my eyes were deceiving me, there in front of me stood Rhoads. A little older, and with an exhausted expression on his face, but there before me stood my son, whom I hadn't seen since, what… her graduation a couple years ago?

"What the hell are you doing here?" was about all I could think of to say, my mind still lost in the intoxicating memories I had just been visiting in my sleep.

Rhoads sat down next to me on that faded old couch and for a moment, no words were coming. Then he turned towards me to look me in the eye as he spoke. His face was so much older now, the lines of a hard life now embedded on his brow, his eyes sullen and tired.

"They called me from the hospital, Dad. I know about Arlo, about what she tried to do," he spoke softly, much unlike his usual loud demeanor. Looking into his once blue and soulful eyes, I could now see how time had become a thief and had stolen years from him, wearing down his heart and weakening his soul. Those eyes no longer belonged to a man of the mid-forties, but to a broken man whose body was now many years beyond where it should be.

"I came when I heard," he continued on, feeling around in his brain for his next words, carefully trying to tiptoe around any smoldering fires that may still be burning within him. He glanced around the living room of the little trailer, now trying to avert his eyes from me.

"Well, I don't know why the hell you even bothered!" I spewed out in anger, even though as soon as those words fell from my lips, I instantly regretted saying them. He looked down at the shag carpet where his feet sat and said nothing, rolling his ankles and gazing at his socks.

"Dad, I just need to know she's OK. I just need to know that she's going to make it out of all of this," he whispered.

I wasn't sure how to react at first. Here sat next to me my son, the child that I'd helped raise, the kid who'd had to become a man way before he should have. I couldn't quite remember when we fell apart, or when he decided that staying gone was the path that made the most sense for him. I knew I had played a part in that. Losing his mama had played a part in that. But it still pissed me off that it was Arlo who was paying the toll for something that I had been responsible for.

I sat next to him, making sure not to look this way as I was trying to figure out what the hell I was supposed to say. How was it OK that he had walked out of our lives and yet was able to just drop back in when he felt like it? I was angry that he wasn't there for the day to day, to raise her, to scold her, to love her. I was mad that he'd missed dances and recitals and class picnics, that she'd always had to take me, her grandpa, to all the things that she was supposed to get to take her father to. I was pissed that the divide between us had become so vast that the only emotion that I could pull from my soul when looking at my own son was that of anger.

"Well, why don't you go over and see her if you want to know so damn bad?" I blurted out, stiffening up a bit.

With a recoil that I could feel, he bristled up next to me as he spoke. "I can't, Dad. I lost the right to that part of my life a long time ago. I don't expect her to welcome me anymore, to hold a place for me at her table for the holidays. I'm just a memory to her now, and that's how it needs to stay. There are too many years of me being gone, of her being hurt and of being abandoned, and to tell ya the honest to God's truth, I don't have it in me to fight for amends anymore. It's just enough for me to keep going, knowing that somewhere in this world, I did something right, that I brought a decent human into this world and that she's doing OK. That's all I need, Dad. All I am asking you for is just that reassurance. Please, Dad. Just tell me she's gonna be OK."

You ever had one of those fleeting moments in your life where you have so much that you want to say, so many things that need to be laid to rest, but then at the last second, you just swallow those flooded words of fire like a bitter pill and stuff them down, somewhere deep?

I had known in that moment that there was nothing I could say to Rhoads that would repair the years of pain we had survived, or to bridge the great divide between us. It had been me who had asked too much of him for so many years, when he had been too young to have that burden placed on him after my leg got crushed, so who the hell was I to ask for anything more from the kid?

As one final act of love for my son, one of the last things I said to him that night, sitting on V's old, faded couch in the darkness, feet nestled into the matted down shag carpeting, I assured him, "She'll survive this, kid. She will survive it like she always has."

CHAPTER 5
LAKE LAPS

I WOKE up the next morning, still on the faded old couch, snuggled right up with Fifi, and Rhoads was gone again. No note, no goodbye, it was just how we did things. I liked to think that maybe he had stopped by the hospital to check on his daughter, but in my heart, I figured he had just needed a little reassurance and to get the hell back outta town.

For the next couple of days while she was in-patient, I tried to stay busy, all the while wondering what the hell we were going to do when I got her back home. This wasn't like she was a little kid anymore, after all. She was a damn adult with responsibilities and consequences for her actions now. She couldn't just run and hide from her problems anymore, and I, for one, was getting too damn old to keep coming to her rescue.

The first day that she was in there, I just puttered in the shop, trying to organize some cabinets, shining up the rims on Elvis, whatever I could do to fill my time. The second day, though, the weather had turned a little cooler, yet the sun was still out, and I had decided to head out to the little Clear Lake to see if I could catch any fish. I grabbed a pole from the shop and dug out my tacklebox. I had to stop at the local Dome Bait Shop to pick up some good night crawlers cause it had been too dry for me to find any outside myself. Plus for a couple of bucks I could save myself from having to bend this old body over to look for them. That had always been Arlo's job.

Sitting in the Dome Bait Shop's parking lot, I peeled back the lid of my Styrofoam container to peer in at the little squigglers. They were some fat and juicy ones. I had to giggle because I could still see a young Arlo, maybe 4 or 5, running around with her little bucket, picking up the worms that would slither out of the damp earth after a good rain. She would step gently through those fat little suckers, carefully picking them up one by one and dropping them into her bucket with a nice fat plop. She never had a fear of worms, slithery things, or things that would bite. Her biggest fear was only that, somehow, she wasn't enough in this damned world.

I snapped the lid back onto my little container of worms, rolled Elvis' windows down, and headed towards the lake. Our little lake was a thing of wonder. At only fourteen miles around, it wasn't that it was huge. In fact, only the small end had ever been dredged, leaving most of the lake at a depth of maybe six to ten feet. The dredged area was a good bit deeper, though, about twenty to twenty-five feet deep, and that always seemed to be where we had better luck fishing for bass. The catfish seemed to like the reedier, shallower waters.

But our little lake was where the local kids learned to drive around her shoreline, all two-lane roads. It was also where you could cruise around to think about things, work life's problems out. We called it "doing lake laps." If you were upset and needed to think, do a lake lap. If you were taking your sweetie out on a date, do a lake lap. Hiding away for your first sip of beer? A lake lap would take you to the open fields where you could hide and sip to your heart's content. Too many times in my life, I've found myself just crawling around her shores, trying to clear my head or just being called to her beauty.

The thing about Clear Lake was that it wasn't clear at all. What a ridiculous name for such a muddy little lake. It seemed to fit her though, because a dirty little lake would belong in a gritty little town. She was deep enough to swallow the secrets that people tried to keep buried out there, and I am sure that, in addition to tossed wedding rings, empty beer bottles, and the occasional missing pair of sunglasses, our little lake has probably lost a few people in her depths as well. We'd almost lost Arlo that way once when we were out fishing.

It had been a muggy hot day, and we'd had our fill of fishing in the shallow waters where nothing was biting. So we decided, against V's advice, to head over to the deeper, dredged part of the lake. V never liked us going out there because she knew Arlo was still young and not the best swimmer yet. I'd made sure that she had her little hot pink life jacket on, snugly snapped around her when we decided to venture over that way. She was chattering to Bast all the way over, betting on who was going to get the biggest catch.

Once we'd made it to the deep part, she had gotten hot and un-snapped her vest. I figured it had been a calm enough day on the water, and we were just sitting still fishing, not trolling, so she should be OK. We'd been out there for about half an hour or so when she had a little tug on her line.

"Bobo! Look! It's jumpin'! I think I got somethin' on there! Help, Bobo, I don't wanna lose him!" she hollered over to me. I hurried over to her and took a hold of her little pole, and there was definitely some-thing pulling on there. I stood up to gain a little more leverage, my back now to Arlo. I could hear her talking to Bast, excitedly wondering what kind of big one they were reeling in.

In all the excitement of trying not to lose whatever it was on the other end of her line; I didn't realize that one of my little fishermen had jumped ship. I'd glanced over my shoulder in time to see her hot pink vest fall to the seat of the boat and watched as the top of her head of unruly blonde curls slowly slid beneath the surface. I had no time to think. With my heart in my throat and a sheer panic that had taken over my guts within seconds, I dropped her damn pole and dove into the water, clothes and all. I am so grateful that the motor wasn't running because I hadn't even thought about what would happen if one of us were knocked into the blades or, even worse... if the boat took off with-out us.

Although the day had been warm, the water hit my body like a plate of ice, pausing the senses and momentarily making me lose my focus. I came up for air, took one giant gasp, and under I went, kicking and flailing around, grabbing for her hair. The oddest thing is that when I caught her only a couple of feet beneath the water, she wasn't fighting the current. She wasn't flailing her arms about wildly or kicking at all. She was simply sinking, like a doll that had gotten accidentally tossed into the wake.

Growing up around the lake, it never bothered me to open my eyes in the murky waters. It wasn't like a pool where there were chemicals to burn, just dirt and grime that made it cloudy. You couldn't stand to have them open for very long, but to keep from getting all discombobulated beneath the surface, sometimes when you were catfishing or swimming very deep, you would open your eyes just to get a glimpse of where the sky was so you didn't lose your way. It was no surprise to me then, that when I clutched on to a hand full of her precious curls and came face to face with her, her eyes were open, staring right into mine. What shocked me though was the smile that sat on her pursed lips. It was just damn creepy.

Once again, we'd had her checked out at the hospital, and once again, she had said that it was that damn Bast's idea. She said that on the way out to the deep part of the lake, Bast had been talking about swimming and how she wasn't a very strong swimmer yet, but that if she just jumped in and totally relaxed, her body would then just float like a dead bass. She hadn't believed him, so he bet her five bucks that it would work. Then she bravely jumped overboard when I wasn't looking.

If you ask the doctors though, they all called it something else—a call of the void—which was when a person is drawn to jump into the unknown like off a bridge, or the edge of a building, or even the urge to swerve off of a road just to see what would happen. They say it's the thrill of the unknown and it's the body's very primal urge to find out about consequences of the unknown.

As they explained it though, most people who feel this "call of the void" thing don't actually act on it. Their common sense and functioning brain kick in and they realize that they could die and avoid the outcome all together. They said they rarely saw it in children as young as Arlo, but that it definitely happens from time to time.

Now, my girl swore up and down that she'd only jumped to win the bet, and we left it at that. We fished again and again, many times after that and never once did she jump in again, or even take her vest off while swimming. I put the time in though to make her a stronger swimmer.

I started by taking her out a little deeper and a little deeper, always right next to her. I knew she had to be comfortable swimming underwater, just in case she was ever to "fall off" of a boat again. We finally made it deep enough that I would actually have her take a deep breath and I would yank her down beneath the water with me, a few feet deeper each time, then let her go and watch closely as she would swim back towards the surface. By the time she was eight or nine, she was able to dive to about ten feet in depth and make her way back up with not much of an effort. While I felt the fear of her drowning had passed, I would never be able to forget that smile that crept across her face that day in the lake, the empty green eyes that had held no expression. Those eyes would haunt me for many nights through the years after that.

I had pulled up to the lake in the early afternoon sun, just in time to see the old Madame of the Lake push off the shore. She's an old paddleboat that had been restored for visitors, equipped with a little bar and a refinished upper deck for site-seeing. With her paddles painted a deep red and her bows a bright white, aligned with shimmering fairy lights on the outdoor deck on the top, she actually was a pretty appealing attraction for visitors. During the warmest of summer months, the Madame would host three tours a day, charging guests twenty bucks a head to grace the little muddy lake on such an esteemed way to travel.

As I got out of the car and went to grab the fishing gear out of the backseat, the Madame's horn just about shot me right outta my skin. My heart paused, making me frantically cough before I began to giggle like a school kid again. I headed on down towards the closest public dock, happy that I didn't see anyone else out there fishing just then. I just wanted a little peace, a little time to sit in silence with only my own brain to bug me. I didn't feel much like entertaining anyone else.

The stress of the last few days surely hadn't left me in the best spirits, and I could feel the ache in my heart settling into my bones. As I perched myself on the edge of the dock, reaching for my little squigglers to stick onto one of my hooks, I could hear the laughing of the people that were having a good time touring the little lake upon the Madame. Oh, how I miss the sounds of people enjoying life. Hell, I missed the sound of my own laughter. With a less than focused tremor in my hands, I successfully got a little squiggler attached to my hook and cast out the line as far as I could throw it.

It had been early afternoon, with little to no clouds passing overhead, but the breeze was forgiving. I held the old pole loosely while slowly reeling it back in and felt a heavy exhaustion settling in. It was getting a little harder to cast the line out, but I figured that I was just tired.

Sitting on the edge of the well-worn and splintered old dock, staring down into my reflection bobbing on the surface, I thought about what that doc had said about Arlo the time that she had fallen off of the boat... the call of the void. A chill rose up my spine and screamed down both arms, making my muscles seize and the hairs on my skin stand on end.

In that single painful moment, I felt completely and utterly alone. I had gotten lost staring into my reflection, questioning why in the hell I was still standing, what my purpose even was on this dust ball of a planet anymore.

As I let out a weighted sigh and actually hesitated to draw in another gritty breath, a strange thing had happened. While I was staring into the dark murky water below me, a dark tunnel began to cloud my peripheral vision and the sun began to become blindingly bright straight ahead of me. The bright ball of fire on the horizon warmed my soul, and I began to feel at peace. Where my arms had felt painfully chilled only moments ago, a new sensation, a warmth had begun to crawl up them, making its way towards my back. I could feel the heat radiating towards me and felt compelled to move towards it, out into the calm waters. It was as if this warm light was coming directly towards me, and I needed to duck under in order to go into it... I wanted to go into it, so mesmerizing, so peaceful, so.... The sound of laughing from the old paddle boat startled me and ripped me back into the moment.

"Shit!" I grumbled at no one in particular, with the stark realization setting in that I had just dropped my damn old pole into the water. Only the splash of the pole, and the fear of losing the expensive, yet second-hand, reel had brought me outta my funk. As I scrambled to lean over the dock, reaching for the pole, the chill had returned, the warmth had left, and all that I had been left with was the fading laughter of the tourists on the lake.

"Bobo! Hey Bobo, is that you?" came a voice I instantly recognized from down the dock. I didn't even have to turn around to know who was making her way towards me. I had known that voice since she was just a little kid, hanging around with her brother and Rhoads, eating homemade popsicles V used to make out of fruit punch from a can in my front yard on sticky summer days.

"Well, hey there Sheriff!" I exhaled, out of breath from grabbing my pole.

"Still don't sound quite right when you say that, Bobo," Mindy Lee laughed. "You doing OK? I mean, you look pretty tired..." she trailed off in a less intimidating voice.

"Oh, I'm good, girl, I'm fine. No reason to worry about this old dog. I still got a lot of fight left, ya know?" I forced a laugh from my gut while wiping the sweat from above my brow. I hadn't thought it had gotten that hot out, but I was sweating like a pig at that point.

"So, what's got you out here thinking this time?" the question came outta nowhere. This girl had always shot straight from the hip, standing there with her thumbs in the hoops of her belt buckle, shifting her weight uneasily from side to side.

I cleared my parched throat, now focusing on the small gal that still looked like she was dressed for Halloween every time I saw her in uniform. Her blonde hair was pulled tightly back into a bun, much like V used to wear, and her gun that rode on her hip looked too heavy on her slight frame, with no hip for it to really even ride on.

Glancing down at the dock in sheepish remorse, I blurted out, "Oh, damn Methodist Hospital. They are keeping her for another seventy-two hours again, but just the seventy-two. That's all they can do. You know her... always fiercely barking, but never a bite. I gotta go back and get her in a day or so, just waiting for the call," I answered, accompanied by a sudden light-headedness that made me want to sit back down on the dock. She must have seen the panic sweep over me because she too-quickly popped a squat right next to me.

"Whoa there Bobo, ya sure you are feeling OK? You are looking kind of pale..." she hesitantly whispered in a hushed tone as she wrapped one arm around my shoulder. The warmth of her arm awakened my heart again and for just a second, it was like she was a kid again, not a sheriff worried about an old guy like me, but just the neighborhood kid who was worried about her neighbor.

I was taking a few deep breaths, trying to slow my heart rate which had begun to pummel my chest, then decided that maybe I needed a pop, a little caffeine for that damn light-headedness. "I think it's just a little low blood sugar is all, you know, that and the stress. I'm just tired," I spoke, turning my face back towards her. The look of worry quickly washed off her brow and her emerald green eyes danced with the shimmer of the water.

"Oh! Let me run to the car, I have a cooler!" she half shouted and was off running before I could get another word in. Watching her little legs carry her swiftly down the dock, I remembered how good she had always been in track as a kid, which made me giggle a little. She may not have been big enough to cause much damage to anyone, but her mighty little spirit and fast little legs served her well in the force.

I felt like I was miles away from that moment, so far away from the old splintering dock that I was resting on. I watched her as she heaved the cooler out of the trunk of her car and carried it towards me on the dock, walking with her hip hitched out while trying to balance the thing on her slight frame. I couldn't help but chuckle. In my heart, she looked like a kid still playing dress up.

"Here ya go, Bobo, let's have a pop!" the Sheriff that still looked like a kid said as she grabbed a couple of pops out of the cooler and plopped them on the dock next to me. With an angel's grace and a toddler's excitement, she kicked off her boots and socks and rolled her pant-legs up to her knees.

"Well now, what the heck are you doing, girl?" I laughed while grabbing one of the pops off of the dock. I couldn't get that damn lid unscrewed fast enough, and by God, that first icy cold slurp about cut my throat like razor blades on that warm day.

As her bright pink painted toenails dipped down below the lake's surface and she settled herself sitting next to me on the dock, she laughed. She laughed like I hadn't heard a young girl laugh in years and my heart had begun to ache for those days back when. The days when the kids were still young, and V was still by my side. The days when my body didn't defy me, and I could make better sense of the world. I was tired of being so alone. It had been so long. Sitting out there on that dock, sipping that icy pop and hearing her childlike giggle, I just wanted it all back.

I hadn't realized that I had begun to cry, and this childlike sheriff was too polite to call me out on it. Instead, we sat in silence for a few more minutes, just sipping our pop and listening to the sounds of the water lapping up against the rocks on the beach's retaining wall. I could have sat there all day, and I felt like she probably could have too, but life still had to keep moving on.

"Feeling a little better now, Bobo?" she asked in-between the last few sips of her pop, turning her face towards me and meeting my eyes in a gaze of genuine concern. I was locked in there for a minute. Her gaze had such a familiar hold, caring yet authoritative, pleading yet humble, like my V.

"Let me follow you on home, Bobo. I just want to make sure you get there safely. I think this weather and the stress of things lately has really gotten to ya..," the little sheriff pleaded while shaking her toes off and trying to wrestle her socks back onto her little damp feet.

I just stared at her for a moment, watching as the sun bounced off of the water and reflected onto her face, nearly blinding her and making her squint as she spoke to me. She reminded me of a toddler with her face all scrunched up in frustration.

I simply laughed again and told her I was fine, that it must have just been the low blood sugar, and that I would be OK making my own way back home. She helped me gather up the fishing gear and walked me back to the car. I can still see her standing there at the back of her cruiser, staring at me in disbelief, waving at me as I drove away. Of course, the girl wouldn't take no for an answer and called me at least three times that night after I had made it home just so she could sleep better knowing I hadn't croaked yet, at least not on her watch.

CHAPTER 6
LEARNING TO FLY

ON THE third full day she was in there, I had to try to keep moving to keep from going crazy. That morning, after feeding Fifi some well-deserved tuna out of the can and scratching her around the ears a little bit, I just stood in the center of the living room of my old trailer, staring out the window, searching for answers. I really didn't know where to turn or how to handle Arlo after I brought her home. For years, we have played the cat-and-mouse game, and I am always there for her when she falls. But I am getting old. Hell, she's getting old enough to know better.

With a heavy sigh, I stood there, bare feet nestled into the thick blue, now matted shag carpeting that had been lovingly picked out by V so many years ago but had seen better days. Standing in our little living room alone, I felt the enormity of life weighing heavily on my shoulders and pushing down into my heart. This wasn't how I had thought our lives would go. I had been left alone for far too long and still had too many years to go on this damn dust ball.

As I stared out of our bayed window in the little living room, I watched as the wind picked up the dried dirt and began to spin the dust dizzily in the distance. I let my mind fall away from the despair for just a few seconds, imagining a time when life was still stable, when V was around, and when Arlo was still too young to be too wild.

I could see her sitting out there on her little metal swing-set under the forgiving shade of the old sycamore tree. She must have been only eight or nine, hair tightly pulled high on top of her little head into a ponytail by V. Rhoads was on the road working all the time, so we were helping out with Arlo a lot back then. But it didn't bother us none. In fact, that girl brought so much laughter into our home that it never felt like work when we were supposed to be caring for her. She had always been a bit of a wild one.

My ears could still hear that giggling Kermit the frog voice hollering out for me to come out and push her on the swing. I could remember yelling back at her that I would be out there in just a minute. I had been hanging some heavy crushed blue velvet drapes in the dining room off the kitchen that V had found second hand in honor of the King himself. I could hear her chattering away to Bast in the distance, carried in on a cool breeze through the fraying window screen that had been graciously letting the flies in, only to get stuck onto the yellow tape hanging from the ceiling in the living room. I had just turned my back to fasten another screw into the wall for the drapery rod when I heard her bellow out a gut-wrenching yell. She had gone from giggling and chattering away to hysterically crying within seconds.

The air in my lungs began to suffocate me, and my heart began to fill my ears. Fear had clutched its ungodly claws around my throat as I painfully turned towards the window. For a split second, my eyes and brain were unable to connect and figure out what the hell I was staring at with my mouth hanging open. In the few seconds that I was frozen there, this is what I remember watching move its way towards me...

The green and silver metal swing set with the rusty crossbars and slowly leaning slide stood behind where Arlo now lay in a crumpled pile towards the side of the slide. At first, there was no motion, just the bellowing cries coming from somewhere beneath that crumpled pile of curly hair and green terrycloth jumper that V had picked out for her that day. By the time I had made it out the back door, the crying had stopped... which was almost spooky. I like to think it was the shock of what had happened that calmed her down, but no matter. What I saw next was still spooky as all hell.

As I flung open the screen door and hopped over the three steps that led out of the trailer, my soul took a hold and stopped my body in its tracks. Maybe it was out of fear. Maybe it was out of disbelief. It ain't no matter why. I just know that I froze still as a popsicle when I saw her.

In the hot summer sun, with dust whirling behind her, this pint-sized doll was calmly walking straight towards me, no words escaping her lips. The way she was standing was what threw me off and took me a few seconds to process my mind through. As she was walking towards me, slowly and effortlessly, her right arm just kind of hung funny out to the side. I could see the crimson stain on her terrycloth jumper and trailing its way down towards her fingertips. The only way I could explain what that arm was doing was... well... it just dangled off the side of her little body.

She was calm as she could be, but when she got closer, I could make out the tears that were still spilling out over those green eyes, and the shocked look of desperation in her little dirty face. All at once, she started shouting at me.

"Ouch! Bobo, it hurts! It hurts Bobo!" she howled as she made her way to right where I had been standing. Out of instinct, or maybe just out of fear, she didn't reach with her other hand to feel what was going on at the source of that pain. She only stood there, crying and staring at that damn dangling arm.

I screamed for V, who I had left inside holding the curtain rod up. Out she flew, knocking into me in the process. Like she was on autopilot, V just knew what to do. I tend to freeze up in situations, getting confused easily and all panicky. But not V. She calmly told me to get the car, calmly grabbed some ice, put it in a washrag, then calmly held Arlo all the way to the hospital as I drove.

I remember little of the twenty-five minute drive, only the sound of V's voice soothing the girl and the way the blood transferred onto V's pretty light blue blouse. Arlo was pretty worked up, carrying on about Bast, angry that he took off after she fell.

"What on earth were you doing out there, dolly?" I could hear V asking her in such a hushed and gentle tone.

"We were just playin'." Arlo began, "We were waiting for Bobo to come on out and push the swings and do the ice cream twister... you remember what that is, don't ya, Nonna?"

Even today, thinking back on those times, on her innocent little voice on that hot summer day, I choke up thinking about that talk. That girl was meant to be outdoors, always had been that way. If she wasn't unearthing worms and burying treasures, she was falling down rock piles and scraping her knees from falling off her bike. But she always wanted this old man around. The ice cream twister was named so because of her love of the chocolate and vanilla twist soft-serve we would get on our rides home from the quarry at the little drive-in that V used to work at.

She would sit in the little plastic board of the swing, and I would twist her around and around until the swing chains were nice and tight and her little rump was about waist high off the ground. Then I would give it a little push and let go. She would spin and spin and giggle until it stopped... then want to do it all over again.

"Of course, I remember, little dolly. Go on," V cooed, coaxing the rest of the story from the broken little body sitting next to me.

"Where was Bast when you jumped?" V asked, rolling down the car window with the hand crank and letting some of the gritty air make its way through and settle on our skin. You get used to feeling the grit in your teeth and dust on your skin out here in Oklahoma. The winds may come and stir everything up, but dust settles on us all.

"Well," her little voice went on, "we were waiting and then Bast said he thought I could fly. He thought I was small enough and smart enough that I could fly. I told him I didn't think so, so first, HE climbed up and stood on the top of the slide and jumped off! Guess what??? He DID look like he flied a little bit," Arlo continued, stopping only to adjust the ice on her arm and look V right in the eye as she said. "So, I thought I could do it too, cause I ain't letting no boy think they can do something better than me, not even Bast!" she huffed.

"Him was standing next to the swings, telling me I could do it, shouting that I was so brave. I was gonna do it! I was gonna fly for sure! So, I climbed up to the top and sat there for a minute cause it's really scary to stand on the top of the slide. But I did it! I stood up and got dizzy and scared and right when I was going to jump, that darn slide wobbled to the side, and I fell off. I fell right off! Didn't get no chance to even fly," she almost whispered, looking down at her bare tanned toes, which had a full day of dirt and mud lodged in between them and under her toenails.

"And then what? Where was Bast then?" V prodded the now whimpering little girl.

"Him was gone Nonna. As soon as I screamed, him was gone. And I never got to fly," she huffed again. "And then my arm hurt real bad, so I got up and saw Bobo!"

With a panicked hesitation in her voice, she blurted through tears, "Is my arm gonna fall off, Nonna? Am I gonna be OK?"

"Honey child, that little arm will be just fine! You are a tough and brave little bird; I just know it. You get that from your daddy, ya know…" V said, calming the girl.

Her daddy. My son. Although there is a distance between us now, it wasn't always that way. And he WAS brave. And he WAS strong. And they were two kinds of the same bag of wonderful. In another life, maybe we will get it right. Maybe we won't have to go through everything that we had to. Maybe he could just grow up being a kid and not have to take on such responsibilities. In another life, maybe we can get it right.

But that day in the car, whatever had gotten us to that point didn't matter. I was getting things right this time around. I was taking care of business for him now, which happened to be an eight-year-old ball of fire with green eyes, a mop of curly blonde hair, and his fiery attitude and sharp humor.

I don't remember much else of the car ride, just the closeness of the three of us in the front of that car in the summer heat, grinding the grit between our teeth as the breeze blew in off the gravel road. She sat right between V and me, like always. When we used to go to town and stop for a burger, right between V and me had always been her spot. From there, she knew she had both of our full attention, plus she could see any car that passed by, just waiting for the next Volkswagen to troll on by so she could smack either of us (usually me) in the arm and shout out, "Slug Bug" and whatever the color of the car was. These were simple pleasures.

While I can't recall too much of the ride, I DO remember what happened when we got to the hospital. When you bring in a little girl wounded like that, in such a horrific way, you can bet damn sure you will get the side-eye from each and every damn doctor and well-meaning nurse. Seemed like no matter how many times Arlo told her story, there was always one more nurse or one more doctor waiting to hear her version again.

Meanwhile, they were taking x-rays and trying to figure out what to do about that busted up little arm. She whimpered with every X-ray because they had to move that little arm into so many different positions between those X-ray plates to be able to see it clearly. She may have whimpered a little, but that little girl handled it like a champ.

She's always been a little scrapper, a little tougher than she really meant to be, but that was born out of necessity. From the day her mama had her, she came out fighting to survive. I suppose when your first breaths of air on this earth are only taken forcefully and through struggle, it's a hell of an introduction to life. Makes sense to me now why this little specter of wild hair and bone could raise so much hell without lifting so much of a dainty, yet dirty, little finger.

Turned out, thinking she could fly caused a pretty good break in that little arm. Arlo ended up breaking the bones right above her elbow, as well as right below. She had to have pins placed just to get the mangled little arm to heal right. I can remember sitting in that little waiting room on the hard purple chairs that time had faded to gray, watching the ceiling drip water into a spot on the floor when she walked out with V, all smiles and a bright pink cast on her broken little wing. It would take more than a little wing damage to keep that bird grounded, that was for sure.

For the next six weeks, and right in the middle of the unbearable summer heat, we weren't supposed to let her get that damn cast wet. V knew that there was no way to keep an Oklahoma kid outta the water in the middle of the summer. Bless that woman, she followed that child around the rest of the summer with bread bags and twist ties to cover the arm up as best she could so that Arlo could still have a somewhat normal summer. She even fashioned her an "itchy stick", as Arlo called it, made from an old wood spoon wrapped tightly with a bulb of gauze on the end, so that she could reach down beneath the cast to get a good scratch in when the creepy-crawliness set in on that dry and healing skin.

Bast never did come around the rest of that summer. In fact, we hadn't heard his name uttered again until that fall, when we got the call from school that Arlo had gotten herself in trouble at school for socking a kid in the lip. When I asked her why she did it, she said the other kid kept calling her weird and saying she had no dad and calling her trailer trash. Arlo had had just about all her little heart could take, so she cocked back and smacked him, closed fist, right in the mouth. I have to admit, I giggled when I had to drive to school and pick her up, thinking of little Arlo pounding some snot-nosed do-gooder right in the kisser. That a girl, my Arlo!

I had asked her who had she ever seen fight like that, or where did she learn it, and of course her answer was Bast. Bast the troublemaker may have been good for a little something after all. I guess I started to warm up to the idea of Bast hanging around a little more after that, if no other reason than he gave her confidence in a world where she needed the backbone to brace herself against all the things that life had already stacked against her.

That was a lifetime ago. It felt like, as I stood there in the blue shag carpeting, staring out the front window, putting off the inevitable. She wasn't a kid anymore, and I was getting too old to keep chasing her down and trying to tame her. At some point, we had to learn how to just be. At some point, she had to learn how to settle that wild heart and make a life for herself, cause the good Lord knows I won't be around forever.

Fifi let out a contented meow from the gallows of her full furry belly, resting comfortably now on Arlo's old bedspread I'd draped over one end of the couch. That bedspread had now faded to a soft pink with torn roses and stuffing, or whatever you call that crap poking out from the inside. I wanted nothing more than to curl up in contentment myself and just stay there a while, letting her purrs lull me into a false sense of security and allow me to rest peacefully for a few blissful hours. I let out a sigh and turned to make my way to the door. There would be no finding peace today. Almost as if I was subconsciously trying to pause time, I kind of hung out by the door, where V had planted some indoor plants years ago. They sat in a built-in planter on top of a half wall that served as a divider between the doorway and the living room.

Standing there staring at the empty planter, I couldn't actually remember how long ago it was that the plants died, or why I never had bothered to replant anything else in there after V had gone on. It just sat there empty now, still full of the black potting soil that had dried almost to dust now. If I tried hard enough, though, I could still see it full of life, with V's blooming Christmas cactus spilling over the sides and Arlo's Christmas stocking tacked to the side of the half-wall, just waiting for Christmas morning.

I turned to glance out at the empty living room that sat in a deafening silence now among all the loud memories that were roaring in thunderous claps through my mind. Arlo and V having tea at the side table, V decorating her white aluminum Christmas tree with her blue plastic ornaments in front of the bayed window, playing cards with the kids at the table. I could see Arlo home sick from school, laying on V's couch while munching on store brand soda crackers watching daytime soapies with V, Rhoads hanging out in the kitchen hoping there was one maple Long John left in the box that I would pick up from the little bakery over on Main Street on the days that I would take a load of garbage to the dump. Yup, for as much pain as this little trailer had endured over the years, it'd sure had a life well lived, too.

I suddenly patted my shirt pocket that held Arlo's treasure and turned to limp over to the shelving unit in the dining area just off the kitchen. Maybe I should set it there for safekeeping for one more day, until she's home. We had built shelves there a lifetime ago, first for V's treasured tea sets, then space was made and eventually taken over by Arlo's growing collection of rocks and other trinkets she would collect while roaming about out in the wild.

I stared at one of V's remaining tea sets, the one that was a cream bisque that had fading roses on the front of the teapot and gold painted spout and handles. Those old, worn handles had been cracked off and re-glued more times than I could count. Out of all the fancy tea sets that V had collected, that particular one was always a favorite. It's the only set that she would use with Arlo when she was little, filling it to the brim with hot chocolate instead of tea, then adding a nice side of store brand chocolate wafer cookies, one of their favorite treats.

How V had come to purchase such a fancy set was a whole other story, one that made a smile creep slowly across my lips yet again, while I was standing there with Arlo's rock in my hand admiring that old teapot in all of her worn out glory.

V had admired that tea set in the window of a little five-and-dime in the next town over right after we'd been married. Hell, we couldn't afford it, and she wouldn't have ever even asked. But every time we went over into town to grab supplies, I would catch her glancing at it wildly through the storefront window, checking to see if it was still there.

That little five and dime had been coming up with new ways to advertise and attract attention to itself from the surrounding tiny towns. The summer after we were first married, V had heard that they were going to hold a rocking chair contest. The idea was that you had to sit in their storefront window rocking away, taking no breaks and keeping that old wooden rocker moving along. You just had to keep going, and the last one rocking would be declared the winner and walk away with a prize of one hundred dollars.

You should have seen the determination in that woman's eyes when she sat in that chair, in that storefront, for a total of fourteen hours and eleven minutes, with not so much as a pee break. Looking through that storefront window at her, I could see that grit and grace even back then, the same grit she'd handed down to her granddaughter. When that woman had her heart set on something, she forged ahead until she got it.

Blinking back hot tears while staring at that little teapot that V had lovingly carried home after her big win, I rolled the little treasured rock around in my fingers a few more times and decided to drop it back in my pocket, keeping it close until I could give it to Arlo myself. I spun around and headed back out the door to go work on Elvis for a few hours to pass the time.

CHAPTER 7
WEED MANIFESTO

NOW YOU may think that after all the life that this old man had managed to live and all the nightmares that I'd survived in my waking hours that there wouldn't be too much that I hadn't seen or that would surprise me anymore. I tell you what, though; you couldn't be further from the truth.

While I was blissfully trying to catch a few winks of shut eye after coming in from a good couple of hours of shining up Elvis in the garage, I must have had one hell of a dream, cause when I came to from my stupor, I shot off of that old couch with the faded roses and hightailed my ass to the back of the trailer to where her room sits. Well, it had actually been her daddy's room, but over time, the need for Arlo to have a place to stay became more important than keeping it a shrine to a son I barely knew anymore and who would rarely make it home.

One afternoon after V was gone and I had only time on my hands and emptiness in my heart, I spent a lonely Saturday night packing up his old drag car models and drawings of cars that he'd spent hours doodling and replaced them all with Arlo's rock collections, stuffed animals and paintings that she'd made. It was that simple. I had packed away and moved out one heartache to let another one reside in its place.

Anywho… like I was saying, I don't remember much of what I had dreamt of when I fell asleep late that afternoon after burning off time in the garage. I can remember that Arlo was in it, and she was begging me to get something from her room. Then I don't remember much else except that by the end of the nightmare, her entire room had folded into itself and fallen into a great dark crater, almost grave-like. In a confused and feverish fit, I woke up and sprinted to her room in the back of the trailer, not knowing what I was looking for, but half expecting something awful to happen when I opened the door. I put my hand on the thrifted antique brass doorknob that V just *had* to have and curled my arthritic fingers tightly around it, pausing before I entered.

Right as I went to push the door open, I heard a loud thud coming from right behind the door, even feeling the vibrations of the weight hitting it through the thin veneer of wood into my body. My heart seized and my breath became shallow and stalled in my throat, which had become dry from all the dust swirling around in the trailer since I'd once again left the windows open.

In fear, I stood there in the doorway to her bedroom, trembling as sweat began to bead across my forehead and crawl down my temples. I had still been half awake while staring at the door and trying to sort out what was real and what had been a dream when I felt a small head nudge into my right calf. Damn cat just about took my breath away and knocked me over all at the same time.

"Awe Feef…." I exhaled and let out a little relieved sigh. I knelt down to grab her and stow her under my arm as I made my way into the comfortable, yet small little room that held so many memories and seemed to unlock the floodgates of our past. Somehow, not being alone made me braver. Even if all I had to protect me now was the ragged, half blind, three-legged furball.

As soon as we made our way into the room, she leapt from under my arm onto the bed that still was covered with the thrifted white chenille bedspread that V had always kept on it in the summer months. My eyes began to dart quickly around the little room, and it was no surprise to find that we were completely alone. Hell, I don't know what I thought would be hiding in here waiting for me. Instead, it was just me and Fifi.

I walked in and sat on the bed, smelling the clean scent of the bleach that V had taught me how to water down and use when washing this bed cover, always ensuring that it stayed crisply white. To the right of the bed sat V's old stereo cabinet, filled with her old records, and on top of that sat one of her favorite porcelain pitchers and bowls. It was a garish rusty red in color with a smoke gray overcoating, and in the dead center of that thing was the face of a gray poodle.

V had always loved poodles, and when she saw this monstrosity at a tag sale, she had to have it. For years it sat in our dining room on a shelf next to the dinner table. Arlo had grown up around that thing, always being careful not to bump it or knock it over. By the time she had reached her teenage years and her Nonna was gone, she sort of became attached to it and claimed ownership over that gnarly looking thing. That was Arlo, though. Much like her Nonna, she could find beauty in just about anything and anyone. Forgetting about the thud that had just scared the wits outta me for a few seconds, I stood up and instinctively walked over to the little rusty red pitcher and bowl.

I glanced down at the top of the American Walnut-stained stereo cabinet and noticed a dust ring that was out of place, meaning that the pitcher and bowl had been moved recently, also exposing my lack of housekeeping skills. As Fifi was purring on the bed, kneading her paw into one of the pillows, I gently tipped the pitcher to the side and glanced over the porcelain lip. What caught my eye made me bust out in laughter and left me a little stunned… although why should I have been?

My big, old, weathered hand would never fit into the delicate lip of the pitcher, so I tipped the contents out onto the top of the stereo cabinet. A lighter with a glittering Elvis emblazoned on the front with rhinestones, a key with a palm tree keychain, and two joints now lay before me. That girl. The fun never ends.

I picked up one of the joints and lighter and sat back down on the old chenille bedspread. "She's still up to her old ways," I said to no one as I rolled the joint between my fingers. I could remember the first time she'd gotten into trouble for this. I mean really, in the land of awful things and the broad spectrum of available street drugs, pot was at the bottom of the list as far as being dangerous. But still, at twelve, it was something I didn't want her doing.

The biggest problem was that her introduction to the mind-altering and heart numbing substance had actually started with us, her grandma and grandpa. It's not like we were big potheads or anything. But when I fell into that rock crusher, it left me in a lot of pain that I just had to kind of fight through for many years.

Then came along the magic of legalizing cannabis for medical reasons. Now, when I first had the idea, V was staunchly against it. "Like hell, Bobo. We did not escape the hippie era unscathed just for you to sit around in your golden years getting high," she would tell me. But then that sweet woman fell sick. The chemo treatments and cancer itself had become so painful as it metastasized into her spine that she would quietly just sit in tears. It wasn't until all treatments had been exhausted and she had entered her hospice phase of life that I was able to talk her into some herbal relief. She had been braving the pain for so long; I think that she just wanted to finally find some peace.

So, it was us, Arlo's grandparents, who had initially brought pot into the house. V would only use it when Arlo was at school, so we figured she hadn't caught on. After V left us, I had used it a couple of times, and whether you want to say it was because of my grief or physical pain remains to be decided. I didn't even really like it; I hate to lose control of my senses. But Arlo always seemed to chase a perceived calmness in a world that had continually thrown chaos in her direction.

She was twelve when I caught her hanging out in the fraidy hole with Bast, puffing away and trying not to cough as that sweet oil coated her young lungs. She had only smoked her way through half a joint when I caught her, but her eyes were half opened, and she was babbling about the leprechaun on the cereal box and how he was going to attack her if she fell asleep. With one hand in a bag of chips and a diet pop between her legs, she sat sprawled out in an old lawn chair down there.

I could laugh about it now, sitting on her old bed, holding that old joint in my hand. She wasn't a kid anymore, no longer my responsibility after all. Still, there I sat. My fingers fumbled with the old Elvis lighter that used to sit on V's dresser, and I lit that sucker up. With a big inhale, my body recognized that sweet taste and I felt a warm and welcome tingle reach clear to my toes.

I stood back up while taking a second hit and reached to put the hideous pitcher and bowl down onto the floor so I could open up the old record cabinet. I grabbed the first record out of its sleeve and placed it on the turntable, lining up the arm and needle. The old speakers crackled and came alive as the voice of a young Elvis filled the room. After the third drag of that sweetness, I placed the pitcher and bowl back in the cabinet and I flopped backwards onto the bed, not realizing I had grabbed that old key that had been sitting next to the joint, and laid there staring at the ceiling with it in my hand.

"Hmm... hmmm. Hmm..." I could only hum along as his majestic deep voice filled the room and the early afternoon sun danced along the walls, throwing shadows onto the ceiling. Fifi sauntered over to where I lay and jumped onto my chest, where she then commenced with her nap and purring. In that moment, in that lonely and empty trailer, I felt a warmth I hadn't known in a while. Maybe it was the sun. Maybe it was the decent pot Arlo had left behind. I was enjoying just lying there with Fifi, listening to the King's low voice rumble into my ear while a forced calmness reached into my soul.

"The little green leprechaun from the cereal box..." I giggled to no one as I lay in my splendor on the old chenille bedspread. I opened my eyes and turned my head towards the wall closest to the door. First, my glossed over and hazy eyes focused on her painting of a seashore that she had made years ago. Actually, I think that was one of the ones that she painted after her first attempt on her life back when she was, what... maybe sixteen? She had painted that one in the treatment center, one of her first attempts at watercolor art. It was good, though, for a kid who spends her days in the dust and rocks, to be able to imagine a seashore that was so lush and alive.

I laid there and thought about how it really was kind of a half-hearted attempt on her life that time, too. She had been having a tough time in school and was hanging out with Bast a lot, smoking the pot that she thought I didn't know about. Kids were tough on her. She was a quiet kid in school but had a feisty temper and was easily riled up. Somehow, with the heartache of her daddy being gone, her mama being too busy to be around, and losing her Nonna V—along with just the "normal" teenage girlie stuff—she got it in her head that she was just done. Or it could have just been a cry for help, cause when I came in from working in my shop that night, there she lay in the hallway floor with a half empty bottle of naproxen and a partially empty bottle of pain relievers spilled out next to her.

It was me who had to drive her over to the ER; me who had to wait in the clusterfuck of a waiting room while they pumped her stomach; and me who was there to pick her up days later after she had told all the counselors precisely what they needed to hear so they would let her go home. Out came my smiling girl, gripping this framed artwork under her wing that never had healed quite right. How something so beautiful could emerge from something so dark and painful never made sense to me.

My eyes then drifted from the painting to the door, down to that antique door handle that V had loved, and then my brain kicked in. "What WAS it that I heard when I came in here?" I thought to myself, reaching somewhere from the back of my mind to recall that memory from just a few moments ago, pre-pot-induced fuzzy glow. I pulled myself back up into a calm and seated position, and when I did so, the key that I hadn't realized I had in my hand scratched my palm with the pressure. I sat there in silence for no more than a few seconds, staring at the key before flinging it in my pocket and looking back towards the door. It was only then that I noticed there was a small patch of paint missing from the upper center of the door. A quick glance downwards and I soon realized why.

The hook that had been affixed there with that double sided sticky crap that was supposed to hold just about anything had fallen onto the floor, the culprit looking to be a large leather satchel bag that had now spilled its contents to the floor and was wedged against the wall as I had pushed my way into the room.

I slowly stood, setting what was left of the joint back down on V's old stereo cabinet, and crouched over the spilled contents and satchel on the floor. As my arthritic hands glossed over a few old photos of Arlo and her folks, the images immediately stung my heart. That girl hoards every memento of a now distant and unfamiliar life. There were a few cosmetic compacts, lipstick, a couple of girly products, and a couple of notebooks scattered about. I gingerly grabbed one and flipped the dog-eared black cover open to reveal foreign handwriting sprawling all over the pages. Some of the writings seemed to be more like journal entries, while some seemed almost like song lyrics. I flopped it back into the pile and flipped open the second notebook, a smaller one that was newer and had a pink cover. This handwriting I recognized.

Reading a few of the pages as my eyes burned and my senses were trying to stabilize themselves once again, I realized what I was holding. Arlo had been looking for a way out. I just didn't realize that she had originally planned to take me out with her.

The manuscript that I was so feverishly flipping through was a detailed manifesto of how to end all of this—she planned to kill us both. Now although there was no way of knowing if this was a recent plan or something she'd concocted years ago out of teenage piss and vinegar, I suspected that the first notebook with its foreign penmanship must have been Bast's. But I knew the free-flowing script that I was looking at was surely Arlo's. The way she had a habit of not picking up her pen when she crossed her T's, or the swirls that she made on the first stroke of her S's were dead giveaways. Glancing only quickly over the sprawling wrinkled pages, I got the feeling that she wanted to be done with this world but didn't want to go alone, also not wanting to leave me behind to fend for myself.

Although reading over a partially completed framework of the planned construction of my own death did make the hair on the back of my neck stand up, this wasn't the first time I'd danced this dance with my girl. When she was about twelve, I woke up one night with her standing motionless at the foot of my bed holding a knife and speaking in a voice that was so unlike her own... almost childlike in comparison. She just kept staring blankly at me and repeated over and over that the aliens were coming for us, and we had to go.

Although my heart was in my throat, I'd had no reason to fear the girl up until that point, so I calmly got up, grabbed the knife from her limp wrist and put her back to bed, chalking the whole thing up to a nightmare. After all, the next morning while asking her about it over her bowl of cereal, she didn't even remember doing it. Night terrors, they said, bad dreams, hallucinations from a lack of sleep and stress.

This, though... this was different. I had spent so many years watching that girl pick herself back up out of the darkness and soldier on that I had come to believe that she was indestructible. She had been doing so well, holding her own the past few years since Bast had disappeared. She had been planning a future, working part time in the mattress factory like her mama had and putting herself through some classes to work her way towards a career in law enforcement. It wasn't until she walked in on that ass-hat Derrick and her so-called best friend that her carefully constructed life built out of grit and fragile ego had come careening down around her into a pile of ash. And now all of her old demons had come back to set up space in her heart.

For a girl who had built a backbone out of equal parts of grit and grace, she was still so fragile, still so easily swayed into thinking that she came from nothing and had nothing to offer. We didn't talk about the incident too much, but she did tell me once that when she walked in on the naked asshat laying on top of her beautiful best friend, she felt that her life had been a lie, like she knew somewhere within her that she wasn't meant to live a life like that, in the big city, married to a soon-to-be attorney. She said that her soul would be forever tied to a different life, one that had meant she would never quite have enough and always had to fight to survive, and that she was just tired of the fighting.

Now, just because she had grown weary of fighting, by no means had she meant that she wanted to take me out with her. For all I knew, this manifesto had been written years ago, maybe after V left us. Maybe after her daddy stopped coming back. Maybe after her mama started dating the new guy with the new family and got a new outlook on life that Arlo no longer neatly fit into. After all, she was lying in that hospital bed right now, and she never attempted any harm towards me before she put herself there. Although *had* she really put herself there? She just kept begging for Bast, asking for him, as if he would either be her savior in backing up her story, or the one holding all the answers.

Damn Alabaster. Damn that kid to hell. I have tried through the years to be kind, to be understanding, to be gracious. When her world was falling apart, by God's sweet grace, she had found him, and many times I think he was all that kept her going. When the kids at school were being relentless towards her, picking on her for her clothes and for everything that she wasn't afforded, he was a kind face in an unkind situation, and for that I have always been grateful.

As they grew older, though, it was as if being singled out and clinging only to each other had made them even more caustic together. The ideas, the trouble, the darkness that had begun to embody them far outweighed any light that he had brought into her world in the early years. I was happy that he took off right before graduation, and Arlo had gotten busy making her own life, steps into the right direction towards a stable, yet fragile future.

So why was it then, that the minute all hell broke loose in her life and she came home to the trailer, he had to come for her and cause the dark floodwaters to rise in her heart all over again? Why did he have to stifle all progress she'd made on her long journey to get the hell out of Freedom?

Whenever she had written it, at least she had chosen a loving way to end me. According to what I was reading, standing there in the middle of her bedroom with my feet buried in the old worn carpeting, I understood that she at least hadn't wanted to shoot me or stab me or hurt me intentionally in any way. I don't think pain or vengeance was what she was after.

From what I had quickly read, she had wanted to poison me, slowly, by adding a little antifreeze at a time to my beer. If that took too long and I was showing signs of pain or sickness, she then had also laid out a semi-detailed trail of ideas to put pain meds in my nightly coffee to knock me out. If that STILL failed, she had thrown around the idea of rendering me at least unconscious with the pills, then gracefully holding a pillow over my face to end me before she took her own life.

Although I had always had an inkling that she may have been out to get me, seeing it scrawled out on paper in her loopy writing still made my guts sink. This world had become unbearable without my V, and I was now being haunted by the thought of being left utterly alone without the girl, too. Maybe she had been on to something... maybe we should have gotten out of here together while we had the chance.

Maybe that was just the decent weed rattling in my head. I shook off the cobwebs in my brain, blinking a couple of times, and stuffed the notebooks back into the binders. I gently put the notebook back behind the door on the floor and then put the old Elvis lighter and remaining blunts back into then garishly red pitcher and bowl with the smokey toned face of a poodle on the front. As I started to leave the room, a thought had hit me out of nowhere... the key! That damn key... I *had* seen it before, and I knew *exactly* what it went to.

Fifi hopped down from the bed and followed me from out of the room in the back of the trailer towards the front door, where I grabbed my hat and reached down to scratch the back of her ears one last time. "It's OK, Feefs, be back in a bit," I said to the little wobbly cat with questionable eyesight who happily stretched out on the shag carpeting back in the living room, all three legs reaching for different directions.

Walking out that front door, breathing in the grit that was swirling around in the air on just another random hot and windy afternoon, I limped down those couple of steps that would lead me towards a future that I wasn't sure of. She's my blood, my heart. I had no reason to fear her.

Instead of walking towards my car though, my body turned on autopilot once again, and I let it lead my heart towards the fraidy hole. My heart was pummeling in my chest, unsure of what was behind that door. I have no good memories of that place, and my soul wanted to retract as soon as my fingers touched the handle on the old door. Holding my breath, I reached into my pocket and pulled out her key that hung from the little palm tree, opening that damn door one last time and stepping back into my own fraidy hole...

CHAPTER 8
TREASURES AND TERRORS

THE MINUTE that I let that old door creak open and took my first tentative step into the old fraidy hole, the fear settled and choked me at my core. As my eyes tried to scan the inky darkness of a sealed room that sat bunkered half underground, and my arthritic fingers hastily fumbled for the pull-chain to flip on the light bulb, my lungs were barely allowing me to take an apprehensive breath.

It was so stupid to be so scared, and I knew that. I tried to reason with myself that when you have been outrunning pain and demons for so long, the body's natural reaction is to react to the past, and this old hole had one hell of a hold on me still. My fingers finally found the old pull chain and gave it a tug. With a slight buzz of current suddenly running through the elements, that old dusty bulb began to illuminate the decaying hole. I don't know what I had been expecting to see in there because it was only the old ghosts of the past that haunted my heart. But I didn't understand why Arlo had carried the key around, where her head was, or what she was hiding in here.

The stuffiness of that sealed storm shelter was broken by the breeze that was now blowing in at my back, almost willing me to take another step inside. I plodded down the remaining couple of stairs and glanced around hesitantly.

Upon first glance, all was as it had seemed just a few months ago when I had checked on the ration supply in there and killed off all the creepy crawlies that had gotten in. I looked towards the small shelf that held the weather radio and a couple of water jugs, then glanced over towards the other wall, where the old blankets and towels sat in their plastic tub. That's when I saw it, the thing that was out of place.

I cautiously walked over towards where the plastic tub of blankets and towels sat and noticed that there had been another tub, a larger black plastic tub that now sat there, out of place and shoved into the corner with an old green tarp hastily draped over the top of it. As I stood in front of the tub of the unknown, questioning what it may have kept away from prying eyes down there in the darkness, I realized then that there were only two people who had access to this place, and the key was last being held hostage by my girl.

"Oh, honey… what have you done now…" I whispered to the stale air, the whisper echoing right back at me, startling me to even hear a voice in all the silence that had engulfed me in that old dingy hole. I didn't have the courage to open the lid of the bin, not just yet. Instead, I slid over a bucket that was sitting by the entrance, flipped her upside down and popped a squat, just sitting there in my fraidy hole, staring at the plastic bin of unknown treasures or terrors that sat before me, letting the solitude of the place eat away at my old bones.

My eyes then darted past the bin and paused, affixed on a familiar part of our past—the old toy robot that had been loved for years, then hastily left behind on a shelf for safekeeping at some point, never to be picked back up by her innocent hands again. There was a time when she had carried that thing everywhere, an old toy that had been her daddy's.

When she had first found it, it was full of dirt and grime from Rhoads playing with it in the gravel piles and dragging it through the dirt, as little boys tend to do. Arlo could see that there was a certain beauty hiding under all of that dirt when she was about six or seven, and dug it out of its previous resting spot, an old damp box full of some of his odds and ends that got left behind out in the shed. She had taken it to V to lovingly clean up, and what they couldn't make shine with a little soap, water, and vinegar, they did with some old model car paint to breathe a bit of life back into it.

That day, while sitting on that old bucket in my fraidy hole, I swear I could see the life still clinging to the soul of that old robot, even if it was just a small shimmer coming from its lovingly painted eyes.

Blinking away at the dust that had been swirling around in that hole, my mind had been triggered by that old robot and I could taste the fear and pain that this old shelter still housed. One of the last times I can remember her clinging to that damn robot was when she was way too old to care about such things.

"Bobo help!!! I'm so sorry Bobo…. Help me!" my mind was able to bring that terrified voice right to the forefront of my brain, oozing the terror back into my soul, much like I had felt on that day she broke my heart.

I could feel the uneasiness, the nauseousness that would settle into my guts and remain there for years after. There are things in this world that the heart and mind just cannot comprehend… things that forcefully embed a dark impression upon your soul… that burn into your mind because your eyes have had no choice but to watch the horror unfold. There had been no option to look away.

Tears crawled effortlessly down my cheeks as I sat in the dimly lit cellar on that old bucket. Pain licked at my heart, and I wanted to throw up then, just recalling the bitter ugliness from that memory.

She had been about fourteen. I knew she had been late coming home from school, but she and Bast were usually out on some grand adventure, so being late wasn't generally a cause for alarm. I had been tinkering in the garage on Elvis, puttering with a new headliner that Arlo had picked out, cause the old one had begun to sag with age and rip.

As I was reaching into the car with a blade to remove some of the last of the remnants from the overhead area, there had been a blood-curdling scream, followed by the sound of the fraidy hole door banging shut against her cement and stone frame. I had dropped the blade and instinctively limped as fast as I could over to the storm cellar. I could hear her cries screaming my name for help. It took this old guy only seconds to get to her, and only those seconds had separated me from what our lives were up to that point versus what they would soon become after.

I had heard struggling behind the door, a shuffling, then just Arlo sobbing. There was nothing in this world that could have prepared me for what lay right behind that door. It was worse than having my leg ripped off in that damn rock crusher. I could have had my heart ripped out just as well at that point.

Sitting on that old bucket, the heaviness of the room and weighted memories finally had gotten to me, and I started to sob. A person can only bury pain for so long. At some point, the sickness and fear and exhaustion just have to spill out so that you can keep moving on. I cried in silence for her. I cried for myself. Mostly though, I just cried for the life that she might have had, if I had only been a few seconds faster getting to her... damn leg. I put my head down into my hands while sobbing, while sitting there on that bucket in my fraidy hole, and just let it all come flooding back into my heart...

There's an emptiness that both veils your heart and leads your soul when you are put into emotionally damaging situations. When a person is exposed to something so shocking, so profound, it's almost as if the soul leaves your body and assesses the situation from above, trying to make all the broken pieces fit together and make sense in order to appease the heart.

I remember the shock. I remember throwing up as soon as the day was over. What I don't remember was ever making a clear thought or decision. I don't recall actually making any type of plan... merely being thrust into a fight-or-flight situation, focused only on remedying the situation at hand. I also cannot remember much of what I said to her that evening or of having any fear of getting caught. But I do remember her pain. I remember her screams coming from the fraidy hole, and I damn sure carry her pain with me, even all these years later.

Sitting on my bucket, I couldn't fight the return of what had assaulted my heart that day. I quit relenting and let myself remember, let time roll back... The first thing that my eyes were assaulted with when I had flung that fraidy hole door open was my Arlo, sitting in the corner clutching her knees to her chest and clutching that damn robot, its eyes glowing at me in the reflection of the beams from the old bulb.

It's funny the things that etch into your mind, the things that history won't let you escape. I see her green eyes frozen wide open in fear, her rosy cheeks smeared with blood. She was rocking back and forth as blood pooled from her seat beneath her on the cement floor and the lower part of her skirt had the lace torn off. It took my brain about two seconds to realize what had been going on down here in this old fraidy hole.

Before running to where she was sitting, I darted my eyes across the floor, making their way to the other side of the old cellar, unprepared for who would be there and in what state. As my eyes fought in the dim light to make their way, my soft heart broke into a thousand icy shards as I quickly assessed a torn pair of ladies' panties balled up and discarded in the center of the cellar, along with a high school football sweatshirt that had been tossed to the side of the room and now lay by the old lantern next to the blankets that had been haphazardly arranged on the cool cement floor.

My eyes then locked upon the shivering and half naked football player gasping for air in the opposite corner from where Arlo now sat crumpled in a panic. Becket Donovan. Light years away from where we sat, seemingly in another world, Becket used to be one of Arlo's best friends. They were into Legos and race cars, drawing and burying treasure together. This was only until the life of an athlete carried him off to be adored and placed on top of a pedestal so high that he forgot how he ever got up there, let alone who all he had stepped on as he rose.

By middle school, he had stopped hanging around, and by high school he had succumbed to peer pressure and stopped even defending his former best buddy. Instead, he would join in when kids would relentlessly pick on her, telling her she was nothing and didn't belong in their world. Something strange had happened the summer before her sophomore year, though. Away from school, away from the other assholes, Becket started stopping by, started paying attention to her again. I could only assume at the time that this was how they ended up in the fraidy hole.

This mere boy, this kid that used to sit on my back porch with my granddaughter eating cold lunch meat sandwiches with squished potato chips in them, the kid that I had taught how to change a tire and hold a bat, sat hunched over, bleeding and clutching his chest, pants pulled down to his mid-thigh, gray football tee-shirt now a dark crimson in the center.

As I walked towards where he was sitting, Arlo shouted out from across the tiny room that now smelled of shame and the irony smell of blood, "I didn't do it, Bobo! It wasn't me!" Then, through her sobbing I heard her form the words, "Bast came looking for me and pulled him off me..." her fourteen-year-old voice faded away, exposing, once again, that of an innocent eight-year-old girl.

"This little light of mine..." I could hear her little voice pleading in my ears as I crouched down next to the bastard. No words escaped his lips, only the gasps of his lungs feverishly trying to swallow just a little more air. I leaned in to see the blue plastic handle of the screwdriver prominently sticking out of his chest. While looking down, I could also see his now limp dick that had shriveled, blood streaked. As fury burned through my veins and a deep hatred now took over my senses, I calmly looked up and into this boy-monster's blue eyes, saying nothing as I grabbed that handle and, with all the force I had left in my body, plunged it deeper into his chest cavity. I do remember that I didn't let go. Not immediately. I had the haunting pleasure and curse of seeing the light slowly fade out of his already dead, yet pleading eyes.

I don't think Arlo and I actually ever talked about what led up to that. I don't need to know and it's something she can't talk about if she wants to be able to move on in her life. Instead, we buried it in the past, much like one of her beloved treasures, much like we buried him. All she kept saying that afternoon and into the night, over and over, was that Bast saved her, that Bast had done it. He had come looking for her and he had done it. I asked no further questions, and we left it at that.

Have I ever felt remorseful for taking the life of a youngin', same age as Arlo? Not once. More than anything else, I've felt guilt over the following years. If only I could have gotten to her faster, we wouldn't have been put in that position at all. But there we were... and he wasn't a light kid. He played defensive back, for Christ's sake. We had to wait that night until way into the evening to go bury our treasure. Good thing for us, our small lot sits on the outer edge of the trailer park, so we weren't too obvious when we rolled Elvis out of there in the middle of the night with her trunk full of putrid cargo.

Our water table is very high and we sit in a flood plain, so we couldn't just bury his stupid ass. Instead, we drove out to the quarry in silence, except for V's eight track humming along, the track that lulled us along through the darkness, taking our minds back to better days and bandaging our broken souls for a while. Van Morrison's "Brown-Eyed Girl," which Arlo had become obsessed with, just kept playing over and over. Now, whenever I hear that song, it gives me hollow knots in the pit of my belly.

It had been well past midnight when we pulled Elvis into the back lot of the quarry, her lights off and nothing but the hum of her engine to be heard around for miles. Although the quarry had long been a place where rowdy kids came out and raised a little Cain every now and then, this was before security cameras had really become widespread, at least in the smaller towns. People were more worried about securing stores and valuables than taking the time to bother watching a bunch of dirt and rocks.

Silently, I parked Elvis and slid out of the car, walking around towards the trunk. Arlo just sat, stunned and silent, in her passenger seat. I had intended to leave her out of this part, to spare her the years of nightmares that would then follow her around afterwards, but let's face it... I didn't have the strength in me to drag this predator's sorry-assed limp body up to the platform alone, and I knew it.

Before we had left the trailer, I had her slide on some old muck boots, the same style that all the guys wore out at the quarry. I wore mine as well, figuring that at best, if anything went wrong, all the cops would have to go on would be a couple of workman's boot tracks just like the thousands of others that had been tracked around in the dirt. Besides, we also had the wind on our side to disrupt the sand and prints.

I stood at the trunk of Elvis, my breath quivering in the shallow pit that had become my chest. I stood there stunned for a few seconds and then let my brain once again run on autopilot. I lifted the trunk lid and peered inside at the old Christmas tree bin that held our nightmare. I figured it would be easier to transport him like this, plus there would be no weird drag marks.

"Shit!" I can remember shouting out to no one as a thought hit me like a freight train. It had occurred to me then that if this was to look like a dumb kid messing around, there HAD to be some kind of prints… the lack of his shoe prints anywhere would definitely be a red flag.

With my body numb and in shock and my brain switched back on auto pilot, I opened the tote to reach inside. His head was turned away from me as I reached down towards his feet to untie his shoes. As I went to pull off the first shoe, his limp body had been jostled and his head rolled back towards my direction. It was garish to see a face after the soul had been wiped away, although evil had already come for his soul long ago.

With a shudder of my own body, feeling the goosebumps crawl across my skin from what my brain was trying to process, I wrestled around in the dark a little, feeling my way around, and then stepped away from the body with the shoes in my hands. Another realization struck. My feet weren't going to fit in those shoes. I'd had so many issues with my right leg since the accident years ago that all the pins and plates and parts make my circulation work like shit and my right foot and ankle frequently swell the size of soup cans. This only left me with one option. An option that I hated myself for, but it was the only way out of this hole.

With an empty sickness that had settled into my hollow chest, I walked over to where Arlo sat in a stunned silence. I opened the passenger side door, illuminating the car with the glow of the dome light to find her staring ahead at nothing, saying nothing and void of any emotion at all, clutching her knees to her chest. She still had blood smeared across her face, still smudges of her own blood dried onto her thigh that was peeking out of her shorts. I knew that what we were about to do was gonna break us both. I knew that we had been broken already. There was no going back.

"Arlo, we need to make tracks," I began, clearing my throat to speak over the purr of the engine that I had left running just in case all hell broke loose and we had to take off quick. "It has to look like he was here, goofing around. Hon, my feet won't fit…" I sheepishly murmured as I extended the dead boy's shoes in my hands towards her emotionless self.

She didn't even look at me. I mean, her eyes looked my way, but her soul wasn't in there. She was an empty vessel at that point. With no words, she dropped her knees and stepped up and out of the car. Ever so delicately, she took the shoes from my arms and sat down at the base of the metal grated stairs, pulling her small feet out of the mucks, and sliding them into the dead boys' shoes, one at a time.

I watched in horror as the moonlight illuminated a small grin that had crawled across her dry lips and realized… she had gotten her first true taste of revenge and it looked damn good on her. Disturbing, creepy even, but good. I watched, stunned, as this creature hopped around the base of the rock crusher in shoes that belonged to her assailant. She stared down at them as she effortlessly danced around and around in the dirt, finally making her way back to the base of the platform.

Only after she'd sat down to put the old mucking boots back on did the grin fall from her lips. Yet, as she handed me the dead kid's shoes, the echoes of revenge still shone brightly in her eyes. She scared me just a little.

Still with no words, we went to the trunk. I had one hell of a time getting those damn shoes back on the boy, being sure to leave one un-tied… evidence of either a fall or how he had perhaps gotten caught on something. I leaned in and snapped the lid back on the top of the tote, so we didn't have to look at him any longer than we had to.

I had looked at Arlo then, wanting to tell her this would all be over soon, that this would all be OK. But when my eyes met hers, I couldn't lie. This would never be over. The fraidy hole would never let go of her mind, always haunting her as she slept. Instead, I simply told her, "There are horrible people in this world kid. You just have to stay one step ahead of them. Now help me get this tote up them stairs, would ya?"

With no words to be uttered, she too leaned into the trunk and helped me lift out that old Christmas tree tote. It was not an easy haul, by no means. I went up the grated rusty steps backwards, pulling the old tote towards me as she stood below, heaving that tote up with the strength of a thousand men. The only saving grace was that the steps up to the top of the platform had been divided up with three separate landings, so it wasn't a steep climb. We were able to rest on the plat-forms on our way up. Still, a limp 160-pound body ain't child's play to move around.

Once we had made it to the top of the platform, I needed her to go back down for two reasons. First, I needed her to run back down and trip the switch when I told her to, and secondly, I didn't want her mind to be as violated as her body had been. There are some things that I could still try to protect her from, and what was about to go down was something her mind wouldn't be able to recover from. Hell, maybe mine wouldn't either.

"Now don't forget, girl, when I tell ya to do it, you put your hand into your sweatshirt to flip that switch so there are no prints, do ya hear me?" I hollered over my shoulder as she made her way back down the platform to the base.

The jaws of the rock crusher sat just below where I was standing on the platform with not much of a barrier or safety rail between. I popped the lid off of the old Christmas tree tote and tipped it onto its side on the edge of the platform. His body sloppily rolled out onto the edge of the landing grate with a slapping sound, making the grated metal stairs shutter in the deafening silence of the night. I stared at him for a half a second, and somewhere within my heart I could hear my V's disapproving voice. "It's amazing what humans are truly capable of..."

I pulled the tote off to the side and stood, gripping the guardrail with both hands, giving the body a couple of good shoves with my mucking boots until it rolled off of the platform and landed with a jarring thud on the rocks still sitting in the jaws of the crusher. I looked away as I hollered down to my girl to trip the switch.

One would think that a body would make snapping noises when being crushed at such pressure. One would think that blood would be sprayed all over, or that there would be some kind of screeching from that old machine. But one would be wrong.

In comparison to what that old crusher is set up to crush, a body is just mush, nothing more exciting than a bag of leaves to her jaws. After a few seconds, I shouted out, "Enough, Arlo! Flip her off..."

I couldn't resist the temptation to glance quickly over my shoulder down towards the crushing jaws as I limped away. It was only by God's grace that I had been spared, and that all I was able to see was the bottom of a tennis shoe poking out among the gravel.

Would you believe that she and I have never had another discussion about it? Even when his body made the news, even when the investigation was splashed all over TV and was all we heard about when we ran into town, we didn't discuss it. We also didn't discuss it when the story that the police ran with was that this young buck had been trespassing, messing around, and had either killed himself on purpose or had met with an unfortunate accident that night out at the quarry. We didn't even discuss it when, after his funeral, I could hear her cries coming from the back of the trailer. There are some things in this dark world that I think are best left to sort themselves out. If we were to bring those thoughts back to life, there would be no locking them back up again.

As I sat there in the fraidy hole, sitting on that bucket, staring down at the misplaced tote that now sat before me, I had to ask myself, "What the fuck had she gone and done now?"

CHAPTER 9
NO GOING BACK

WITH A heavy heart, I rose from my bucket and walked towards the elusive, misplaced tote. Some things in life you are just never well-prepared for, but it's like yanking off a band-aid from a scrape, you just bare down, grit your teeth and do it, pain be damned. I first kicked at the tote with my muck-boot covered toe. I breathed a little easier when the tote bounced a little from the force, cause a tote with a dead body doesn't bounce. I popped off the lid and jumped back, fearing what I might find inside.

Looking away, back towards the door, I first used my sense of smell to help me decide if I really wanted to look or not. Death has a scent, ya know… a putrid and sweet scent that stains the air, a smell that is absolutely identifiable and instantly pungent. Sniffing the gritty and stifling air, I was relieved to find that I hadn't smelt that. There did seem to be a faint scent of iron or metal in the air, though, which was always reminiscent of blood.

Under the overhead glow of the old light bulb that was still buzzing with current and flickering, I slowly turned back to the tote. Peering ever-so-cautiously over the side, I saw a pile of clothes. Shirts, maybe a blanket. I didn't get it. What was the big deal here? What was I missing? I grabbed the tote out from the corner and emptied the contents into the center of the damp cement floor of the fraidy hole.

Along with the clothing and blankets and towels that tumbled out, I also heard a muffled thump. My heart skipped beats, and I almost choked on my own spit, along with being strangled by my own throat that was now dry and refused to allow me to take on any further air. I held my breath and gently tapped at the pile with my toe. There *was* something hard in the center of the pile, beneath the clothes.

The clothes. These weren't her clothes; they were men's clothes. I could see the arm of an orange and brown flannel poking out from the pile and another shirt, maybe a light sweatshirt sticking out of the pile too… "Oh dear God…." I whispered in a hushed tone to myself as my brain began to sort out what I was seeing beneath the dim glow of the overhead bulb. The flannel hadn't been orange and brown… it had at one point been orange and cream, and had now transformed to a rust brown, rust… the color of dried blood.

"What…… have you done girl…" I grumbled, kicking the stained men's clothes around on the ground. A ball-cap tumbled out from beneath where the arm of the sweatshirt had been resting. There was no dried blood on the hat, but I had recognized it immediately. The emblem of the giant pot leaf on the front gave it away, as did the bent bill with the worn edge. The hat was Bast's. But I wasn't sure whose clothes they were, though. They seemed awfully large.

As I leaned over to pick up the sweatshirt from deep in the pile, my eyes locked on something that caused my jaw to hang wide open. I had to catch my breath and sit back down on the bucket. With my head in my hands once again, I tried to calm my breathing… breathe in, 1…2…3… breathe out, 1…2…3… in, out… "This little light of mine…" I imagined her sweet voice.

I couldn't get the vision out of my head, and I had to glance up and open one eye to be absolutely sure that I hadn't imagined it. With a fearful and apprehensive eye, I slowly let my gaze fall back over the pile of clothes and scanned quickly for what I had thought I had seen. And there it was.

Poking out from beneath the pile, still partially entombed in the nest of bloodied laundry, was the shiny black butt of a gun.

Immediately, I started to shut down the questions that were mounting in my brain and let my body go back into autopilot mode.

Once again, I was able to rise above the situation as I calmly stood up from the bucket. A person's soul will go to extreme measures to protect the body that houses it. That is about the only explanation I can come up with for why I have handled the darkest of days so gracefully, and why my nightmares don't haunt my waking hours. I just survive. And sitting in that fraidy hole, staring down at that gun, my survival meant getting to Arlo, maybe getting some clarity. Just like that night all those years ago, I decided to protect her, or her and Bast yet again. I would burn the clothes, whoever's they were. That was an easy enough thing to dispose of. But the damn gun. I didn't know whose it was or what it had been used for, but I was betting there would be Arlo's prints on it.

"Awe, fuck!" I let out an exhausted and soul-worn shout into the dim and empty room. That girl. I was continuously cleaning up after her, protecting her, staying one step ahead of her. It's just what I do, what I had always done. She was all I had left.

I snapped out of my shock, out of my anger, and let the autopilot of my soul kick in once again. I gathered the clothes and threw them back into the bin for now, figuring that when I got back home with Arlo, maybe we could sit out by a fire, toast a few marshmallows, and we could burn them. As I went to grab the gun, I noticed something else on the floor that had been twinkling in the dim light of the failing bulb, hiding like a secret under the barrel of the 9 millimeter. I wanted to immediately throw up when I moved the gun and saw what it was… Arlo's engagement ring.

I stopped all thoughts from getting in my way, tossed the ring into my pocket and picked up the gun. I grabbed an old rag from the shelf that held the emergency supplies and, after flipping the chamber open to see that there were no rounds left, wrapped the gun in it. Then I stuck the gun in my waistband, turned to pull the chain for the light and, though unsteady, headed slowly back out of the fraidy hole. I knew where I needed to go, but before I did, I made a quick stop into the shed to grab my hand spade and small shovel. I threw them into the car, then grabbed an old ice cream pail off the top of the workbench and headed over to the side of the trailer where some of V's roses still grew. Frantically, I unearthed a couple of the smaller rose bushes that had begun to grow and plopped them into the pail along with some extra soil. I tossed those into the back of Elvis as well and was off.

I glanced down at the old blue Casio watch on my arm that was hanging out of the window as I headed down that gritty gravel road. I had a little time. It was gonna be OK. I just had to make it to the hospital by four, and it was only a little past noon. As I pulled out onto the blacktop, I hit play on V's old eight track and the speakers snapped and came alive once again. The sounds of BB King's guitar filled the vacuum of silence that I had been ensconced in.

The sun was blazing as I rounded the bend in the road that would take me to where V lay. As always, out here in the middle of nowhere in Oklahoma, the wind was still raging, swirling the grime around in the air, yet bringing with it a welcome relief from the scorching sun. I pulled into the little public country cemetery, slowing down to watch the geese flutter about in the little pond out on the edge of the grounds. As far as final resting places go, this was as good a place as any to be put back into the earth.

V and I hadn't really been overly religious people, though we had tried to walk the line and do for the greater good. I had never been baptized under any religion, and V had been raised southern Baptist. I don't really know if there's a heaven, and as far as I'm concerned, the hell is here on earth. I do like to believe that there is something bigger than us out there, though, and I like to believe that my V is out there waiting for me somewhere, no longer in pain. That's about as far as my beliefs reach.

Before V left us, she had wanted to get all of her affairs in order. Bless that woman, she knew that I would never be able to give her a proper goodbye or manage to lay things out exactly how she had envisioned them. In her last few months, I traveled with her as we shopped for her casket; she didn't want me to spend a lot, but picked out a nice honey oak colored one lined with pink satin and embellished roses stitched onto the headliner, as well as a pink satin pillow for her to rest her head on.

She picked out her outfit to be laid to rest in too, a nice flowery printed blue dress because like she'd said, "I may be dead, but I don't want to look all dark and dreary." There was to be a spray of red roses laid on her closed casket, as well as a vase of red roses next to her at the small memorial service. But that was it, as she was never one to be fussed over and couldn't stand the thought of people staring at her.

We had sat together at the funeral home and picked out her above-ground vault, a rosy quartz color, as well as the bronze nameplate that would forever tell the world where my V lay in peace. Everything had gone just as she had planned, leaving me with nothing but empty hours to fill when it was over.

She had always liked this cemetery, as it sat out in the country, un-affiliated with any local church. It was a real burial place for the locals which was taken care of by a few local farmers who would have their families out on picnics a couple times over the summers to help clear around the stones and vaults. It really was a beautiful plot of land, with Redbud trees that were scattered along the side of the property that would be a glowing purple in the spring, mixed in with bold Cypress trees that would turn a deep rich red in the fall. V's place of rest was in the shade of a Cypress next to some beautiful butterfly bushes that bloomed a deep purple all summer long.

Because this was a little country backwoods cemetery, you didn't have to put up with the hubbub and rules of an in-town cemetery. We could lay flowers and things out any time of year, with no worries that anyone would bother anything or throw them away. We pitched in to pull weeds and watered each other's plants that adorned the graves. No one was pretentious here. No one gawked at anyone. You were simply left in peace, which is what V had wanted. Hell, people have even come over and buried beloved pets next to their graves or plots and no one thought anything of it, which is why my plan would work perfectly yet again.

I pulled the car over onto the small lane next to where V was at rest and limped on over to her, ice cream pail of rosebushes and small shovel in hand while the gun rested comfortably tucked into my waistband. Setting the things down on the ground, I collapsed into a heap in front of her above-ground rosy quartz colored vault.

My heart ached to hear her voice, to smell her soft skin that had always smelled like the lavender scented night cream she would slather on. It felt like I hadn't seen her in years and yet, also seemed like just yesterday that I'd said goodbye, all at the same time. The memories of her are intoxicating and smothering all at once.

Sitting on the dry ground now at the base of her vault, I began to humbly speak into the wind as the family of geese began to notice me and make their way over towards where I was sitting. They were used to people and hoping that I'd brought bread.

"Awe hell, V, it's so damn hard! I knew losing you would rip my world apart, but it's the carrying on without you that is killing me," I wept as the geese looked on. A truck crept by slowly just about then, only acknowledging me with a wave out the window as they carried on about their own business, then faded in a swirling fury of gravel dust down the road.

As I sat there on the dry ground, letting the dirt and grime swirl around me, I reached out to run my gnarled fingers over the cold raised nameplate that adorned the front of her vault. I do good most days, pushing her sweet memory out to the very edges of my mind, in hopes that the pain of missing her doesn't suffocate me. But on these days, the days where I need her advice or the days where life itself weighs down on me hard, I can barely keep the pain out of my heart and the memories at bay. I let a couple of tears roll down my cheeks and let out an exasperated sigh while talking to no one.

"Oh V, I'm still chasing her, still trying to save her and wearing myself ragged. But what else can I do? She has your feistiness still, you know..." I chuckled out into the silence, letting the sound ride out on the wind into the nothingness that was surrounding me. I felt every hair on my body stand up in the sheer loneliness of the situation, and although it was a warm day, there was a chill that was setting into my bones. Sadness and loneliness will do that to a person. You feel it. It's a hollow feeling in your soul and your body feels... well... empty, I guess.

Sitting there contemplating what my next move was going to be, trying to figure out where Arlo and I would go from this point, I glanced around at the geese, who seemed to be a captive audience. "Hey there old friends..." I hollered over their way, acknowledging them and letting my mind wander for just a moment, pretending that my V was still here, still enjoying the tiniest things with me in our everyday life. I could see her sitting next to me then, when we would come out here to put flowers on graves of recently lost friends and neighbors, giggling her menacing little laugh while flinging bread out towards the birds.

It all moves so fast. One minute we were young and full of adventure, then time winds down and you don't know how the hell you got here, to this place, talking to the ghosts of your past and clinging to memories that you're terrified to lose.

I stood back up, brushing my hands on my pants and startling the small captive audience of geese as I did so. Letting my brain default back into autopilot mode again, I carefully used the hand trowel and small shovel to dig a hole to the right of the base of the vault. I knew I couldn't go too deep, cause of the water table, but had to go deep enough for the rose bush roots and for the dark treasure that I would bury there. No one came 'round, and, aside from my geese friends, no one would be any wiser as to what I had done. I let my mind just go blank while I was digging, only focusing on what I was doing, too afraid to allow the thoughts to come in.

When I had what I thought was a deep enough hole, I grabbed the small starter rose bush that was blooming a fiery orange color of blooms and set it into the hole to test the depth. Seemed pretty good to me, so I glanced around once more to be sure that the only witnesses to my depravity were my feathered friends and ghosts of the past that had no tales to tell, and no one to listen to them, anyway.

Satisfied that I had been completely alone out here in the swirling dust and grime, I gently reached into my waistband beneath my shirt to grab the gun that had been wrapped haphazardly in the old rag from the fraidy hole. With trembling fingers, I laid her to rest in the earth, stopping to stare in awe at the darkness that attached itself to her.

"What had she done?" I allowed the thought to crawl across my mind, waking my consciousness from the autopilot slumber it had been forced into. Blinking a couple of times, I grabbed the starter rose bush of fiery orange and steadied it into the hole with my left hand, gingerly pushing dirt back in to cover up the terror with my right. I stopped just long enough to reach into my pocket and grab her engagement ring, then plunging it into the damp dirt beneath the rosebush. Happy with how the rosebush was standing, I decided that the dirt wasn't quite damp enough yet, and I wanted to be sure that the damn thing survived while killing the secrets that lie beneath her. I hobbled back over to the car to get the gallon of water that had been left in the back seat just in case Elvis overheated.

As I stood there gently watering the bush, I quietly began to once again speak with V. "Remember that damn robot she used to have? The one that you helped her clean up and bring to life again? I bumped into the damn thing in the fraidy hole, V. The thing still terrifies me. Don't look right," I spoke to the cold vault that was in front of me.

"Remember the time that she came to us in the middle of the night with that thing tucked under her arm shouting something about how the robots will protect us and that her daddy was trying to kill us all? Remember that V?" I paused for a second, lost in thought, recalling the creepy feeling of being terrified of an eight-year-old.

"You were never scared, though, were ya? You easily assumed she was having a nightmare and just walked her back to bed. I watched the eyes on that thing as she walked back out of the room, though, a little unsure about the whole thing. That was you though, V... saw the good in everybody and blocked out any thought of the bad stuff. That's where I'm at now, V... trying to push out the bad stuff...." I had let my voice trail off and capped the water jug again. I looked around once more at that little patch of land, wondering what other secrets some of its inhabitants took to their graves, what other secrets are buried so shallow beneath the surface.

Wondering if all secrets manage to stay buried.

I stood, placing one hand back on my sweet V's nameplate, and closed my eyes one last time, willing her face to come to my clouded mind. Her hair was tacked up neatly in a bun and her green eyes danced playfully in the light. I could even smell her face lotion on the swirling gusts of grime that were blowing around me. "Damn it, V… I miss ya. Love ya," I whispered as I turned to walk away. I didn't look back, never did. That was one of V's rules that I had come to live by. Stemmed from her losing her own mama in an accident because she'd forgotten something at the house on the way to a friend's for tea, went back to retrieve it, and was killed by a passing tractor on the way back into town. "Never go back," V would always say, and we never would.

I made my way back to Elvis and sat there for just a moment, watching the geese slumber away towards the little pond, content that their show was over. I had no idea what I was in for next, no clue what I was going to do when I brought Arlo home, or even how I would handle the rest of the afternoon. All I knew was that I loved that girl. She needed me, and I was going to bring her home. No going back.

CHAPTER 10
MENDING THE BROKEN

IT BECOMES almost suffocating watching a person try so hard in life and yet fall over and over again based on their poor decision-making skills. I sat at the table, eating my corn flakes for a late lunch, mindlessly staring out the window onto the back porch where she used to ride her little tricycle around when she was a peanut, allowing the pressure to build up on my heart as I sat in the silence of an empty trailer, reminiscing about our past. The silence of living alone is deafening, so it's easy to let your mind search through past reels of time in order to keep you company, make you feel less alone and a little more in control.

As I sat there, the milk clumsily rolling down my chin with each bit of flakes from my spoon, I didn't want to feel the panic that had set into my soul, didn't want to have to face the reality of where we were in life and try to plan the next steps for her. I felt sick, weighed down with a heavy heart, as anxiety settled into my chest.

Today was the day they would be calling me to rescue her, to pick her up from the hospital and bring her back home. With every breath that I tried to draw in, my lungs seemed to tighten and fight me, and my heart felt like it was on shaky ground. I reached for the Lazy Susan in the middle of the table and grabbed the smaller bottle of heart pills that graced my presence. Flipping the lid off and popping one in my mouth, I wondered if I would have had heart problems if my life had gone a different way.

Maybe I wouldn't have needed that damn pacemaker after I'd lost V, or the shunt placed after Arlo first tried to take her own life, or the defibrillator put in not long after she crashed Elvis and decided to move out.

"Bobo… look how fast I can go," I could hear her saying in my heart as I stared out at the now empty cement patio where we used to spend lazy summer and fall days while she zoomed around on her trike, or scooter when she got a little older, or skateboard when she was older still.

"Hey, you, the cats need their water bowls filled again!" I could hear V's sweet voice urging me to put more water in her fancy bowls for all the feral cats that had made their way to us and found a home. That woman had a love for all stray things, and an affinity for mending the broken. The void in my life still echoed out to me every day, a thousand ways, that she is missed.

I couldn't help thinking to myself while I was sitting there that I was failing at this life thing, at how I raised our granddaughter. What would she have done? What advice would she have for me now? My fractured thoughts were interrupted by the slurping sound that was coming from right in front of me. Shaking my gaze from the window where the sun was blissfully drying the tears to my weathered and warm face, I glanced down at the table, only to see Fifi helping herself to my bowl of flakes. "Go for it kid, live your best life while you still can," I spoke into the emptiness of the trailer, patting the old girl gently behind one ear.

I had decided to not just sit in the trailer the rest of the afternoon waiting for the call. It had become too suffocating, waiting for the hours to tick by until I could go pick her up. Instead, I decided to go out and clean up some of my scrap piles and see if I had enough to haul a load in, cause Elvis could use a new radiator… she'd been overheating a lot these days.

I stood up from where Feef had finished my corn flakes and put the bowl on the avocado green counter and grinned. V had always wanted to change that counter out, to make it a royal blue, but it had always been one of those things you just kept putting off until next year, cause it seemed like too big of a job, until there were no "next years" left.

As I headed for the door, I instinctively touched my shirt pocket, realizing that I was still carrying one of her treasures with me. I had taken the little rock out when I did laundry, setting it on the dryer for safekeeping, then grabbed it and threw it back in my pocket when I had gotten dressed that morning. I'd forgotten about it when I was out at the cemetery. I had thought once again about setting it in the window or on the shelf next to V's beloved teapot, where it would be waiting for her when she made it home. But instead, I decided to keep it with me, a small token of the hope that I carried, and planned to give it to her when I saw her later.

I grabbed my old quarry hat from where it was perched on the edge of the hall mirror next to the front door and stopped as I caught a glance of myself while putting it on my head. I was in awe of the reflection that was haunting me from the other side of the old glass. When had I become so tired, so worn out, so old? It only feels like a short time ago that I was with my V, that we were full of life, and that this trailer was filled with voices of laughter carried by the gritty breeze that would swirl around when the windows were left open. It had been a lifetime ago now that her laughter would fill that old trailer while we danced in circles in the little living room to her old eight tracks, Arlo laughing and clapping us on.

Breaking my gaze from the mirror, I defeatedly glanced towards Fifi, now curled up in the living room on the shag carpet, basking in the glow of the morning sun. This trailer, much like myself, had become only a shell of what it once was. It was sad. It was depressing. It was lonely.

But as bad as I felt swimming around in this loneliness, I was also hellbent on making sure that kid would get her ass outta here again. It didn't matter how much it would sting me to push her out, to goad her back to her own life in the little corner of the world that she had built.

It had to happen. Much like myself, the loneliness would suffocate her here, and I wasn't going to let that happen.

I headed out to the back lot behind the trailer where I had my couple of scrap piles set to the side, hidden beneath a tarp. I had separated out the cans, which really never bring in much for money, but I also had a fair amount of copper that I'd been stockpiling, ripping the wiring out of various scrapped parts that I'd picked up here and there along the way.

It's amazing what people will just give away or throw away because they don't want to go through the hassle of separating the shit from the good stuff. I've picked up old motors people were hauling to the dump, just to bring them home and spend a few hours untangling the copper that's housed inside the case in order to make a little extra money.

Arlo was always a good little scrapper. From the time she was about four, she would sit on the tailgate of my old Blazer and we would go on one of her favorite adventures, which she always called ditch diving. I would drive around in the country, looking to see if there was a glimmer of a can in the tall weeds, then come to a rolling stop if I saw something. She would then bounce off the back, dressed in her finest burgundy fake leather "snake boots" as she called them that V had picked up at a garage sale. She would then hop off my tailgate as I came to a rolling stop and pounce into the ditches, grabbing her treasured cans and tipping them upside down, letting any old putrid fluid drop to the ground before throwing the cans into her bucket. Then she'd giggle, toss the bucket into the back and crawl on up to take her spot on the tailgate once again. We would do this for hours, and she would never get tired of it.

Everything was a treasure hunt for that girl, and she was always finding it or burying it. On our ditch adventures, she would come across other things too—an old teapot that had been tossed aside, a forgotten glass jug, even a set of keys once. She would come up with the best stories for these finds because she always was intrigued about what their backgrounds might have been. Her imagination had always been good at running wild.

Today, though, it was just my hands that were doing the dirty work. I grabbed the couple of bags of cans that I had sorted out and tossed them into the back of Elvis. I flipped on the light in the back of my shop and tried to adjust my eyes to the darkened space, searching for my buckets of copper. I found them sitting under the back workbench, two pails full. As I went to grab the first bucket, something else fell to the ground.

"Well, I'll be damned...:" was all I could say to the empty shop. I slowly leaned over, reaching for the small old coffee can that had toppled to the floor, already knowing what it was. Slowly lifting the lid off of the old can, I could see the glimmer of her hidden treasures.

Pop tabs. Nothing fancy, nothing that was worth much, but she would keep her eye out for them and collect them from wherever we would go. She refused to put new ones in her stash, though. They had to have been found in the wild, on the ground, within the grime. Then she would bring them home, clean them up, and toss them in her old can. She had done that for as long as I could remember.

What I wasn't sure of was why they were here? They'd been tucked away on a shelf in the fraidy hole for so many years, right next to that damn robot, I do believe. I poked one arthritic finger around in the small stash to see if there was something else in there that I was missing. It didn't take too long to find it.

With careful hands, I slowly lifted the little pearl-handled knife out of its resting place. I would recognize it anywhere. That little knife was one of the last things that Rhoads had given her before he left for good. They had actually gotten it from a crane machine one fourth of July at our little carnival. She carried it with her, first tucked safely in her pants pocket, then later in the bottom of her purse. She would never let that go... not without reason.

I set the bucket of copper wiring back down and walked out to the sunshine so I could see what I was looking at a bit better. Once the sun hit my soul, I extended the blade of that little blue pearl-handled knife, looking for what I had already assumed I would find. The air failed to fill my lungs and my heart stalled as I stared at the blade that a young girl had once carried, but that a young woman has recently wielded. On the sharp edge of the blade, blocking the shine of the metal, were the rusty remnants of dried blood.

Now, I know. I supposed it could have been from fishing. But Arlo never actually cleaned the fish. There were a thousand things that it could have been from, but my mind wasn't letting me come up with any other answer that would make her want to hide this. What had she done? Who had she done it to? First the gun, and now this? Once again, my heart had that familiar heavy, yet empty feeling and a sickness balled into the pit of my guts again. Here I was, kicking into autopilot one more time to cover her tracks and try to keep the kid on course.

With shaky hands and an unsteady gate, I put the little knife into my pocket and put all the intrusive thoughts out of my mind. It was time to focus, to prepare, to once again cover her tracks. I went back into the shop and grabbed the two pails of copper wiring. They were so heavy that I was only able to move one of them at a time, dragging that damn right leg along a little as I went about doing so.

Once I had those buckets into the car, I turned quickly to head back into the shop one last time, grabbing another two buckets, these much lighter than the copper. These lighter buckets were what I liked to refer to as my scrap crap… the stuff that really isn't worth much, but is more of what was left over when I ripped motors and other things apart to tear out the wiring. At the scrap yard, they call it ferrous because it's mostly iron and steel, so I do make a little off of that too, enough that it's worth not just throwing it away at least. I suppose I look at it like scraping bones for all the meat. You just don't throw things of value away.

As I lifted the second bucket into the trunk of Elvis, I stopped quickly to reach back into the pocket of my dirty old coveralls I was wearing and fumbled around to extract that old knife. I had figured that if I could throw that damn thing into one of the ferrous buckets of scrap and bury it good and deep in there among all the little chunks of odds and ends, it would just get tossed along with a bunch of other scrap into the scrap yards baler, no one being none the wiser as it would then be squished into ugly, yet precise little scrap bales and shipped the hell on out of town.

As I flipped the little knife into the bucket, I felt a nagging sickening feeling come over me as the sun danced off the tip of the blade. There was so much history attached to that thing, so much of Arlo attached to it. This was exactly why it had to go. I had a bit of a coughing attack. Must have been from that damn grit and dirt that's always swirling around out there. I slammed the trunk lid, making the decision that I best get moving.

The drive over to the scrap yard is maybe only twelve miles or so, not an awful drive at all. I listened to V's old tunes as I drove and just kept thinking about what the hell I was going to do when I brought Arlo home. It was a peaceful drive. I remember that the sun had been high overhead as I made my way down the last of the blacktop and turned onto the gravel entrance of the scrapyard. It wasn't too busy. Sometimes you had to wait behind semi loads of scrap and truckloads of canners, but I had been able to pull right on up to the first gate.

"Hey Bobo! Whatcha bringing in for me today?" Gracie, the cute little attendant with bright blonde hair, big boobs and a nose ring asked as I rolled down my window. She was a tough one, that girl. There was a spark in her that was just fun to be around. She could give it as good as she could take it, and let me tell ya what… for a gal like that to be able to work day in and day out with old scrappers and truckers, well, a girlie better have some thick skin. That loud mouth didn't hurt either.

"Hey kid! I got a couple pails of copper wiring…" I began before her smokey blue eyes darted to her clipboard and she interrupted me.

"Is it clean?" she blurted out, all business in her voice, housed in a body made for sin.

"You bet Gracie! Stripped it outta some old motors that I'd come across. Took damn near twice as long as I thought it would, but you know… these old hands can't work quite as fast as they used to…" I said as I nervously wiped my brow from the sweat running into my eye and glanced down at my calloused arthritic hands.

"Cool, cool. What else ya got in there?" She nodded her sweet, unassuming head towards the trunk, smacking her gum as she spoke. I had a loud ringing in my ears that was just firing up and my heart was hammering into my ribcage at that point. The terror and confusion of the whole situation was riding on my mind, and I was trying to not act suspicious, trying to just act like the good old scrapper Bobo that I'd been since the crushing accident had left me with few ways to make decent money.

With a forced inhale that felt like I was drowning in my own body, I shouted out the window, "Couple buckets of ferrous, odds and ends. Got a little bit of nickel in there, but mostly stainless."

"Sounds good, Bobo. Why don't ya pull up to gate two and they'll help you from there," Gracie grinned and ripped the ticket from the little clipboard she had been scribbling on. Right as she was about to hand it to me, she stopped and looked me right in the eye.

"Hang on, Bobo, you doing, OK? You look a little pale," she said as her hand paused midair in handing me the ticket. Maybe I hadn't been as skillful in hiding things as I had thought. Maybe the heat was just getting to me.

"Just a little hot I think, a little dizzy, but I'm OK," I winked at her. She switched the ticket into the other hand and reached into the pocket of her filthy overalls and pulled out a green lollipop, thrusting her cute little dainty fist back through my window.

"Here ya go! Try this… it ain't sugar free, so maybe it will make you feel a little better," she said with a wink and a grin.

"Thanks kid! I think after this I might just head on back to the trailer for a nap. Feeling kind of tired suddenly. But you know at my age…" I trailed off, ripping the wrapper off of the bright green Lolli. I could smell it before it hit my mouth…. apple, V's favorite.

"Take care, Bobo!" Gracie said as she handed me the ticket that was in her other hand and backed away from my window, already focusing on the truck that had pulled in behind me, way too full of pop cans that were spilling all over the place as it drove.

"Damn it, dude! I'm going to have to clean that crap up!" I could hear Gracie shouting and giggling at the truck as I was pulling away, heading for gate two. I still remember how sour that blessed green apple Lolli felt in my dry mouth, and how I had foolishly believed that I was just dealing with terror and low blood sugar. As I sat in line behind another little car, I just kept hearing the ringing in my ears get louder and louder, and I suddenly felt like I was going to puke.

"Oh, for fuck's sake... calm down," I whispered into the air, trying to slow my racing heart and calm myself. "Breathe in, 1...2...3... breathe out, 1...2...3... in and out," I was whispering to no one. I focused on a little voice from my past that became louder and louder until I joined in.

"This little light of mine... hide it under a bucket... NO..." Breathing in... 1...2...3... breathing out, 1...2...3... Damn, this had been a tough episode to control. No matter what I did, my heart did *not* want to settle the hell down. I took in another deep breath and focused my eyes on the line, slowly crawling in front of me.

Finally, it was my turn to pull ahead to gate two. The little guy responsible for gate two wasn't old enough to even drink yet, but a likable kid called Tank. The nickname was funny cause he was just a little dude, five foot four, maybe a hundred and five pounds. He'd been a wrestler in school, so those were a solid one hundred and five pounds. Hence, Tank.

"Hey Tank!" I hollered as he made his way over to take my ticket.

"Hey Scrapman! How ya been? How's that cute granddaughter of yours doing?" he said with a playful grin.

I handed him the ticket. "Still too much for you to handle, Tank. Way too much to handle," I laughed, fully feeling the meaning behind those words. The kid glanced down at the ticket, popped his head back up and asked, "Just smaller buckets today, sir?"

"Sure thing kid, small load today," I answered, almost choking on the Lolli that had popped off the end of the stick and was now aimlessly rolling around in my mouth while keeping my mouth damp at least so I could talk.

"OK, I am just going to grab the roller cart and I will unload ya. Just pop the trunk," he shouted over his shoulder as he turned to get the cart.

"Pop the trunk. POP THE TRUNK? You young kids… geesh! Let me get out and open it for ya…" I remember saying as I opened the door and went to take a step out of the car. These young kids, no idea how older cars worked and how easy their lives had become with technology.

I remember stepping around towards the back of Elvis. I remember leaning down to reach for the trunk lid and glancing up as Tank headed towards me with the rolling cart to load my haul and carry away my burdens. I can even remember instinctively patting my hand over the lump in my shirt pocket, right over my heart, that held Arlo's small treasure. But then it all goes black.

CHAPTER 11
AWAKENING

I DIDN'T want to come back. Once you make your way through that darkness and see the glorious light in the distance… when the pressures that have held you down for so long in this life have been lifted, your soul truly fights the call to come back. I imagined that was what Arlo had felt that day so long ago as she leapt off of the old boat, facing the call of the void. I remember feeling warm and at peace. I remember familiar voices calling to me from somewhere on the gilded golden horizon and how I felt the urge to run towards those voices while ducking beneath the warm, bright glow that hovered from overhead. And then I heard her.

"This little light of mine…" I had heard the faint whisper from somewhere in the distance behind me, out there in the cold darkness of the unknown. "I'm gonna let it shine…" the whisper kept droning into my ear. I had wanted so badly to just be done with this life, to move on to my beloved V. She was only moments away. But the little voice kept nagging in my ear, "Hide it under a bucket? NO! I'm gonna let it shine. Come on Bobo, come back to me," the little voice continued to hound.

It could have been the drugs in my IV they had given me at the hospital. It could have been my exhaustion and my mind just replaying all the thoughts and worries that I'd been held captive beneath over the course of the previous few days. I could have said that it was any of those things and any sane person would buy my story. We aren't dealing with sane people here, though.

I could feel her warm breath on my two-day-old gray whiskered cheek before I even forced my heavy lids to part. I could smell the vanilla and lavender lotion that she used religiously, just as her grandma had taught her to, and my heart instantly recognized the frail little voice.

Turning my head towards the whisper, I let my eyelids fall open just a slit to see my girl, my Arlo, standing at my bedside, tears streaming down her pale cheeks. Her emerald green eyes were a shocking blood red where white should have been and the lids themselves were puffy. Those tired and sad eyes locked with mine for a few moments, willing me to come back, silently begging me not to leave her alone here.

She was squeezing my hand as I slowly drifted away again, frantically searching for the voices that had been calling me beneath the intruding chorus of beeping and alarms that had sounded from the tubes and wires that had been attached to my lifeless body by IVs and sticky pads. I remember hearing her screaming at me not to go, not to leave her, to come back to her. But that was all that I remember.

When I woke up again, I was alone in my hospital room. They had pulled the drapes open wide, and the sun was blazing into the room, lighting up the ceiling. I was counting the cracks on the ancient, probably asbestos-filled ceiling tiles when the nurse entered the room. I would know that voice anywhere.

"Well, hello my sleepyhead! How ya doin' sweet thing?" she cooed as she stood next to me, writing feverishly on her little clipboard while looking at the machines beeping and doing the work. I glanced over at her, noticing that her wildly unruly red hair had been pulled up into a messy bun again, just like when she was taking care of Arlo. She looked so tired, so much older. Once again, she was sweating profusely, but her demeanor remained as calm and cool as a cucumber. Her chubby little fingers kept scribbling on her little clipboard as she made small talk without looking me in the eye.

"You again... what do they have you working on all the floors? You all must be understaffed," I laughed, clearing my throat. She didn't respond, just kept looking at the monitors and scribbling away. It wasn't until I had an itch and went to scratch my balls that I realized there was a serious problem. I couldn't move my arm that far. It was caught on something, I thought to myself, "What the hell?" and looked down towards my side.

There they were. The same flimsy Velcro and vinyl restraints that had been holding my sweet girl down just a few days ago. At least I thought it had been just a few days. The drugs that they give you in those places are a real mind fuck. I had always believed that those pill-pushing docs were getting rich off of those drug companies out there peddling their pills on anyone who would take them.

I tried to panic, tried to will my body to fight the sleep that was suddenly trying to engulf my brain. But out of the periphery of my right eye, I could see that the little chubby red-headed cherub wasn't just scribbling on her notepad. She was pushing more meds into the damn IV. "Well, fuck!" was my last thought before a warm wave slowly crawled up from my toes and engulfed me like a warm blanket, lulling me back to sleep and giving me the tingling sensation that I had just pissed myself. Then again, maybe I did.

Who knows how long they had me out. I don't really even remember waking up, or how many days I'd been in there. I do remember the first argument that I had with the fine Dr. Grady, who, when I looked down at his tennis shoes, still hadn't gotten any blood or piss on them yet. He still looked at me with that deer in the headlights face, just like the day they brought Arlo in here. Hell... had he even left in the past 72 hours? He, too, looked exhausted, like he had lived years in just a few days. I didn't even know how many damn days I had been in there, let alone what Arlo's status was.

"How the fuck does a heart attack lead to me being held here like a whack-a-doodle? Take these damn restraints off of me, boy!" I shouted at the little doc. "I am gonna beat your ass for this if you don't let me go! I need to get to Arlo, you little asshole!" I remember snarling at him as he calmly looked over his notes, standing over by the window in the little sterile room with the cracked ceiling tiles.

There were one hundred and forty-two of them, by the way, and thirty-seven had deep crack lines that I was convinced were going to collapse over me while I was chained to that damn bed. I figured I hadn't lived that long and defeated all the odds that had been against me just to be taken out by a few old cancer-causing asbestos ceiling tiles. It was just another thing that pissed me off about the whole situation. I was agitated, and rightfully so. No one would give me any answers and I was sure as shit sick and tired of being spoken to as if I too was a youngin'. Damn them all.

"Bobo, it wasn't a heart attack..." the deer-in-the-headlights little doc began to say before I cut him off.

"The fuck it wasn't! Doc! How long ago did you get out of school? I know you are still wet behind the ears and all, but Christ! Even I can figure out what happened to me! I had been under all of that stress and felt like ass for a couple days. Well, even longer than that! I had chest pain and a hard time breathing. I remember getting out of the car to lift the trunk lid... and that was all I could remember. What the hell happened then if it wasn't a goddamn heart attack?"

I could hear a loud sigh escape from the little doc's lips before I caught him rolling his eyes and running his fingers casually through his already thinning and prematurely graying brown hair. He grabbed the little brown doctor's stool from the corner and wheeled it over to the side of my bed. It took him a few seconds to figure out how to form the words that were about to hit me harder than that damn rock crusher ever could have all of those years ago.

"Bobo, you almost successfully ended your own life," he sheepishly muttered under his breath, avoiding my eyes and rolling his ballpoint pen around in his fingers as he spoke.

The air seemed to be sucked out of the room with his words, and my head began to spin. There was a deafening ringing in my ears that had successfully drowned out anything else that he was trying to say. After the initial shock had begun to wear off, about the only words that

I can actually recall him saying was something about my medication and I had been taking excessive amounts. "Bullshit" was all I could think of, but didn't dare utter another hostile word.

I knew all too well how this worked; I had seen this play out with Arlo time and time again. The more you deny and get hostile, the longer they can hold ya in there. The way to win at this particular game was to play nice and give them the answers that they wanted to hear, and as long as you can get a doc to sign off saying you are no longer a threat towards yourself or anyone else, they let you go again.

It's a proper game of cat and mouse, a way to soak the insurance system in my opinion, and a royal pain in my ass. I just let him keep droning on about the drugs in my system, that my meds were at toxically high levels and that with all the stress that I'd been under, it sure looked like an "end of life" attempt from where they were sitting.

That night in my hospital room though, my mind began to wander... back to the manifesto that I had found in Arlo's room, back to me smoking the joint on her bed. Had I imagined any of that? At one point, *had* she actually wanted to die and take me with her? I kept trying to remember how many pills I was supposed to be taking and what time of day I was supposed to be taking them. There was nothing I had done differently to land me here, under this label of a supposed "suicide watch."

Sure, I had been depressed. Who the hell isn't these days? Was I lonely? Yes. Was I sad? Some of the time. Did I live in the past a little too much? Maybe. But did I actively try to end it all? Hell no! I had been feeling just fine until Arlo showed back up at my door, and even after that, I figured I was just feeling shitty from the stress of it all and the emotions of the past being stirred back up again.

I laid in bed that first night with the crisp white sheets that smelled like bleach pulled up under my neck, staring at the dark ceiling in a new kind of terror. I knew I hadn't purposely done anything to myself to end up in here. But blood tests don't lie. So, what the hell was I left with for an answer? Am I slowly going crazy, forgetting when I took my pills? Arlo? Did she do something to my pills? Did she really want me dead? Bast? What the hell. I slammed my eyes down tightly, willing my-self to go to sleep before the paranoia manifested from being in that hell hole got the best of me.

The first therapist that I spoke with the next morning was kind enough to have the restraints removed after determining that I wasn't a threat to myself. She was a young thing, with kind, almond-shaped brown eyes and long, mousy brown hair that fell over her shoulders. She smelled like laundry detergent and her glasses had a small crack in the frame right above the bridge of her nose that I couldn't stop staring at when she spoke. I supposed that made me look like I was a little nuts, staring like that, but that's what they wanted anyway, right? To vilify me and make me look damaged, make themselves look like the heroes. Plus, the meds they fed you in that place took your guard down, lifted your veil, and you were an open book to their line of questioning. And boy, did the questions just keep coming.

The second therapist that I spoke with wasn't as pleasant to watch, but she was still nice enough. Her approach was through art, so we sat at a little Sunday school-like table, her sitting across the table from me as I slowly and methodically worked on gluing little seashells to the top of a little wooden box. I thought it was fitting that I was making a little treasure box in that place while I was trying so hard to watch what I said, avoiding spilling Arlo and my secrets of "buried treasures" out to anyone who would listen or threaten to up my doses of medications.

As she asked me about my past, about Rhoads and V, about Arlo and the situation we were in now, I just kept focusing on the tiny purple shells and how the school glue got gummy around their edges, making it look like sea foam... like the shells that were in Arlo's painting of the seaside when she'd been in that God-forsaken place doing her "art ther-apy." Poor kid. As my therapist droned on about safe choices and the need to have a nurse come do home visits to assess my medications through a locked box now, I just continued to nod my head in agree-ment while I was actually thinking about my poor girl.

How many times had I put her in a hospital like this? How many therapists had that kid sat and bull-shitted her way through conversations with, telling them exactly what they wanted to hear? Had it ever done her any good? She was twenty-two now and still on the run from herself. It was during this therapy session, the second day that I was in there, that something unlocked in my mind beneath the veil of murky medication, and I blurted out, "Oh God! Where is Arlo? I was supposed to take her home!"

I dropped the little seashell that I had been working with and sat staring at the therapist, my eyes frightened and wide. I could feel my hands trembling in fear as the hair on my neck stood up with a sudden fight-or-flight response.

With an all-knowing smile that slowly crawled across her cracked lips that had the remains of this morning's pink lipstick peeling off of them, she calmly folded her hands in front of her, resting them on the table.

"Yes, Bobo, let's talk about Arlo," she began, ever so carefully, almost like her words had just stumbled into a minefield. "Now, how have you been since she has been gone? I know that you told the last doctor that you struggled a bit when she moved after high school. Can you tell me a little about that?"

Staring from across the Sunday school-like table at the little therapist who sat like a schoolmarm, arms folded neatly in front of her, I felt like a child. I felt like I was being shuffled along, being poked at and prodded like cattle until the words they wanted to hear were extracted from my mouth, whether or not I meant them. I was tired of that shit, tired of the games. I honestly just wanted my granddaughter and wanted to go home.

"Look Doc, I was supposed to pick her up and take her home, and since I am in here, I don't know where she is. Can you please just find that out for me and let me know that my girl is OK?" I calmly asked through gritted teeth as my hands were gripping my own legs beneath the table, nails digging into my thighs just to try to appear to be remaining calm. My heart was heaving in my chest, and I wanted to throw up as I waited for any type of answer.

"Bobo, she's just fine. Your granddaughter is fine," the little therapist chided, once again picking up her pen and going back to scribbling down a few more remarks. "What if I told you that in another twenty-four hours or so, you will be going back home together? Would you like that?"

Jesus Christ. This chick was talking to me at this Sunday school-like table as if I were a small child. Still, I had to play the game. In these places, there was only one way out, and getting all bent out of shape wasn't gonna do it. So, instead of raising hell and cussing' her out, I slowly picked up my little purple shell in one hand and school glue bottle in the other and went back to work on the little treasure box. Arlo would like it anyway. She could put her rocks in it, I supposed.

"Yup I would. That sounds like a plan to me," was all I could muster to say in response. We sat like that for a few more minutes I guessed, me working on gluing together my little treasure box, and the young therapist scribbling notes on her little pad while she asked me about my family, about my work at the quarry, about the scrap business. The questions seemed to have no end with that one. As I was trying to steady the final little purple shell on top of the little foamy dollop of glue that I had dropped on the corner of the top of the little treasure box, she caught me off guard with her last question of the day.

"Hey Bobo, can you do something for me? Can you tell me what year it is?"

"Oh, for fuck's sake!" was all I could manage to say.

I kept playing their games though, being good and giving them the answers that they wanted to hear, and, true to their word, at the end of my seventy-two-hour hold, they let me go. I was just tucking in my shirt and grabbing my jacket when I heard her voice from the doorway.

"Hey there!" Arlo's voice shot across the sterile white room. I was startled as I turned to see her standing in the doorway with a new haircut, to her shoulders now, not even long enough to put up in one of V's buns anymore.

"When the hell did you have time to cut your hair, girl? Jesus, I've only been in here a couple of days!" I blurted out. The poor kid looked stunned as the glorious smile fell from her face and she instinctively reached up towards her shorter hair.

"Oh kid, no worries. It looks good on ya! Just surprised me, that's all. How are you feeling? Doing OK?" I asked, standing there, just soaking in all the glory that was her. I hated to admit it, but some of what the therapist had pointed towards was true. I missed that kid. I hated that she lived a couple hours away and didn't get home much anymore, hated that I was left alone in the trailer with only Elvis to pass my hours, and hated that it was now my duty as her grandpa to chase her right back out of town again for her own good.

"I'm good, Bobo, I'm alright," Arlo began as she twirled her shorter hair between her fingers. She stood there for a moment, just looking at me all wide-eyed in silence, like she was unsure of what to say next. I was at a loss for words myself, and for a split second, I almost let fear reach into me where that girl is concerned. I knew I hadn't landed myself in that place on purpose. That hadn't been my intent. I also knew that this was my girl. I had raised her.

There was no room in the already growing space between us to let the fear and doubts begin to creep in, so I nipped them in the bud right then and there.

"You know what they were saying about me, don't ya, girl?" I shot straight from the hip and looked her dead in her emerald green eyes. "They thought I was giving up on it all, thought I wanted a way out."

She said nothing in return and instead just walked over to me, threw her arms around my neck and buried her face in my neck, just like when she was a little girl. "I don't care what they say, Bobo. You would never leave me, and I would never leave you," she whispered, swallowing hard to choke the tears away, chasing them back just as fast as they had tried to fall. A spitfire with an angel's grace, that one was.

She dropped her arms, backed away, and rubbed her bloodshot eyes. "Now, let's get you home! Grab your coat and keys, your seventy-two hours are up!" she said as she grabbed the baggies of meds and the paperwork that the little chunky red-headed nurse had just gone over with me.

"Get me home? That's my job! I was supposed to be getting you home!" I spoke to only the stale air in the room that smelled like rubbing alcohol, disinfectant and had the faint scent of piss, as she was already halfway down the hall. I stopped once more at the nurse's station on the way out, just to be sure that I hadn't forgotten anything and had signed all the forms that they had needed from me. The little chunky redhead wasn't there, but I spoke with the male nurse named Todd, who double-checked once more and was ready to send me on my way.

Turning to leave the nurses' station, Todd hollered after me. "Hold up, I still have a few of your things from when they brought you in, man." Curious, I spun back around again in time to just about bump into Todd, who had jumped up, run around the corner of the nurses station and was now literally so close to my face that I could taste the Marlboros and hours' old coffee on his breath from his recent break.

"Here ya go, sir," Todd shoved a green hospital monogrammed drawstring bag into my arms. I nodded in confusion and begun to shuffle on down the hall to catch up with Arlo. Catching up with her at the elevator, we hopped on inside and waited for a little old lady to roll inside in her wheelchair.

I couldn't help but stare at her fancy sweater that I was sure had to have been expensive. This little old lady was made up to the nines, as V would have said. She may not have been going anywhere but home, but her hair was done, she had a pink to her cheeks and her nails were a dark painted red. I was lost in gawking at the pattern in her sweater, which appeared to be flocks of geese highlighted by little bright blue pools of water that they were all gathering around. She caught me staring at her and winked at me.

"Come on, Bobo, let's head home." Arlo had taken my arm and pulled me back out of the elevator. Had we even moved floors? I must have been too intently staring at that little old lady's sweater and not noticed. As we walked out of the main hospital doors, I blurted out to Arlo, "Hey, when do we have to have you back here to make sure your meds are adjusted and that you're doing alright? Did they tell you that yet?" Arlo stopped dead in her tracks in the parking lot right ahead of me, dust swirling around her, and slowly turned around. With those emerald green eyes looking towards the ground, she sheepishly spoke to the wind, "Bobo, I'm fine. It's all going to be fine. But..." she paused and looked away towards where Elvis was parked in the back of the lot, so no one would be able to door-ding it, of course (that's my girl!), and then her eyes came back to mine. "We do have to be back here at the end of the week for a follow-up though," she exhaled and allowed a half-assed grin to crawl over one side of her mouth.

Seeing Elvis in the back of the lot, I followed her towards the car. Curiosity had gotten the best of me and as I walked, I pulled open the drawstring on the green plastic bag that Todd had given me. I reached into that dark green plastic bag and grabbed for the first thing that my arthritic fingers graced over and yanked it out to see what the hell it was. Stopping and standing right next to Elvis now, my stomach fell, and I threw the object on the hood of the car, reaching back into the bag to see what else I had brought with me to the hospital. My brain registered the second and third objects without even having to see them. Closing my eyes and fighting my lungs to inhale a large breath of dusty air, I threw it too onto the hood.

"Bobo... you alright? You don't look good..." Arlo was hollering over at me from the driver's side door. The world went deafeningly quiet as I stood there next to the car, entranced by the items that now lay on the hood, trying to make sense of what I was seeing.

There, in the dusty and gritty sunlight, there on Elvis' hood in the middle of the parking lot that sat next to the hospital that I had just battled my way out of, sat the little pocketknife with the pearl handle and the old trucker's hat with the bent bill and the big pot leaf emblazoned on the front of it. Next to that sat the little rock that I had dug out of the quarry and carried around to give to Arlo on her return home. What the hell. Why did these things get brought in with me at the hospital? I meant, the little rock, sure... it had been in my shirt pocket. But the hat? The knife?

I could hear her voice from somewhere far away, calling out to me and drawing me back out of the deafness that had encapsulated me in that parking lot. The deafening silence was replaced with a roar of ringing that was stemming from somewhere deep within my ears as I turned to face her. She had run over to my side of the car, placing her arm on my shoulder and stood next to me, leaning her face over into my eyesight.

"Bobo, what's up? You look like you are going to be sick? Like you saw a ghost! You OK? Do I need to go get somebody for ya?" I stared into those emerald green eyes briefly before I was able to shake off the buzzing noise in my ears and blurt out, "Why the hell are they here?" as my heart beat mercilessly in my chest from fear. I swore I was on my way to having another heart episode.

"They who, Bobo? They who? What are you talking about?" Arlo was shouting out, obviously worried about my reaction and unsure of what to do next. I glanced from her back to the hood of the car and said, "Those! Why the hell did the hospital give me those?"

She looked down at the hood in what appeared to be confusion, dropping her arm from my shoulder, exhaled heavily and turned towards me once again. "Bobo, what are you talking about? Your hat and that old pocketknife? I don't know what the hell the rock is from," she said as she reached lovingly for the little rock, clearly intent on rescuing it.

My hat... MY HAT? What the hell was going on? That wasn't my hat, and why the hell was she saying that it was? *Is* she trying to set me up for something? This beloved girl, my Arlo? Did she not know that I would already move heaven and earth for her? What game was being played here?

"What the hell Arlo? What are you talking about? Them ain't my things!" I reached forward towards the car to pick up the hat and shove it back into the bag again. When I went to reach for the little knife, her delicate little hand stopped mine.

"Well, not the knife, but the hat sure as hell is, Bobo. I gave you that so long ago. Don't you remember? It was a joke after I got caught with pot the first time." Arlo stood right in front of me, staring at me in disbelief. I just sat there wondering what the hell she was up to now.

"The knife's not yours though, it's mine. Man, it has been years since I had seen that old thing. You remember when I used to carry it everywhere with me when I was little? As a kid, it always made me feel like such a bad-ass! Where the heck did you find it?"

In that moment, standing there in the gritty sunlight in the hospital parking lot with Arlo, I wasn't sure what to think. What was she trying to do here? How the hell many meds did they give me in there, anyway? I knew then that as much as I loved her, I couldn't trust her. She wasn't well yet, not in her right frame of mind. I would just play along, I supposed.

"The hat?" I asked her with a muddled expression as the beads of sweat began to pool across my forehead and drip over my brow, stinging my eyes. I raised a hand to shield my eyes from the sun, and she did the same.

"No, silly goose. Bobo, you wear that thing all the time. I mean, where did you find my old knife that dad gave me? I thought I had lost it." She stood with her nose crunched up and furled brow in the heat as the grit and dust danced in the wind and swirled all around her.

"Oh! Right, right. I think it was in the garage! I was out there getting some stuff ready to take into the scrap yard and it was under the workbench... in a bucket..." My voice had trailed off, nervous as to what she would say when I mentioned the bucket and how it had been hidden.

She reached for her knife and a smile crawled across her lips once again. The expression clearly changed from one of giddiness from retrieving a childhood memory to one of utter confusion and panic as she glanced back up to me.

"But Bobo," she began sheepishly, "there hasn't been a scrapyard in this town for years." She fumbled with the knife between her fingers, along with the little rock that she had lifted gently off of the hood, staring down at the hot and crumbling asphalt beneath her feet.

It was about then that I decided I'd had enough of playing along, enough of her games. I had half a mind to drag her ass back into the hospital and have her committed again. Clearly, she was not right yet. But my head had begun to pound, and I was tired.

"I don't know what you're talking about kiddo. I had gathered a load of scrap and was hauling it over there to door two when I collapsed. I'm guessing that's where they found me and brought me in," I said, pulling the hat over my head just to shut her up for the time being. I got into the passenger side and slammed the door. She stood out there for a few more seconds before curling the little knife in her fingers, putting it in her back pocket like it had always been there, and walked around and got into the driver's side.

She grabbed the bedazzled palm tree keychain and turned it to bring Elvis to life. "Let's just go home, Bobo. We're just so tired," Arlo almost whispered as she reached for the knobs to the old eight-track player. We said nothing as we listened to V's old tapes all the way home. First a little Elvis, then a little Righteous Brothers, and finally, Arlo Guthrie.

CHAPTER 12
DANCING OVER FLAMES

IT WAS almost evening by the time we had gotten home and pulled Elvis back into the little garage. I was starving, so I headed into the kitchen to see what we could find for some supper. Feef hopped right up onto the counter in her spot closest to the window, and her purring just about lulled me to sleep while I was scavenging through the fridge.

"Hey Bobo, do we have any hot dogs in there?" she asked as she hurried through the little kitchen. She quickly opened a can of cat food for Feef and dug around through a cupboard for one of the ridiculously fancy teacup saucers that V had collected from garage sales to feed the animals on. There was just something so otherworldly funny about seeing cats eat off of fine china. I stared at Feef in all of her glory, chowing down in the sunlight while sitting on the avocado green counter. To her, there was no better place to be.

My peaceful reflection was interrupted once again by Arlo. "Hey Bobo, did ya hear me in there?" she asked again, standing next to Feef, just staring at me with a grin on her face.

"Sorry kid... just so damn tired. Yup, I think we have some dogs in there. Bread OK?" I asked half-jokingly because she knew we never bought buns. That was a stupid luxury.

She smiled and winked back at me. "Grab them and come outside. I will start a fire, OK?" she shouted over her shoulder as she headed back outside. "Behave Fifi," I told the cat, who was still perched in her spot on the counter as I grabbed the dogs from the fridge, the bottle of ketchup and the remaining half a loaf of bread. Right before I made it to the door, I turned back to grab the half-eaten bag of plain tater chips that I knew we'd put between the dogs and the bread, just like we always had, and then I headed outside into the gritty evening breeze.

Arlo had gotten the fire started already around the back of the trailer, next to the garage. She had pulled the two aluminum folding chairs with their fraying orange and white ribbons of unraveling fabric and sat them up right next to the fire. Giggling like a little kid again, she took the dogs and shoved two of them on two roasting sticks she'd found on a shelf in the garage that had been long forgotten about by me. They were designed so that at the end of the stick, it looked like a little metal man standing there and when you placed the dog on there, well... it really looked like it was his wiener. We had found them at a yard sale when Arlo was just a young kid, and she always got a kick out of them.

Grabbing one of the roasting sticks from her, I settled into my old aluminum chair and spent a few minutes just taking it all in. There we were, the two of us, just like we had been for so many years. It had been so long since we had done this, just having dinner and shooting the shit. Staring out across the field behind the trailer, it had occurred to me that we hadn't talked at all about how she was doing, how her time in the hospital had been. She hadn't even mentioned Bast, and I was curious about when she was planning on heading back home and getting the hell back out of here.

Twirling my little man on a stick right above the dancing flames, I stared into the fire, cleared my throat, and attempted to act like everything was normal, that we hadn't both just walked out of the loony bin and back into lives that neither of us were sure of. "So, how are you doing, kid? When are you going home?" It came out a little more bluntly than I had meant it to, but she only grinned, let out a little giggle, and grabbed a handful of tater chips to crumble up onto her bread for her dog.

"Bobo, I honestly don't know why you worry about me so much... I am *just* fine, I'm telling ya. Please stop worrying..." she stopped mid-sentence to carefully move her almost burnt dog onto her tater chip-covered hunk of bread and glob on the ketchup. "As for leaving, Bobo, I have a couple of weeks. We have to be back at the clinic in a few days for a follow-up so I was thinking that I would hang out here until then, and then I'll head back to my own place. I just want to be sure that you are doing OK first," she smiled, staring me down straight in the eye before taking a bite of her dog.

No mention of Bast. No mention of her time in the hospital. At least she did sound like she was planning on going back to school, so that did ease my mind just a bit. But what about how she left things? What was at her apartment to go back to? If she had left in such a rush, full of heartache and anger, what did that apartment look like, and would that trigger her in some way going back there? My mind clicked as my focus returned once again to the little pearl-handled knife, the gun, the bloody clothes, the damn hat I was wearing on my head at that very moment, acting like a goddamn fool.

Looking at my girl quietly eating her hot dog and staring at the fire, I allowed my heart just a sliver of time to question what I actually thought it was that she was capable of doing. Raising a little hell growing up was one thing, but could she have done something to Derrick, her ex-fiancé? All I knew was that he had never tried to reach out since she had been back. Neither had the roommate, that I knew of. Then there was the damn bloody knife, the clothes, the gun, the handwritten manifesto in her room. After all, she did help me with the body all those years ago when things went bad after she'd been taken advantage of. Did I set her wheels in motion to be a murderer? Did I...

"Careful there, Bobo! You lost your wiener!" Arlo hollered out to bring me back from wherever I had gone. Glancing away from the flames and down at my stick, I had lost the dog.

"Man, Bobo, they really have you out of it still. Let me get ya another one," Arlo said, wrestling another hot dog from the plastic wrapper and putting it back on my stick. She did have a momentary look of concern on her face before she reached into her pocket and pulled out a joint. A flicker of wickedness danced in her emerald-green eyes. She sat down in her little aluminum chair and pulled the Elvis lighter out from her pocket, flipped it open, and lit it up. She settled back into the chair and inhaled one big hit before slowly exhaling back out again, sitting in silence, staring into the flames. She then reached back into her pocket to pull out the little rock that I had rescued for her from the quarry.

"You know, Bobo. I'm not sure that I am where I am supposed to be..." she spoke into the flames before taking another hit, methodically holding her breath before relaxing and letting the smoke twirl back out of her nostrils and mouth like a beautifully defeated dragon. She gently rolled the dusty pink rock between her fingers of the other hand, rubbing the smooth edges as she stared into the dancing flames.

Rolling the hot dog off of the stick and onto my bread and pile of tater chips, I asked her the one thing that had been eating away at my heart. "Arlo, you never have felt like you have belonged anywhere, so where exactly is it that you think you are supposed to be?" I asked, calmly, before taking a big bite of my dog.

Man, that was a good hot dog. I didn't realize how dang hungry I'd been. When you're in the hospital, time is different. You have no concept of how long you're in there, when you last ate, or even if you need to take a piss. Machines and medicine do everything for you in there. They override your brain and your thoughts. They make your body run on autopilot, which I've had a lot of experience with.

"I mean, I just feel like I'm out there trying to find my way. But where is my place? I belong on rock piles and in fishing boats, running through ditches and swimming in lakes. I'm just not a city girl. The only place that I'm ever pulled towards is home. Here, with you," she said matter-of-factly to the fire before taking another drag and turning to pass me the joint. I hesitated.

"Oh, come on, Bobo. No one is here to care anymore, or make a fuss," she whispered, and I knew full well that she was right. I took the joint, sat back, and inhaled the sweetness while thinking about how much V would be so against me sitting out here, smoking a joint with our girl.

But that was unfair now, because V hadn't lived *this* life. She hadn't known *this* Arlo or experienced the loneliness that had suffocated me these last few years. Life wasn't fun anymore. There wasn't much to look forward to anymore. Maybe I *had* wanted to let go of it all. Maybe I *had* tried to end it all. Something went off in my brain, electrified, and came to life. Had I taken too many meds on purpose? Why wasn't any of this making any sense to me?

Completely forgetting what we'd been discussing, I blurted out to Arlo, "Where did you say it was that they found me?"

I had caught her off guard, as she had been staring at the fire too, trapped in her own thoughts, rolling the joint between the fingers of her right hand and the little treasured rock in the fingers of the left. It took her a few seconds to string a coherent thought together. "Before they took you to the hospital, you mean?"

"Yeah, when I was brought into the hospital, who found me? Where had I been?" I asked. It had dawned on me that she had told me that the scrap yard had been gone for years, but I had just been there. That was my last memory. So what was she up to? I was trying to catch her in her own web of lies.

"You were here, Bobo, in the garage. It seemed like you had been looking for something in there and passed out, slumped over the hood of Elvis. You were lucky that Dad stopped by and found you..." she trailed off, turning back to stare at the fire, which had begun to simmer down to a slow burn of crackling embers.

She hadn't flinched. The words rolled off her tongue just as easily as the truth would have. What she was saying had made no sense though, cause I knew Rhoads had stopped by just long enough a few nights ago to be sure that Arlo was OK, and then he was off into the night again. I could feel my old heart flipping around wildly beneath my rib cage while I was trying to think of the next thing to say. I had loved this girl fiercely and to the best of my ability, but clearly, she was not stable. Clearly, she wasn't OK.

I only hoped that the doctors would see that in a few days and change her medications again, like they had in the past. She just needed her meds adjusted so that her brain could run on autopilot again. What was I going to do with her until then, though? I couldn't have her running around here. God knows who she would talk to or what other things she would drum up. Plus, I didn't really trust her. As awful of a feeling as that was, I just felt like she was out to get me, to end the both of us. An idea came to me then, one that I let spill from my lips before I had fully put a plan together.

"Hey kid, let's drive to your place and get some of your things if you're planning on staying here for a couple more days. That might be a fun little trip! I need to get out of here, anyway. It would be a nice little drive. You can drive Elvis." The words poured out of my face before I could stop them.

Her response was less than ecstatic though, more that of a young teen than a 22-year-old woman. "Sure, Bobo. Sounds good," was all she said while sleep had begun to invade her brain and she was nodding off by the fire. I reached over to grab what was left of the little joint being held by her limp little fingers, kicked back in my lawn chair, and puffed away that night until a blissful sleep found me, too.

I dreamt of a different time that night by the fire, a time that was easily accessible when my eyes were closed and my heart and brain could just relax and run wild. Funny how the brain does that, escapes time and space in your sleep to transport you back to a simpler, happier time. I had always bought into the theory that your soul was always one step ahead of your body and that it was always acutely aware of what your body needed, whether that may be sleep, food, forgiveness or even just a little peace and quiet. That night by the fire, I really believed that my spirit had been broken and that I was spiraling down a dangerous fraidy hole of my own, starting to question my own decisions and dangerously close to teetering on the edge of my own sanity.

It came as no surprise to me later then, that my soul led me into a blissful sleep, as the smells of the lingering, smoldering embers wafted through the gritty air and lulled me deep into silence. I was transported back to her, my V, back to a time many years ago when we had been at our wits' end with this kid and we were completely at a loss as to what we were supposed to do to help her.

Sitting around our little kitchen table in the trailer, having a plate of V's spaghetti with her homemade sauce (the secret to the sauce was a little French dressing), watching the evening game show on TV and trying to guess the letters as they popped up on the screen, there was a familiarity and warmth to the whole scene I traveled back to.

Once again, Arlo hadn't shown up for supper and we weren't quite sure what she was up to or when she would be back. She would never stray for too long, but if she was with Bast again, she could stay gone a couple of hours, out there somewhere, digging around in the dirt and grime, either trying to find the treasures that she had buried, or looking for brand new hiding spots to bury the new ones.

She would have been right around ten or so then, and V had recently been diagnosed with cancer, yet at that point, we had been blissfully unaware as to how far it had progressed. At the time, she had only viewed it as a minor setback, although scary as hell, and was too tired to argue about our granddaughter's current whereabouts.

Just the week before, Arlo and Bast had been in trouble for sneaking into the old barn up the road and trying to steal an old four-wheeler to go joyriding. A couple weeks before that, the police had graced my little patch of a front lawn when Arlo and Bast had skipped school and hadn't wanted to get in trouble so they'd concocted an elaborate story about a white van with no windows attempting to lure them in, and how they had narrowly avoided a kidnapping. The stories were endless, the choices that she made were always wrong, and as a young adolescent girl, there was no end to the emotional outbursts and tears.

In my heart, I could still feel the safety at that dinner table that evening, sitting across from my beloved V, twirling my fork in her homemade spaghetti, knowing that if all else failed, we were at least in it all together. She had been my anchor in this world, my sanity and peace in frantic and disturbing times. Looking across the table at her, watching her chew her noodles and guess the answers to our game show while the red sauce dripped down her chin, I felt calm in the simplicity of it all.

"But what are we going to do with her, V? She's running wild, and it's only getting worse. How can we protect her when we don't know where she is?" I questioned, looking back down at my plate, twirling the fork in the noodles. I kept twirling my fork as her voice lulled my worries, the reason that sleep had blissfully carried me back to this memory. I needed to remember her voice, her heart, and her wisdom.

"She's a strong-willed child, that's for sure," V had begun while glancing away from the TV and back at me, still been twirling the noodles around in the sauce on my plate. "But our girl is destined to take the harder roads in this world. She always has been. She has to make mistakes and learn. That's her only way out of it. All we can do for her is to be here when she comes back, because she will always need a soft place to land. The world is so hard and unforgiving, and although she will want to run, raising hell all over, her heart is good. She will find her way, but it will be on her terms only. Ain't nothing you and I can do about that," she had said, pausing to wipe her chin with a paper towel. "Just remember Bobo, she's not a bad kid. She's just been dealt a bad hand. All we can do is help her deal with the cards she's been dealt. We can't change them."

Ahhhh. My V. My light in the darkness. Had she been so naïve about her granddaughter, or was it truly as simple as she had alluded to back then?

Help her deal with her cards. Help her deal with what she had been given. I could do that. I have been doing that. I would continue to do that. Somewhere that night, nodding off in front of the fire, my purpose had been redefined and my soul lit once again by the flame of my V. I would wake up holding on to that feeling, once again willing to follow Arlo right into the fraidy hole one more time.

I don't remember how we had gotten back into the house that night from our slumber by the fire, but when I woke up the next day, Arlo was already cleaning the kitchen, the cat had been fed and she was out in the garage, tinkering on Elvis. After I poked my head out to see where she was, curiosity got the best of me, and I made my way to her room. It still looked as it always had, although the bed hadn't been made, of course, and the stereo cabinet was open. She must have been playing V's records again. I peeked into the garish red pitcher and bowl to see the sparkle of the lighter glaring back at me along with the little pink-toned rock that I had secured for her. This was her treasure trove for safekeeping, her hiding spot once again.

I sat down on the bed and rested my head in my hands, staring at my feet. I was thinking to myself how foolish I'd been, fearing that my own granddaughter was out to get me. This was my Arlo, our Arlo. I just needed to get her through the next few days and it would all be better... just get her to her follow-up appointment with her doctors. Maybe they could adjust her meds again, just get... My thoughts trailed off as I lifted my head and noticed something that made the hairs on my arms and on the back of my neck stand up, like they do when something is horribly wrong.

The bag was gone. That heavy leather bag that held the detailed manifesto outlining a young girl's hopes and dreams—and her plans to derail our lives, was gone. I glanced quickly at the floor and around the room but saw nothing out of place. Only the heavy leather bag with her well-laid plans was missing.

"Bobo... where are ya? You coming?" her voice came from the back porch. Hurriedly, and with confusion, I got out of her room and headed back down the hall towards the back porch where my granddaughter was waiting for me. My heart was racing once again, and I was trying to calm my panic as I met her face to face at the sliding glass door.

"You don't look great, Bobo... you doin' OK?" she asked, putting her hand on my shoulder. Swallowing the dry lump that was now nestled in my throat and trying to calm the tremor that was threatening to make my hands shake, I croaked back, "Just tired, kid, that's all."

"I don't know Bobo... you are all sweaty and pale, not looking too good. Why don't you rest a little and we can leave later on this afternoon? Maybe you need some more of your meds? Can I go get them for ya? Let me just..." she trailed off, heading out to the kitchen to grab my pills. I would be lying if I said that the thought didn't cross my mind that my own granddaughter was trying to overdose me with my own meds. I would also be lying if I were to say that at that point, I actually cared.

CHAPTER 13
ROAD TRIPPIN'

AS WE walked out to the car in the mid-morning sun, I still wasn't feeling in tiptop shape. I had decided to let Arlo drive. She smiled and gingerly crawled into the driver's side of Elvis, put the key in the ignition, and fired her up. A mischievous grin crept slowly across her face as it had a habit of doing, like no time had passed, and she was fiddling with the old eight-track player as I entered the car.

I could hear John Denver's "Rocky Mountain High" come to life through the crackling speakers and for just a tiny fragment in my mind, I could have sworn that our dear V was along for the ride, perched in the back seat, nestled in with her wide-brimmed sun hat and red lips, just like when we taught Arlo to drive, when she was obviously much too young to be doing so. But V knew by then that she might not make it, that her days were numbered here on this unforgiving mud ball that we lived on, and by God, she didn't want to miss any of the milestones if she could help it.

When the car backed out and headed out of the drive, I turned to Arlo, who resembled her grandma so much these days, although her hair was now not long enough to sweep high into a bun. She had it pulled up into some sort of a clip thing with loose pieces falling around her face. She seemed to have aged years in just a few days, but I reckon a haircut and stress can do that to a human.

"Hey Arlo, remember when Nonna V and me taught ya how to drive?" I asked, feeling the warmth of the sun on the side of my face as I turned to look out the window, imagining those carefree days so long ago. The barren and cracked land that held the salt flats appeared in the distance, and I noticed a flock of geese slowly making their way overhead.

Nine. There were nine. One more odd goose out. My brain began to relent into a hazy exhausted and medicated bliss, and somewhere in that haze I vaguely remember trying to sort out what may have happened to that flock of geese, why the one traveled alone at the end of the formation, yet still hung on to the flock. I had wondered... until her voice summoned me back once again to the present time in the car. I had been so close to the edge of sleep... so close.

"Oh my gosh, Bobo! It was hilarious! Remember how you and Nonna pretended to be cars and made me try parallel parking between the both of you out at the quarry? Thank God that woman was quick to move, cause I just about ran her over!" Silence fell upon the car as she went on, "Hell, I was only what, ten? It was the damn year of cancer, wasn't it? Goddamn I miss her, Bobo. She seemed to always have the answers, always holding us all together, ya know? What I would do just to be able to lean on her now..." I could hear Arlo saying from somewhere far off on the horizon as I leaned my warm head against the cool passenger side door window and closed my eyes.

I had been more exhausted than I had thought, and I just couldn't fight the heaviness that was pushing down on my eyelids and my heart any longer. A peaceful sleep had finally found me in the car that day, on the way to Arlo's place.

Arlo's place. That sounds so strange now. Arlo's place. For what felt like that girl's entire existence, Arlo hadn't a place that she fit into.

I can remember when she was just a little peanut and started staying with us overnights when her mama was working, or for weeks in the summer when there were no babysitters, or at least no money to pay the babysitters. She had always enjoyed the simplest of things, like V's homemade freezer pops made of the cheapest fruit punch that came out of a can. I can still taste that biting metal flavor on my lips with that first bite on a wickedly hot day.

We would sit outside in our ragged lawn chairs, and I would let her "help" me with whatever I was working on, whatever it was that was keeping me busy that day. When she was about four, I had her set up at a little station in the yard with a gallon pail in front of her and a stack of old computer switchboards. I showed her how to use the little needle-nosed pliers that were almost too big for her small palms to take the tiny bits of copper-coated filament out of the board and separate it into another bucket. She had been fascinated as to how things were joined together, and even more intrigued to learn how they could be ripped apart. She had always been a great little scrapping buddy.

Arlo always liked to keep her mind busy, kind of like me, I guess. It wasn't good for either of us to let ourselves just sit idle, so we would always have something in the works to pass the time. We had to. Really, there weren't many kids around where we lived, so she spent a lot of time either just alone or with V and me. We loved every second of it though. My heart still listens for her to come barreling through the front door, telling me about her day's greatest adventures or what plans she had come up with for the Jav when she got older.

Nodding off in the car, my overactive brain and straining heart were able to relax. Gone were the pressures of trying to defend her, to save her from whatever she may have done. Gone was the panic of my own mental stability and the dread of getting older. In the car that day, it was just me and my granddaughter going for a ride, not knowing where we would end up, but knowing that we were in it together.

I had been lost, listlessly floating on an ocean of memories. I'd settled in nicely somewhere around the time when she was about eleven or so, us sitting in the backyard on those damn, worn-out old lawn chairs listening to a ball game on the radio while shelling some corn for V for supper. I could remember the smell of meatloaf wafting from the broken screen in the kitchen window, and I could hear the undeniable crackle of the old radio speakers as the excited announcer delivered the play-by-play. Looking over at Arlo, she seemed to be content, seemed to be at peace for now, shucking the sweetcorn and ignoring the outside world for a little while longer. It was hot. The sun was becoming unbearably hot on my forehead, and I had begun to feel sick.

I heard her from the echoes somewhere before my eyes could adjust to actually see her. "Bobo, hey Bobo. We're here," came her voice from the driver's side of Elvis. My burning eyes shot right open, almost not wanting to leave the simpler times I had been visiting in my sleep. I stared at her in confusion for a moment before glancing around quickly.

"We are where, exactly?" I asked, not recognizing a damn thing that I was looking at around the car. My neck was starting to ache from the weird position that I had fallen asleep in, which she noticed as I was rubbing my neck.

"My place, Bobo, my place. Hey, you doing OK? Let me get you some Ibuprofen." Her voice trailed off as she grabbed a bag from behind her in the back seat. I sat staring out the side window at brick buildings that I didn't recognize, trying to come out of my stupor and figure out what the hell this kid was up to and just how the hell long I had been out of it.

"Arlo, where did you say we were? I feel like I just fell asleep. We can't have made it very far in that time," I still just sat, mesmerized by the foreign building out of my window. She had grabbed the bag from the back, spun back around in her seat, and was now rifling through it, searching for one of the many pill bottles that I could hear clanging together in the bag. Her fingers finally found the bottle of Ibuprofen she was searching for, and she popped off the top.

I will not lie. When I went from staring out of the window and my gaze fell back upon my granddaughter, there was a brief moment when I looked at the bottle in her hand and my heart froze. For a millisecond, I let myself wonder if what she was about to hand me was just Ibuprofen, or if something a little more sinister was going on. Did I trust her? Was she actually out to end me, to end us both?

"Here Bobo, take these," she said, handing me a couple of little red pills and a bottle of water from the back seat.

"I don't know that I really need 'em, kid. I think my neck was just kinked from leaning against that damn window for so long. I really don't think..." I trailed off before I was interrupted again.

"What do you mean, Bobo? You weren't out that long. I don't live *that* far from ya. Now here... stop being proud and just take the dang pills, would ya?" she said, thrusting the pills into my arthritic hand. As I stopped arguing and sheepishly took the pills, my mind was racing all over the place. What the hell did she mean she didn't live that far from me? She'd lived a couple hours away from me for a few years now, ever since she graduated from school and hooked up with Derrick. Oh, God... Derrick. And what had become of him? What was I about to bear witness to at this apartment?

I looked down at the little red pills, then back out the side window, still not recognizing where the hell we were and not knowing what this kid was up to now. Fine. I would play along. I was getting too old for this shit and I was tired at that point. I threw the little red-coated bastards in my mouth, staring back out of the window of Elvis, hoping they wouldn't kill me. Then again, maybe I had hoped that they would. Fuck.

"OK, Bobo, here's the plan," she began, while I was still only half listening while fighting to get my bearings and make sense of the little brick building I was staring out at from the passenger window. I could not wrap my head around this place and I knew that something was very wrong.

"We have to be a little quiet going in, Bobo, cause my neighbor is a blabbermouth," she started. Wait... so she didn't want the nosy neighbor to know we were there? Why? What was this girl trying to hide? "I just don't want to get stuck talking with her, that's all. We will never get out of here then," she said as she flung her bag of pills back into the back seat and grabbed her mint lip balm off of the dash, rubbing it across her cracked lips as she spoke.

"Now, I really don't plan on taking much, so when we go in, you can just have a seat in the living room and I will grab some stuff from my room and we can be gone again, OK? I want to be back home before it gets too dark out." These were the words that came from her mouth, but what I heard was more like, "Don't touch anything, don't snoop around, and I'll be right back."

She climbed out of her side of the car, then opened the trunk to retrieve only one empty tote to take in with her, the lid bobbing around from side to side. "Come on, Bobo, let's do this," was all she hollered over her shoulder as I steadied myself getting out of the car.

I watched her head up into the entryway of the two-story brick building that seemed to house four apartments, based on the mailbox that hung outside on the stoop. She turned right into the entryway, placing the tote on the floor while she was fumbling through her pockets. I guessed that she was looking for the key. She looked flustered as I called out, "Above the door frame kiddo." She froze, staring at me for a moment, then sighed and stood on her tiptoes to reach above the frame.

I didn't know where the hell I was. I didn't know for sure whose damn apartment this was. The one thing that I did know was that all my life, I had been the poster child for losing things. Keys especially. I also always wanted our home to be open to Arlo, so when she was very young, we would hide the house key in a planter or under the front rug. As she grew taller, the key eventually made its way above the door. I suppose, somewhere in my exhaustion and drugged state, my timelines collided, and I thought we were back at the house, years ago.

Instead of feeling bad about it, I had to grin and giggle when I realized I had rubbed off on our girl, as I watched her retrieve her key from above. At least I guessed somehow this was her door. I just didn't understand the whole situation. I helped that girl move in years ago. I can tell you what street her apartment was on. There was a poplar tree out front, and the front door was orange. She had been on the second floor; I had thought it to be the safest. This place, whatever it was, was *not* it. Since I had slept the whole way there, I didn't even know what the hell town we were in, let alone how far away we were from home. I would have to try to pay more attention on the way back.

As I slowly followed her up to the door, I realized that I needed to brace myself for whatever was in there. I knew that when she caught Derrick with her roommate and threw them both out, things hadn't ended well. I expected that there had to have been arguing, screaming even. I expected things to be thrown around, plants overturned, maybe pictures broken. These were the original things that I had expected to see. That was what I would have expected to see in her apartment before I had found the gun, and the knife with the crimson rust on the delicate pearl handle.

That was before I discovered the bloody clothes and the damn hat that I was still foolishly wearing on my head that she was trying to convince me was mine, just to throw me off of her trail. Oh, my girl, what have you done?

I stood in the doorway with my hand on the frame, peering into the apartment, as she had disappeared somewhere into the back. My ears were screaming with my heartbeat in my head and I felt nauseous. I was terrified to look around, scared to step inside. I had half expected to see blood spattered across a wall, broken shards of glass scattered around the floor. But there was none.

I stepped inside for a better look around and saw nothing out of place. There was a fern in the windowsill, Fifi's empty crystal food and water bowls over on the floor by the fridge (although much larger than what that little cat would need) and the quilt that V had sewn for her years ago, folded and tossed over the love seat, covered in animal hair. Nothing really seemed to be out of place. There was surely no sign of a major struggle that went on in here.

I walked towards the kitchen and I could hear her shuffling around in the back of the apartment. "Ya need any help back there, kid?" I shouted, not meaning for it to be as loud as it came out. Immediately her little face poked out of a doorway down the hallway with a stunned look, her green eyes wide, as she put her fingers to her lips and whispered back loudly, "Bobo... shush. Remember? We are trying to be quiet. Do you want to grab my med box from off the top of the fridge out there?" Then her face disappeared back into the room at the end of the hall as quickly as it had appeared. I could hear her jostling things around back there and decided to just do as she had asked of me.

Limping into the foreign kitchen, I noticed the pictures that were stuck to the front of the fridge with her little plastic alphabet magnets that she had always gotten a kick out of.

Standing silently in front of the fridge, I stared at the photo of Arlo with V taken years ago in front of the Ferris wheel at the little town carnival for the Fourth of July celebration. She must have been around eight or nine there in that photo, grinning ear to ear and hanging on to a stuffed cat she had won by picking up a little faded rubber duck from a blow-up pool using a fishing rod. That effort had earned her a prize that matched the color of the duck.

She had loved that little stuffed cat so much. The poor thing had seen better days, though. I quietly chuckled, thinking of V throwing the dirty thing in the washer and being shocked when she went to take it out and the dang leg had fallen off! V had to do a little animal surgery on it really quick before the kiddo got home from school. I don't think she had ever noticed the jagged stitch marks that her loving Nonna V had carefully mended that little leg back on with. Or if she did, she never said anything and loved the little mangled creature just the same. Yup, those were the days.

I glanced around at a few other photos, some faces that I didn't know. There was a picture of her standing with her mom and dad at graduation and another with them together at another ceremony that I couldn't place, and it took me by surprise. I could count on my hand the number of times Tara and Rhoads had been in the same room together since their divorce all those years ago, and I couldn't for the life of me figure out when the hell that picture was snapped.

It looked like Arlo was getting some kind of award or being presented with something. And then there was the way she was dressed in that photo. Her hair was a little shorter, much like it was now, but she had on some goofy looking dress pants and dress shirt, nothing like what she would normally wear. There were a few other people in the background too, smiling and seeming to have a good time, all dressed kind of like she was.

I moved up even closer to study the picture, and I noticed something else that was odd. Rhoads and Tara… they didn't look well at all. They appeared to be tired, maybe older looking. I felt like my tired eyes were playing tricks on me as I leaned right into the picture and made the chilling discovery that Rhoads had grayish hair and his eyes had creased and wrinkled around the edges. Tara's too. What. The. Hell.

"Did you find them, Bobo?" Arlo half whispered and half hissed from the back of the apartment. I backed up from the fridge, rubbing my eyes and cleared my throat. Damn eyes. They were watering now, and I couldn't honestly tell ya if it was from being tired, from emotions wearing me down, or from the panic that I was slowly losing my mind. I glanced up above the fridge, where next to a couple of boxes of cereal, I saw her med box.

"Yup, got it!" I softly responded to the voice down the hall. I reached above my head to grab the lime green box of pills from their resting spot, pulling them down towards me and knocking something else loose, causing it to come crashing down to the floor, its contents now loosely rolling around on the scratched beige linoleum tiles.

I squatted down, because let's face it, bending over ain't what it used to be, and came face to face with what I had knocked loose.

There was a small green cardboard box that was well worn, and scattered all around the kitchen floor now were the contents, which appeared to be nine-millimeter shells.

"You OK out there?" The faceless voice was quietly calling out from the back of the apartment.

"Just fine, Arlo, just fine," I shot back, quickly and perhaps more loudly than I had meant to. I sat in my squatted position, staring blankly at the bullets, trying to make sense of it. Why were these here? She didn't own a handgun that I knew of. She…

"Oh, dear God," I slowly exhaled out, quietly to no one as visions of the gun in the fraidy hole came rushing back in a flood of memories that I didn't want to go back to. Could these belong to the gun that I had meticulously disposed of out at V's serene resting place beneath her beloved rose bush only days ago? My arthritic fingers were shaking as I hurriedly attempted to grab all the little roly-poly bastards and shove them back into their box.

"Almost got it all, Bobo! Be out in a sec!" Arlo quietly hollered, again, from somewhere down the hall. I wanted to puke and my head was a whirling aching mess at that point, but I had tried to gain my wits about me once again and stood to tuck the little box back above the fridge, next to the bag of kibble that had been stowed there.

Breathe in... breathe out... (this little light of mine...) Breathe in, 1...2...3... Breathe out... 1...2...3.. (I'm gonna let it shine...) I had been standing silently in the center of the kitchen, staring blankly at the linoleum on the floor, counting the craze lines on the tiles with the lime green med box perched beneath my arm when she walked back into my sight, shoving a heavy tote with the lid securely fastened on it.

"Hey Bobo, you don't look too good. You don't look too good at all!" she blurted, stubbing her toe on the tote while running towards me to take my arm. "Let's just sit for a minute Bobo, no rush!" she said, walking me slowly over to the dark green microfiber loveseat and sitting us both down.

"What the hell, Bobo? I leave you for just a few minutes and you look like you've stared death right in the face! What's going on with you? Maybe this was too much too soon. Maybe we shouldn't have come here... maybe we..." She started to panic, eyes wide with fear.

"Oh cripes, kid, calm down. I dropped your med box and when I went to pick it up, I just got a little lightheaded was all. Nothing to be getting your undies in a bunch over." I had turned to face her, forcing a smile upon my blank face. She sat next to me, staring blankly, almost as if she was trying to look into my eyes and read what the hell had been rolling around in my brain.

"Well, why don't I get ya some water, Bobo? You hungry?" she was already halfway to the kitchen before I could answer.

"Hey there, kid, this was supposed to be about me helping you out. You don't need to be making any kind of fuss over me," and I was breathing in, 1...2...3... and out, 1...2...3... (This little light of mine...) In, 1...2...3... and out, 1...2...3... I sat there on the loveseat, almost in a haze of confusion. What the hell was wrong with me and why wasn't anything making sense? I had almost built up the courage enough to question my dear Arlo about the mysterious bullets when she reappeared with a couple of orange round tablets, a can of pop, and a bag of tater chips.

"Here ya go, Bobo. Sorry I don't have more to give ya, but I'm wondering if your sugar is low and maybe this would help ya out. She spoke sweetly, holding out her offerings to this failing old man. I sat the tater chips in my lap and grabbed the pop with one hand and the couple of chalky orange looking tablets with the other. Last time she gave me red tablets, weren't they? Wonder what the hell the orange ones were gonna do to me.

For a few whole seconds, I debated hiding them under my tongue and then spitting them out when I excused myself to take a pee. But in that moment, looking into her lost green and lonely eyes, I figured that if she was dancing on the edge of this world, not knowing if she wanted to hang around or not, then hell, I may as well join her. I wasn't gonna spend my time obsessing over whether or not my granddaughter was trying to kill me. Let what may come, come, as V would always say.

I popped those little orange bastards into the back of my throat and washed it down with a little bit of pop. I had been kind of hungry. Hell, maybe my damn diabetes was acting up again. This didn't really feel like my heart this time, so I had been a little less worried about it. I pulled open the bag of tater chips and sat there, next to my Arlo, snacking away like she was a kid again, both of our hands covered in the salty crumbs of goodness, taterchip oil glistening off of our fingers. These were the good times. I had made a mental note that this is what the good times felt like.

Like all good times, though, it had to end. We had to get going and head back home again. After we ate and sat there for a few more minutes, I begun to feel less panicked, a little more calm, but very tired.

"Do you need me to help you grab anything, girl? I can carry the bin for ya if you want to grab anything else..." I began to ask, when she immediately cut me off with a shocked look of intrigue and terror on her face.

"No, Bobo! Don't you go anywhere near that heavy old tote! I got it!" She almost raised her voice and barked the orders at me. Well, that was intriguing. Why didn't she want me near that tote? Why didn't she want me to go anywhere near the bedroom in the back of the apartment? Oh God! The bedroom! That was probably where it happened! That would have been where she would have found Derrick with the roommate! Shit, shit, shit. Maybe I just didn't want to know...

She calmly threw her head back and laughed. "I mean, I am perfectly capable of grabbing that dang tote, Bobo. I don't want you fussing over me and worrying about me in your weakened state. Let me help you for once, OK?"

Staring at her, I couldn't help but to be lulled into a false sense of security and wanting to trust her with my whole heart. She was an extension of us, V and I. Her hair, her looks, her heart. All V. But her fire and attitude and will to survive, world be damned, that was like looking into a goddamn shattered mirror.

CHAPTER 14
AND WE MEET AGAIN

ARLO STOOD and glanced around the little living room. "I think I'm good, Bobo. I'm just gonna run and pee quick and we can get going, OK? Just sit here for a minute and eat a few more chips. I want you to be able to make it to the car so we can head back. Don't rush getting up," she sweetly spoke towards me, but I couldn't miss the careful, yet disturbing sideways glance that she gave that damn tote she had dropped, still sitting at the edge of the hall and the little kitchen. She quickly took off down the hall, and in the time it took her to get to the bathroom a few feet away and shut the door, I had already popped up off the love seat myself, limping my way as quickly as I could over towards the bin.

I hesitated there, with my hand on the lid, not entirely sure that I wanted to peek inside. My body was achy and warm and my head was beginning to throb again. Listening for any sign that she would be coming out, I tried to control my racing heart and labored breathing. With trembling fingers, I reached for the lid of the tote to ever-so-quietly peel back just the corner to take a peek inside.

The toilet flushed from down the hall and I could hear the water running in the sink. My eyes tried to focus on what she could possibly be hiding in the tote. At first glance, I could only see a sweatshirt that had been thrown on the top of the pile within the tote, one of her favorites, but when I quickly lifted that off, I could see a couple of photo albums that had been tucked neatly beneath it. Relief filled my body as I heard the water shut off, and right as I was about to close the lid, I swiftly pushed one of the photo albums to the side, exposing the greatest horror that I could imagine.

There, beneath the photo albums that presumably had held years of precious memories of my girl, beneath the ragged old sweatshirt that she had thrown in, and nestled on top of what seemed to be a few more clothing items, was a hand. A fucking hand! I don't know if the hand that was peeking out from the clothes in the bin was attached to an arm, or anything else, but I had no time to find out. As I rushed to flop the sweatshirt back over the top and went to snap the lid back down again, my eyes caught the sight of dark, rusty, dried blood that had been sprayed across the front of the sweatshirt. I could hear Arlo coughing from down the hallway as I snapped that lid back down and sat on the closest chair near the door, an old wooden dining chair.

She came out of the bathroom all smiles, like there was nothing to hide. Like she hadn't just spent an hour packing a bin full of God knows what to haul the hell on out of here. What the hell had she done? How many bins had she already taken out of here? Her smile fell and her eyebrows raised in deep concern when she noticed I was sitting almost slumped over now in that chair, struggling to catch my breath and even stay awake.

So damn tired. Breathe in, 1...2...3... Breathe out, (This little light of mine...) Breathe in, 1...2...3... Breathe out, (I'm gonna let it shine....) I glanced past her towards the back bedroom, which she had made sure that I hadn't been into yet. What was she hiding in there? What had she done? Did I even want to know? I didn't think my heart or my sanity could take the pain of what may be hiding beyond that bedroom door.

My eyes were once again getting heavy, and I had begun to sweat again, unsure whether it was the stress of it all, my heart, my meds... who the hell knew? All I knew was that I was sitting on a dining room chair staring at my granddaughter, who may or may not have killed someone and who may or may have been trying to kill me too.

"Jesus Bobo, what's gotten into you? I knew we shouldn't have come. I knew this was just too much too soon for you. Let me grab the last few things. We need to get going," she grumbled as she was hurrying to get her shoes back on, glancing around the room, grabbing odds and ends of paperwork and things as she went. She went over by the door and grabbed a plastic tote bag from a hook, quickly cramming paperwork and unopened mail inside. Then, she ran back into the kitchen, and I couldn't help but wince a little as I saw her swiftly open a drawer, grab a couple of folding knives and shove them into the bag. She was also frantically opening and slamming cupboards, grabbing all the medication bottles that she could find, tossing them in as well.

She walked over to the fridge, and right as she had her hand on the handle, her toe kicked something and it rolled across the faded and cracked cream-colored linoleum floor. Sweat was rolling down my back as she knelt down to pick up what she had kicked with her toe. As she stood up, she held the bullet between two fingers, looked up at me, grinned and said, "sneaky little bastards."

She then reached up on top of the fridge, grabbing the tattered green box that held the rest of the bullets, and after dropping the rogue bullet back in, tossed it in her tote too. She made no mention of the bullets as she opened the fridge, grabbed a water bottle, and walked back over to me. Her steps were slow and deliberate. Heal toe, heal toe. Although it was only perhaps six feet from where I had been sitting, I felt like she was methodically calculating her next words, her next moves as she made that walk.

I have never feared my granddaughter. Arlo has been many things in her life. She has been confused, lost, left out. She has felt out of place, like a nuisance, and of no value.

I have come to her defense in the middle of the night when she needed me. I have sat across the desk from asshole teachers and principals whose agendas were only to protect the reputations of their schools, not to defend and protect their more quiet, awkward students, the ones who weren't of any value towards their precious sports teams or GPAs.

For years, I have seen that girl battle her own demons while trying to find her way... her path in this godforsaken world. Never once did I think she would turn on me. Never once did my brain need to tell my heart to put up a shield, to protect myself from what she had become. Never once had I ever thought I wouldn't be able to help her, to protect her, to lead her forward in this world so she could get the hell out of our trailer court and on to a better life. Never once... until that day.

She knelt in front of me as I sheepishly hung my head. I was weak. I was tired. I just wanted to go home. With a tongue as sharp as her old pearl-handled folding knife that her daddy gave her, now spattered with crusty crimson, she let the words flow out of her mouth like volatile lava, ebbing down a mountain, swallowing everything in its wake in a fiery inferno.

"Bobo," she began, placing one hand on my knee and looking right into my exhausted eyes. "I'm not sure what's going on with you, but I'm going to get you home now. You aren't well. You aren't well at all, and frankly, you are scaring me," she whispered with a sharp tongue as she thrust the water bottle into my hand. She then fished around in her little tote bag until her fingers fell upon an unmarked orange medication bottle of pills. Red pills. Again.

After popping the top off and gently sprinkling one, two, three pills into her hand, she then reached her hand out to offer them to me.

"I'm OK kid, I don't think I need..." I began, but I was quickly cut off by her insistence.

"Jeepers cripes Bobo, you ain't getting any better if you don't take your damn pills. Now just take them! Please..." she trailed off, her face falling into a desperate contortion of pain and pleading, which left me unsure as to whether she was actually trying to help me or end me. I just didn't know anymore. Somewhere in the past twenty-two years, I had lost where the lines started and ended. I no longer knew who was trying to save whom, or who wanted to be saved.

"OK, Arlo, OK," my arthritic hands shakily took the pills from her small hand and threw them back into my throat, washing them down with the water. I sat for just a second, still fighting the room that had been swirling around my head, trying to keep my wits about me. She smiled, softening her grip on my thigh and stood back up.

"Let's get you out to the car, Bobo. Let's go home," Arlo whispered, opening the door.

"Let me at least help you get your things out to the car. I could help you with the tote," I offered, knowing full well that I would be met with an unwavering resistance.

"No!" she was quick to whisper back, now that the door was open., " Bobo, I told you, I got it. Let's just get you to the car and then I will come back in to get it. Here, if you want to help carry something, take this.." her voice trailed off as she reached back around to the other side of the door, grabbing an unfamiliar coat. She lunged it into my arms and held my arm as we headed back out the door.

It really must have been a sight to see us shuffling back to the car. At that point, my head had gone from spinning to feeling like it was in a vice, and all I wanted to do was block out the light and sleep. Her little voice had been sweetly chattering all the way back to the car as we walked arm in arm. I couldn't recall a damn thing that she was talking about. All I knew was that her voice, my Arlo's voice, was the one thing that I could count on, the one thing that had always been a constant in my world and that would lull me into a false sense of safety.

She helped me into the car, where I then sat quietly as she opened the trunk, tossing her bag in before heading back into the apartment for the dreaded tote. She's a small thing, so it was no surprise that when she came back out, she was struggling with the weight of the tote. Actually, she had given up on carrying it at that point and was bent over it, shoving it across the yard to the back of the car. When she made it to the trunk, I could hear her straining to try to lift the bin. I hand-cranked open the window and hollered out, "Need help, Arlo?"

There was a hesitation before I heard a sheepish "yup" coming from behind the car. Slowly, I slid off the coat that I had been holding on my lap and started to get out. As I did, something fell out of the coat pocket onto the floor. I leaned down before getting out to grab whatever had escaped.

There, on the floorboards of Elvis, my gnarled and cramped fingers gingerly picked up a set of shoelaces that had been tied into a little messy ball of a knot. Tied to one end was what I believed to be Arlo's engagement ring. At that moment, all the air was sucked out of the car. How was this possible? I had already seen that ring back at the fraidy hole days ago! Why was it here? And why the fuck, upon closer inspection, was there blood on the laces?

I frantically shoved the wad of shoelace and the ring back into the pocket, then dropped the coat back onto the seat before stepping out of the car. I had made my way to the trunk of the Javelin, where Arlo stood, nervously stepping side to side. I leaned over to grab a side of the tote and the damn thing barely budged.

"Christ, Arlo, what the hell is in here? Do we really need all of this… whatever it is? Maybe you could split it into a couple of totes, or…" I nervously spat out before once again being cut off.

"No, no, it's just some heavier books and stuff in the bottom, Bobo. It will be fine if we just lift it together. I can always take the stuff out little by little, but I just want to hurry up and get it in there so we can get home. How are ya feeling?" she asked. Her pacing had stopped, and she was staring at me curiously.

There were so many scenarios that were playing out in my mind, so many questions that I wasn't sure that I wanted the answers to. Instead, I let out a deep breath and said, "I'm OK, kid. I'll be fine. Just tired. Now come on, you lift that side and we should be able to get it in there."

I had to shut off my brain. I had to kick into autopilot once again, just like that night so many years ago at the quarry. When your brain kicks into autopilot like that, your emotions dull and even fear becomes numb. We each grabbed a side of that old tote and after a couple of tries, heaved it into the trunk of the Jav. After I reached up for the lid of the trunk and slammed it shut, an icy trickle of déjà vu ran up my spine as I slammed it down and turned to look at Arlo.

She just stood there, staring down at the trunk lid, breathing shallowly. Methodically, she broke her stare, forcing a smile to once again crawl across her cracked lips. Her eyes turned to meet mine like nothing had happened.

"OK, Let's get going then!" She forced the smile to stay in place as she walked back to the driver's side door. I knew, though. She couldn't hide the fact that she too had just felt the déjà vu. She had just felt that flood of memories return from long ago from that night at the quarry. It didn't matter that we had never spoken of it again. Truth was that it had happened, and our guilty conscience, no matter how justified, still liked to kick in every now and then to remind us that we are human, and that no amount of ignoring he past would bring logic to what we had done, nor would it erase it from our memory.

Back in the car and finally headed home, Arlo once again messed with the eight-track knobs, trying to find the music that would drown out her thoughts. I was exhausted and had caught a little chill from sweating trying to get that damn tote into the trunk. I pulled that old, worn, leather jacket up over myself and finally stopped fighting the heaviness that had been weighing down on my eyes.

With my eyes closed, the world once again disappeared. It stopped spinning long enough for my nausea to die down. I could hear her in the distance, singing along to her Nonna's old music, just like when she was a kid. I could picture V sitting in the back seat, loving the joyride and singing right along too. I swear, I could almost smell her lavender-scented face cream.

"This is a pretty nice jacket, kid. Where'd you get it?" I blurted out over the music, not really focusing on the answer. I was so warm suddenly, from my toes to my head, just about to enter a blissful sleep that would hopefully carry me all the way home, when the words that I heard come firing back at me plunged me into a darker abyss.

With the giggle of a teenager, Arlo stopped singing long enough to answer, "Bobo, why are you being so silly today? You know whose coat that is! I only wore it all the time way back in high school! Isn't it great? I found it out in the fraidy hole when I was digging around in some totes! I figured since he was planning on moving in with me, it would be a fun surprise when he got here!"

Swirling again, my head could make no sense of what she was saying. *Who?* I don't remember that damn jacket from when she was a kid. I don't know who the hell she was talking about moving in with. What was wrong with me? It felt as though I was falling into a sleep that I couldn't wake myself up from. My chest was tight again, making it hard for me to even breathe, let alone throw these questions out there to her.

"Breathe, Bobo, breathe!" I could hear her shouting at me as I felt the car pull over to the dusty shoulder, wheels coming to an ungraceful and forced stop. She had stopped the car and turned towards me, taking my face in her hands. "I think it's a panic attack, Bobo, like when I used to have them! Remember when you and Nonna V would tell me to sing my song and breathe?"

I forced my eyes back open to stare into the eyes of the child that I loved so fiercely, so effortlessly, yet was also now so terrified of. What was happening to me?

"Breathe, 1...2...3... Breathe, damn it!" she was screaming into my face now.

"This little light of mine... 1...2...3.... I'm gonna let it shine... 1...2...3..." I could hear in my screaming ears, unsure if it was a voice from my Arlo now or from the past that was forcing me to pay attention and try to breathe.

"This little light of mine... Breathe, 1...2...3..." I could clearly hear the Arlo who was sitting right next to me in the car chanting in a sing-songy little voice. I turned to look at her and saw that she looked frightened, panicked even, her green eyes pooled in tears.

"Please, Bobo... grandpa please..." she pleaded as the wind picked up, swirling the dirt and grime around the car. I could see beyond her, through the window, that a flock of geese were once again in the sky, seemingly once again an uneven number. "This little light of mine... 1...2...3..." she kept right on singing.

I had begun to count in my head, focusing on slowing down my breaths, willing myself to breathe in a more gracious pattern. With my head still spinning, my ears ringing, and the nausea returning, I took a few more deep breaths and settled back into my seat.

"It's OK, Arlo, it's OK. I'm OK," I said, relaxing back beneath the old leather coat.

"Jesus, you scared me. Let's not do that again and just make it home, OK?" she pleaded, still visibly shaken as she turned to put the car back in drive and pulled back out onto the road.

"Just a long few days, that's all," I half whispered, listening to my heart pound in my ears and still working to calm my breathing down. I leaned my head once again on the cool glass of the passenger side window and let the sound of the humming of the tires over the rutted out blacktop carry my thoughts back to another place. I tried to stare out into the vast openness of the salt flats, searching for the missing goose, but my body was fighting my urge to stay awake. Before I nodded off completely, giving in to the meds that I suspected were responsible for my rapid and sudden incoherence, the warm jacket once again misfired a fleeting thought in my mind, causing me to blurt out the question of which I feared the answer.

"Nice jacket, kid. Whose did you say it was?" I asked once again, barely staying awake long enough to hear the answer. As my eyes slammed shut with the heavy weight of meds, my mind had already begun to drift back to the trailer, back to when she was a kid, even before the "accident" at the quarry. We were in the kitchen and V was making her potato salad—always add relish and a little mustard—that was her secret! Arlo was at the table playing with her robot with the creepy eyes. I had come up behind V, putting my hands around her waist, sinking my head into her shoulder with my eyes closed, just taking in the scent of her lavender face cream.

"They're coming to get us, ya know," Arlo was muttering from the table. "I said, they are coming to get us," I heard her say again, this time with a more menacing force. My eyes shot open, darting over to where she was playing, noticing the damn robot had begun creeping towards me on its own.

"What the hell?" I blurted out as I was cut off by Arlo shouting, "Aliens! Aliens Bobo… they are coming to get us!"

In my nightmare, I quickly turned from watching Arlo and the creepy robot back to V, looking down at her hands as she was peeling the potatoes—always peel away from yourself so you don't cut yourself. The ring. The ring looked so familiar, yet not at all. It was Arlo's ring! I dropped my arms from her waist and backed away. What was happening? Why was this happening?

As the little robot with blinking eyes kept advancing towards me and my panic started to come back, I heard out of nowhere her voice, Arlo's voice, coming from the car that I was still riding in. Yet my mind wanted to go home, go back in time and find peace, go back to V.

"The jacket? Well, you know, since we decided to move him in with me, I thought it would be fun to have that there for him when he came home! That's why we had to be quiet, ya know? His name isn't on the lease and I don't want anyone to know he will be there, so I have kind of been avoiding the landlord about the whole thing, in case she sees him. She has seen me moving totes in and out enough times already. I think she's getting suspicious," she giggled, and I could hear her fiddling once again with V's eight-track player.

I felt paralyzed, maybe by meds, maybe by fear, but I couldn't speak. I could do nothing more than lay there, head pressed against the window, longing for this all to be a dream, longing for all of my geese to be in the flock again in a nice flying pattern, when she spoke the words that threw me off of the ledge and into the dark abyss.

"Bast, Bobo. It's Bast's coat. He's coming back."

CHAPTER 15
PIT OF HELL

FOR THE rest of the ride home, I believe I was dancing between reality and an unconscious state, not really knowing where I wanted to be. I could hear her singing sweetly for most of the ride, aside from when she was talking out loud about how she didn't think that the little bit of medicine that she gave me would knock me out that fast and that she only wanted me to relax. At least I thought that's what she had said in my reality. And I had thought that she was alone.

There was also an undefined moment that lived somewhere in the darkness of my mind that I was still unsure whether it really happened or if it was just a byproduct of the exhaustion and the drugs. From somewhere beyond my nocturnal state, I can remember the car stopping and the driver's side door opening, allowing a gritty gust of wind to fill the interior of the car. The all too familiar grit settled on my lips. When I licked them, I could immediately taste the salty, grimy quarry dust, the comforting, yet alarming taste of home.

Things get fuzzy for me though when I try to think back on that night because like I said, I was exhausted and drugged, slipping in and out between a foggy consciousness and a dreamworld that was filled with warm memories and sweet horrors of my past. I think I remember the sound of Arlo rustling around towards the trunk of the car, and I know I remember her yelling out a firm, "Damn it!" before stomping back over to the driver's side and reaching into the backseat to retrieve her bag. I forced my heavy eyelids open just enough to see her pulling a pair of men's tennis shoes out of the bag with no laces before hearing her whisper to no one, or maybe it was someone, "Almost forgot about the footprints," as she clumsily kicked off her shoes and stuffed her feet into the obviously too big and well-worn shoes that once belonged to a living, breathing man. I didn't even have to watch the rest, to witness the monster of my own making. I had done this. I had set the blueprint in her mind that now allowed her to operate on autopilot.

She was out there in the night, beneath a lazy summer sky, stomping around to lead them off of her trail. She was out there in the grit, in the dust and rock piles she had always called home, to bury her treasure. At one point in her life, she had loved him. Derrick had been the one who was going to lead her out of this town and on to their next big adventure.

They had met right after high school, purely by coincidence, at the local lake while she was fishing off of a dock. He was an avid outdoorsman, knew all there was to know about hiking, geocaching, hunting and fishing. It was his zest for adventure that ignited her spirit and his smothering love that extinguished all of her insecurities she had about the world. For the first time in many years, she finally had felt like she belonged somewhere to someone, finally had a road map of life laid out in front of her. And she stuck to that plan.

Arlo had wanted to go into law enforcement and enrolled in school, moving in with the roommate. While she was at school, he was working as both a fishing tour guide and a sales attendant at a tackle shop. He would drive the two hours up to see her on the weekends, every weekend, and they would hike, fish, and just explore. It was during this time that I can honestly say that she was at her best.

Unfortunately, the man who provided her with the highest of highs ultimately drug her into the deepest pit of hell. Although they had just gotten engaged and were already planning out the wedding, one day her class was canceled and she went back to her apartment a little early on a Friday. That's when she walked in on him and the roommate, frolicking in bed. I cannot tell you exactly what went on in that little apartment that day, or what became of the roommate or the fiancé. I had never heard from them again, although I never really talked to them much in the first place, so what the hell did I know?

When she called me to tell me she was heading home for a while, I knew her spirit had been broken and it was over. I knew the old Arlo would tearfully return, and as luck would have it, Bast wouldn't be far behind. Misery loves company. What I do know, was that we had ended up at the quarry. Again.

I sat in the car that night, exhausted and unable to rouse myself to move, to really care about what was going on around me. I felt the car jostle about as she was lifting something heavy out of the trunk, and I could hear the clanging of the cold metal stairs as something heavy bounced its way along or was being heaved along. There was a short, yet deafening silence before the unmistakable growl of the rock crusher came to life, followed by a grinding sound of something being caught in her jaws. But then I heard something that I hadn't been expecting. She started growling along again, followed by a slow grind, then started up again.

A shocking realization easily came to the forefront of my mind after all the years of working out at that place. The jaws of the crusher weren't getting caught on anything. Someone was throwing something in there, slowing it down, and speeding it up again, and repeating the sequence. Starting, slowing and speeding it up again. But why? What would the point of that be? Nothing would look like an accident. Nothing would look like someone had fallen in *if* that's what she had done with Derrick's body.

Unless. My mind recoiled back to the quick flash of what I had seen in that tote at her place, the appearance of a hand reaching out of the pile of clothes and photo albums. All I had seen, all I could have seen, was only a hand. Arlo had said the landlady had run into her moving totes out already. But yet she hadn't brought any home, so...

I gasped in a half-conscious state, gagging on the chalky gritty dust that entombed the car and drifted into my nostrils, realizing what she had done. She wasn't trying to make anything look like an accident. She was making him disappear, part by grisly part. I started to cough as the crusher finally slowed, then churned to a silent halt, followed by the sound of the metal stairs creaking once again, beneath the weight of her small feet. I pushed my eyelids open once more just to see her clear the final landing, the tote now clumsily balanced out in front of her, clearly with nothing left inside. And her feet were now bare.

I let my heavy lids fall once again, giving in to the medicated coma I was about to blissfully enter as she got back into the car, sliding her own shoes back on. She reached over to my side, pulling the jacket snugly up under my chin once again, and started the car. She hesitated for a couple of minutes, and before I drifted off, head still leaning against the cool glass window of the passenger side door, I heard her softly begin to cry.

I woke up to her tapping me on the shoulder. "Bobo. Hey Bobo, we're home," she was whispering into my face. My head was still pounding as I forced my eyes to open. "Let's get you inside. You hungry?" she questioned, stepping away from the car and walking towards the side door of the trailer.

"Wait… what about your stuff? Don't you want to get it out of the trunk?" I shouted out, not even stopping to gauge the impact of what I was saying until the words were already gone. But without hesitation, she just waved an arm in the air. "Nah, that can wait until tomorrow," she shouted, followed by the loud clang of the door slamming shut.

I sat stunned, momentarily, trying to sort out in my brain what the hell had just happened. Slowly, I got out of the car, absent-mindedly clinging to the leather coat as I headed towards the trailer. I could hear her rummaging through the kitchen as I stepped inside, happy to see a friendly and familiar face as Fifi met me at the front door, surely upset that we were late to dinner. Dropping the jacket on the chair by the door, I scooped up that little three-legged wonder and nuzzled my face into her fur as we headed for the kitchen.

"You really need to go shopping, Bobo," I heard her voice coming from behind the open fridge door. "There's really not too much in here.

I'm thinking maybe a bologna sandwich and tater chips? You need mayo too... you're out," she said in a manner so calmly that it almost broke me. Had I helped to create someone so sinister, so evil, so brokenhearted that she was able to carry out such dastardly and wicked deeds one minute, then calmly talk about lunch meat and mayo the next, like nothing was wrong? Had I done this to her, made her autopilot setting so easily accessed and manipulated?

"Grab a bowl for Fifi," was all I could say. She turned towards me rolling her eyes, "Fifi is just fine, Bobo," she huffed as she went back to rummaging through the poorly stocked fridge.

"She's hungry, Arlo, just look at her," I said, holding out the little ball of fur towards her. Arlo glanced up from what she was doing, laughed, and went to grab a bowl for her.

"She likes the fancy bowls, the crystal on the fluted stems," I teased, and heard a giggle from where she was digging through the cupboard.

"Fine. Here you go, Bobo, for Ms. Feefs," she exhaled, holding out the bowl. I put Fifi down on her spot on the avocado green counter next to the sink facing out of the window. I reached into a cupboard for a can of cat food, but found none, so I opened a can of tuna fish instead, dropped it in the fancy bowl and set it next to my three-legged buddy. "There ya go, Feefers, there ya go..." I sang to her, patting her on the head.

"Great, OK, come on Bobo, let's eat," Arlo said as she took the sandwich stuff and chips over to the little dining table. I grabbed a couple of paper plates.

We ate mostly in silence, my head still pounding and unsure as to what to say to her. "How you feeling, kid?" was about all I could think of to say. After all, she had been in the hospital before I had gotten there, and I really hadn't asked her too much about it. Then again, that was just us. When the shit hit the fan, we really didn't talk about it. We just let it go.

"I swear, Bobo, I can't believe that after everything you have been through in the last few days, it's still *me* that you're worried about. I told ya, I'm good, nothing to worry about here," she half mumbled, biting into her sandwich. All at once, she grinned while staring over my head. I knew what she was looking at.

Directly behind me was a photo of my V. I had it etched in my brain from years of sitting at this table, staring at it. It was from when Arlo was a peanut and we had taken her fishing. V had her hair pulled up into a bun and a blue satin scarf tied around her head, with little dark, loose curls falling down around her ears. Her lips were a bright pink, and I had snapped the picture as she sat at the edge of the dock looking out over the water as the warm glow of a setting sun entranced her thoughts. Right after I had snapped that picture, something had tugged at her line, pulling it into the water, causing her and Arlo to laugh as I dropped my camera and leaned to grab it, dang near falling into the water myself. Those were the best of days.

"Hey Bobo, we should have a dish of ISH cream," she giggled.

With an instinctive smile growing across my lips, I immediately replied, "That's a great idea… ISH cream it will be," and jumped up to hobble to the freezer. Opening the freezer door and reaching in to grab one of my constant supplies of quarts of old-fashioned vanilla ice cream, I hadn't noticed the tears that were welling up in my eyes.

V's love of simple things had always included a dish—never a cone—of "ISH" cream. V's dad had always called it that, so that was what she knew to call it. After he had passed, it was her way of keeping his memory alive. So on that night, in V's and my trailer, my granddaughter and I had a dish of ISH cream for V, and forgot about the rest of the world.

Before we headed for bed that night, Arlo had stopped by my room to say goodnight and bring me my evening pills. With a calmed heart, yet still feeling unwell, I took the pills with no hesitation, hugged her goodnight, and laid down with Fifi, hoping to dream of a better tomorrow.

She hesitated at the door, turned around and whispered, "Love you Grandpa,"

"Love you too Arlo Marie. Give 'em hell," I whispered back as she closed the door, leaving only the dim hallway light to creep beneath the door, illuminating the glowing orange carpet that V had so dearly loved. I heard her walk down the hall towards the bathroom, pulling a load of wet laundry from the washer and starting the dryer. I fell asleep that night to the comforting humming of that old dryer, and then the water running in the shower, a sound I had missed. A sound that meant I wasn't there alone.

When your kids or grandkids grow up, you realize just how much the simplest memories mean to you. When you are in the thick of raising them, loving them, helping them grow, you never think that it's the minute, day-to-day things that you'll pray to dream about each night, just to have those feelings again, that connection, that closeness. You spend your life protecting them, putting them first, and fiercely loving them, then they do their job and grow up and leave. As they should.

But at night, if you are lucky, your mind just might fall back and echo memories to you from the darkness, allowing you to hold their tiny hands in yours again, feel the warmth of their hot breath on your face waking you up in the mornings once more, or hearing their little voices call from the swing, begging for just one more special twisty push. I hear her all the time. My days are mostly filled with useless ways to pass the time anymore. But my nights? My nights belong to her. To them.

She's four, snuggled up next to V on the couch under her quilt, shoving her little jammie covered feet in my face, "Rub them Bobo, my toes are cold," she would giggle. She's six, standing at the edge of the dock, patiently waiting for me to worm her fishing pole. She's eight, laying on the couch with a fever, just wanting V to rub her head and make it better while watching the game shows on TV. She's ten, crawling up a pile of rocks out at the quarry, calling for me to come see the best one yet. She's ten, holding my hand at V's graveside, dropping petals onto her grave.

"This little light of mine..." I could hear the words calling from the darkness, stunning my heart through the silence. Then a giggle. "I'm gonna let it shine..." The little voice had grown from a whisper to a louder, closer voice. "This little light…" I could feel the warm breath on my cheek and instinctively opened my eyes.

Stunned, I saw the face of my Arlo, my now grown Arlo, hovering inches above my face. The glow from the window illuminated her damp hair, which was hanging loose and long, dripping down onto my chest. I could hear the welcome hum of the dryer in the background. I was no longer sleeping. This was no longer Arlo.

"Hide it under a bucket? No!" she hissed at my face, continuing to sing. Confused and in a dazed shock, I pushed her away, leaping off of the opposite side of the bed. I stood staring at her as she reached over and flipped on the light.

"Bobo, what the hell? Are you OK?" she shouted, standing there, on the opposite side of my bed, scratching her head.

"Me? Why the hell were you hovering over me? What are you trying to do to me?" I hysterically shouted, no longer able to control my composure.

"Bobo, I got out of the shower and you were hollering in here about something, I was just coming to see if you were OK! Jesus… just go back to bed!" she shouted, spinning around to leave the room, slamming the door as she went.

Stunned, I slowly shuffled around the bed towards the light switch, clicking it back off again. "Christ," I had thought to myself, "What kind of drugs was I on?" I sat back down on the bed, threw the covers over me and laid back down, listening to the welcome white noise of her hairdryer running down the hall.

Instinctively, I once again reached out and felt that Fifi had jumped back onto the bed, and once again, I wasn't alone in the dark. The sheets smelled of bleach, just how V had taught me to do, and I could hear the low buzzing sound that the old electric alarm clock made as it sat perched on the bedside table next to V's watch that she had laid down there one day, never to be picked up again. I closed my eyes once more, begging for a catatonic sleep to find me and bring peace to my soul one more time.

She's three, sitting in her car seat with chubby little toes kicking wildly into the back of my seat, excited about her kid's meal and French fries, eager to get her hands on the plastic toy. She's five, crying on the soccer field because it was a coed league, which V and I hadn't realized, and Arlo refused to play with the boys, screaming and staring at the both of us with terrified eyes as tears flowed down her cherubic cheeks with her balled-up baby blanket pulled up beneath her chin in disappointment. She's six, cautiously sitting next to the car, skinned knees covered in band-aides, watching me change a tire, just waiting to hand me a tool, a flashlight, a beer, anything that she could.

She's nine, baking cookies in the kitchen with V, running me in scoops of dough when V had her back turned, giggling the whole time. She's twelve, barely speaking to me, but still making a point of locking her arms around me every night to tell me goodnight. She's fourteen, laying in a hospital bed, begging me not to leave her, begging me to stay…

"Bobo, hey Bobo…." I heard her voice once again call from somewhere in the darkness. I had ignored it and tried to focus on my dreams, not wanting to leave the memories behind. She's three, sitting on the curb waiting for the Fourth of July parade to start, sticky from the Push-Up Pop she just ate, blue juice trickling down her chin and dripping onto her belly. She's four, running through the living room with her baby doll on her hip, chasing the dog. She's six, lining up her toy cars all over the back stoop, polishing them up with an old shop rag, calling me over to look at her favorite ones..

"Bobo, you awake?" a voice threatened my peace as a sliver of light from the hallway cut across the room, urging me to open my eyes. I still fought the urge, clinging to simpler times. She is eight now, decked out in a helmet, squealing as she races the neighbor's four-wheeler up and down the road. Now she's nine. Cautiously pulling plugs from circuit boards and dropping them into the bucket on a sultry afternoon next to me in the backyard while listening to the local ball game.

"I think he's sleeping Bast, I don't know…" I heard the words echo from the hallway. The door pushed open a crack more, and I was once again pulled from my escape, from the world that I had been so desperately trying to hang on to, the memories that gave me my only comfort. I ever so gently forced my one eye to open, lifting my lid just a crack... just enough to see her silhouette in the hallway turning to speak to someone who was on the other side of the door frame.

"Bast, what the hell am I supposed to do now? Are you ready?" The words ran like a toxic stream of acid from her sharp tongue as my mind raced to make sense of what I was hearing, my breath silenced by the stunning revelation of who was now in my trailer.

Bast was home, and he had come to take her with him.

CHAPTER 16
THE JUMP

YOU THINK you know your kids, or the kids that you raised as your own. You know them because they grew up under your roof, lived by your rules—for the most part—and were taught the basic values in life like love, respect and honor. You managed to raise them in a corrupt world spread across an unforgiving landscape built of hate and prejudices. You sacrificed in order to push them further ahead. You instilled in them the courage to move forward when the world was against them, to be better than what was expected of them. Your children, and grandchildren, become who you have built them to be.

That is, unless their paths are altered and their hearts become manipulated by the wrong person at just the right moment in time, when they are at their most vulnerable. Then the comforting shag rug gets pulled out from beneath your slightly unstable feet, and the world, as you knew it to be, crumbles like the rocks in the crusher.

I felt my loyal Fifi leap on me before I saw her coming. My eyes met hers, now frantic and wide as the light from the hall illuminated the wild terror and stoic confusion that contorted her angelic face. She settled onto my chest, standing guard and watching the commotion that was unfolding in the bedroom doorway. I could feel Feefs' body, tensed, lying right above my heart, and as she guarded me, there was no content purring vibrating from her now, only a soft growl that emanated from her little throat, aimed at the one other person who loved her as much as I did.

I lay there panicked, my heart racing beneath my dear Feefs. I had to think that my stress was what made her turn on our girl, the person who rescued her and gave her another shot at life. Seeing me, her current caretaker, the only person who she could depend on and trust in this world anymore faltering and trembling in fear must have been why Fifi was so quick to turn on the one who loved her first, the one who had saved her. Because in the end, I guess it didn't matter who had rescued her; she was in survival mode, doing what seemed to benefit her the most, and to hell with the consequences.

I continued laying there, holding my breath until I was ready to pop, too terrified of my own granddaughter to even move. Had everything that I worried about, everything that I assumed of her, been correct? Did Arlo want to take us both out of this world?

The door continued to open and before she stepped into the room, Arlo half whispered over her shoulder, "Just get ready, Bast, I got this... then you can take him." Fifi, sensing that Arlo was up to sinister things, arched up on my chest and hissed, but then settled almost immediately as Arlo dropped a hand on top of the little furball's head and scratched her ears, sitting down on the mattress next to me. Fifi had begun to purr, comforted if not still confused, as I lie there, silently wishing that I could escape into my head again, trying to conjure up the warm memories of her youth, of a more loving and stable time.

Instead, the darkness did not want me, and I remained anchored steadfastly into my reality, mercilessly pinching my eyes closed, not wanting to see her face. I didn't want to see the desperate or confused look in her eyes. I didn't want to face who she had become.

"Bobo, you awake?" she whispered in my ear, her warm breath hot on my cheek, just like when she was a little kid. "Bobo, we have to get up," she spoke a little louder.

Acting like I was stirring from my sleep, I pretended to pry my eyelids open and seem confused as to why she was sitting there, although I knew damn well what this was coming down to. Gently pushing Fifi off of my chest, I sat up and came face to face with her.

The girl whom I had raised, the child whom I would give my last breath to, was staring me right in the eyes with the look of a deranged soul, no mercy dancing in her mind. There was no soul behind those emerald-green pools that were blankly staring back at me. I glanced down to see her holding something. Her fingers curled around something that shimmered just a touch in the slice of light that was licking its way through the darkness from the hallway light.

My spine electrified, and every hair on my body raised on point as my mind clicked into focus, realizing what she was grasping: the little pearl-handled knife that Rhoads had given her. The little pearl-handled knife she had hidden and I had found over and over again. The little pearl-handled knife that carried traces of secrets that should stay buried. In shock, I shoved her away from me and stumbled out of the bed, ending up cornering myself over by the window as Fifi sat at the foot of the bed, looking on, watching the end play out.

"Jesus, Bobo, you're gonna hurt yourself! Just calm down," she spoke into the half-lit room as there was rustling and movement happening behind her in the hallway. She was speaking, but her words were being drowned out by a loud ringing that was screaming in my ears, I suppose out of fear, or maybe from the fight-or-flight rush of adrenaline that you hear people talk about. My heart was pounding so forcefully beneath my ribs that I thought a heart attack was imminent. I began to panic, my thoughts flooding so fast and so aggressively that I could no longer keep them bottled up any longer. If she had come to destroy me, I sure as hell wasn't going to cower in a corner and make it easy for her. Damn it, I was going to fight.

"After all that I have done for you! After everything that V and I have done for you all these years! Arlo Marie, what the hell are you thinking? Pull your head out of your ass and wake up!" I launched into the first of a few tirades, wildly fluctuating between sobbing and screaming, standing next to the window in the corner in my pajama pants and old undershirt, still veiled beneath the darkness of the room, only the glow of the hallway light illuminating the show that we were putting on, and at that point, probably loud enough for most of the neighbors to hear.

She launched off of the bed herself, sending Fifi flying off and running under the bed for shelter. There was a desperate anger in her voice as she calmly spoke, lashing into my heart with each word that she meticulously uttered. "Bobo, I love you so much. So, so much. You know that I do. But we can't do this anymore. This is no way to live, no way to exist. It's just too hard, too..."

I didn't let her finish as she was making her way over to my dresser, carefully opening the second drawer from the top, knowing full well what was in there.

"Goddamn it kid! Life is hard!" I was shouting then, oblivious to the neighbors' hearing and, at that point, not giving a shit if they did. "It's hard, and it hurts and we just keep moving on. It's all we can do! It isn't like we get a choice in this! It isn't like I chose for V to die or Rhoads or Tara to walk away, or for you to be stuck with me! But these were our cards, kid! You don't get to make the call on this. You can't just say that we are done!" Out of breath, I trailed off, no longer focusing on my words, but now watching in horror in the light of the hallway as her little hand reached beneath my socks in the second drawer and pulled out my trusty nine millimeter and sat it on the top of the dresser. She reached back into the drawer, presumably looking for the loaded clip, yet said nothing.

"Please Arlo, my sweet girl. Don't do this! Don't do it honey..." I was crying, crawling back up on the bed to get by her, planning on sprinting past her and towards the door. Just as she was spinning around to see what I was doing, I felt my bad leg give out from under me as I leapt, my body defying me and reducing me to a crumbling heap on the floor. My body collapsed, and my heart and fighting spirit went with it.

I had no defense left. Humbly, I sat there on the bedroom floor, on the shag carpet that V had lovingly picked out a lifetime ago. I sat there on the floor of our little trailer, the humble home that used to ring with her voice and smell of whatever V was cooking. I hung my head in my hands, closing my eyes, feeling Fifi cuddling in next to my bad leg. I sat there, on the floor of our little home where all of my best memories began, and where I tried to race back to every time I closed my eyes. I sat there, blocking out Arlo's voice, blocking out what was about to happen.

I could hear the voice of a seven-year-old Arlo calling me into the darkness, "This little light of mine…" Breathe, 1…2…3… I ran my arthritic and trembling fingers through Fifi's whisper-soft hair and could feel her body begin to warmly vibrate against my leg. "I'm gonna let it shine…" her little voice called out. Breathe, 1…2…3… I continued to sit there on the floor of my home, body defiant and the end near, no longer in a panic, but ready to finally be at peace. I kept stroking Fifi's fur and allowed myself to block out what was about to happen, trying to find my way back to the darkness. Back to where my happiness lay.

"Hide it under a bucket?" Little Arlo giggled and ran, mischievously begging me to follow her. She was eight now, sitting on the edge of the patio eating a golden piece of summer sweetcorn, butter rolling down her chin. She was ten now, once again by my side in the garage, saying nothing, but watching every move I made while working on the car, V's eight tracks filling the air around us. Sitting on the floor of our trailer in the dimly lit room, my mind swirled, flashing moment by glorious, hard-fought moment in front of my eyes, every sweet memory that I had hung on to, every painful reminder that V was gone, my Arlo could no longer be saved, and the end was coming for me.

"No!" she giggled again from somewhere in a field, now about eleven, while plotting out her latest treasure map, trying to figure out where she last buried her stash of stones and goodies. "I'm gonna let it shine…" Breathe, 1…2…3… "Let it shine… let it shine…" she sang. The memories flashed faster, more like a dizzying carousel that made my head spin. The mood of the memories was now darker, somber, and twisted.

She was ten, sobbing as we sat next to V one last time, her precious little hand in mine, gently kissing the Nonna whom she had loved so much a final goodbye. She was twelve, lying in a hospital bed with bandaged arms, swearing at me and telling me she wanted to die. She was thirteen, screaming at me from down the hall, promising me that it was Bast's idea to run away, not hers.

She was fifteen, waiting for me at the police station, promising me that it was Bast who stole from the local grocery store, not her. She was sixteen on the front stoop of the trailer after running away for a couple of weeks and showing back up again, like nothing had ever happened, saying nothing, but wrapping her arms around my neck and giving me a big hug.

Breathe, 1...2...3... This little light of mine... She was fourteen, huddled in the corner of the fraidy hole, trembling with fear and uncertainty, staring up at me with pleading pools of emerald green eyes as her attacker sat slumped over in a heap only feet away, gasping for one last breath, that damn little robot from her childhood staring with its fire red eyes, just a few feet away on the shelf where she had placed it all those years ago.

A struggle from the hallway and the clash of rising voices pierced through my darkened world and I felt myself falling back into reality, back into the trailer, back onto the shag carpet that I was sitting on, head in my hands, gently rocking back and forth as I stroked Fifi, eyes pinched tightly closed, trying to block out the pain of what was about to come.

"Bobo, Bobo, can you hear me?" her now adult voice was rising above the commotion in the hallway, trying to find its way to me, but I was fighting like hell not to let her in. I was desperately trying to get back to my memories, to where I wanted to be. Breathe, 1...2...3...

I never thought that I would feel more alone in this world than when I lost my V. That was the emptiest, darkest existence that I could have ever imagined. To love someone for so long, to have your soul entwined with theirs for so many blessed years, and then to be left to walk alone without them, well... it was a cruel twist of fate.

But I had my Arlo. My girl. And together, we weathered many a dark night, many nights by the fire, many nightmares along the way that shot you out of bed in a cold sweat. But we had made it through, her and I. I had almost gotten her out of here, almost pushed her on to a better life, in a better world that was a hell of a long way from Freedom.

But this was a new feeling of being alone. This was the bottom of a barrel that I hadn't even imagined existed. As I sat there on our shag carpeting in our little trailer, lost within my own head, I wept. I could feel the sting of tears filling up my eyes that were being pinched tightly shut out of sheer will because I didn't want to remember her this way.

I felt a shudder run its course up from the base of my feet, icing its way along the back of my legs, crawling up my spine and making my teeth chatter with fear. My ears stung with a high-pitched droning scream that I couldn't silence but was grateful that it was blocking out most of the surrounding sound. Breathe, 1...2...3... I would not think of her this way. I would not look at her. The memories that called to me in the darkness, the visions that came to me when I needed to escape. Those are what I would carry with me into the next life. I refused to see Arlo any other way.

Her voice broke through the screaming in my head, broke through the sound of my own sobbing, of my own heart being shattered, "God, I really hate to have to do this, Bobo, I do! But you have left me no choice!" she whispered, her voice closer to me than before, her breath hot upon my cheek once again.

I was no longer a man of great faith. I was not sure how anyone who had lived the life that I had battled could actually believe in a higher power. For what would be the point of putting someone through such great pain and agony only to let them live mercilessly through so much heartache for the rest of their time on earth? But in those final few moments, with Arlo by my side, I had no choice but to believe, to believe that love would transcend all of this and that somehow, we would all find our way back to each other again.

Shaking, sitting on the trailer floor, our humble little home, on our shag carpeting, I kept my eyes pinched tightly but stopped stroking Fifi's fur just long enough to reach out and feel around to grab the hand

of my granddaughter sitting next to me. Breathe, 1...2...3... I sat in silence, praying to a God that I wasn't even sure existed for a
granddaughter who, now, only existed in my heart.

The screaming in my ears quieted down. The violent shaking of my
limbs and chattering of my teeth had calmed, and my heart had slowed.
I could feel the tears freely streaming down my cheeks, tracing their
way around the two-day-old stubble. Echoing from somewhere in the
distance, from many years ago, her little voice called for me once again.
"I'm gonna let it shine" was the last thing I heard, in her innocent little
seven-year-old voice, right before they jumped me.

CHAPTER 17
SAVING US ALL

I STOOD there in the front of the room for a quick minute, nervously messin' with my belt buckle. Speaking in front of people never came easy for me, and I had already been talking for quite a while. It's not a simple thing to do, you best believe me, but when you get asked to help some kids that were like my Arlo, you just simmer down and do what needs to be done. Nervously, I glanced at the clock and then back around the room, quick-like. Clearing my throat, I said, "'Scuse me just a second," and my hands were shakin' like a leaf while I took a sip of water. I calmly looked back down at the notecards I had written to remind myself of what needed to be said.

"Sir?" I heard a small female voice come from somewhere in the back. "Can I ask you a question?"

I tried to see who was speaking, but there were so many families that had shown up and packed the room that I wasn't sure where that small voice was coming from. "Of course, ma'am, go right ahead," I responded to the faceless voice in the back.

"Well…" the small voice started out, "If I may ask, how old was Arlo when you knew she was affected?" The question stung my heart without it meaning to. While trying to come up with a decent answer, my mind reeled back through years of memories, almost like flipping quickly through an old photo album.

I can see that sweet girl laying in her hospital bed begging me to take her back home to the trailer with me. Back further, I can see her grinning and leaning on the hood of Elvis, dressed in her gold prom dress. She was sitting at the police station waiting for me to pick her up, scared to death. She was lying next to me on a train car out by the quarry watching fireworks after her mama left. She was running towards me with a broken arm. She was sitting next to me crying after we lost V. The answer came to me as clear as day. "Ten," my voice quivered as I replied, "She was ten."

"And what brought it on, if you don't mind me asking? I hope I'm not overstepping?" came another faceless voice from somewhere in the back as a hush fell over the crowd. They all wanted to feel normal. They just wanted to feel less alone. I tried to remember that these families were frightened too, just as I had been. They were thrown down their own fraidy holes and were trying to fight their way back out, but they were looking for hope to do it. I guess we were supposed to be that hope.

Again, I cleared my throat and continued on, calmly now, speaking to this room of families that had just been given the same diagnosis that my Arlo was labeled with all those years ago.

"Well, from what we know, and I reckon what you all have been told as well, it's brought on in part by traumatic events. In Arlo's world, the biggest traumatic event of all was losing her Nonna V. That shook that child. It messed with us all. But Arlo was so young back then that she just couldn't make sense of that loss. That was the first time she was triggered, when she was truly diagnosed," I answered while thinking about those first few days after we lost my sweet V.

It hadn't been hard on just Arlo; I don't know how I made it through those first days myself without her. That wasn't the first time that she had mentioned Alabaster, though. He had begun to appear when she was very young, maybe five or six years old. Back then, I had thought it was just an everyday imaginary friend. At first, I had thought a new friend would do her some good, get her mind off of her loss. But it didn't take too long for me to realize the truth about her beloved Bast.

"Although they say that trauma can be one cause of bringing it on, DNA can have something to do with it too, as I am sure you have also all been told," I continued on. This was where I reckon I should tell them about me. "I was also diagnosed, just like Arlo, but a little later in life. I have heard that there is a likelihood of this disease running through the dad's side of the family, but there's not a lot of proof of that yet either." Those words were hard to get out. I looked around the room nervously again as I collected my thoughts. I just wanted them to know it would be OK, that their families would be able to make it out of this too, like we had.

"I look at the diagnoses like this... it is almost like a perfect storm needs to happen in order to shake up your brain a bit and stuff it into the fraidy hole. Now, we are from Oklahoma, so we all know that a fraidy hole is a dark and confusing place to be during a storm. But as dark and confusing as it can be, there is a safety to it. As long as you stay in that hole while you are scared, you are supposed to be safe. And what do we do when we are in that dark hole, usually with not much light? We make up stories and things to make ourselves and our kids feel better and forget about the storm outside. That's what this illness is kinda like... a scary but safe little fraidy hole," I said, realizing that I was staring down at my cards almost the whole time and starting to fidget with my feet.

"So, with my Arlo, she already started with a couple of strikes against her. I had already been diagnosed, and she had a rough start to her life. Heck, that girl's rough start happened at birth when her and her mama both almost died! I think her sickness stayed away, or at least was very minimal, though, until she was about ten, right after her Nonna V died. That was when her talking about Bast had intensified, and he had gone from just a childhood buddy friend to more of a force in her life." I kept talking, not really even looking up.

I was talking with such speed now, almost like I wanted to get all the words out so I could just be done. I kept reading from my notecards and kind of noticed that the room got really quiet. I carried on though, Fifi standing loyally by my side, leaning into my leg. After all we had been through, she had really bonded to me and I started taking her everywhere I went, kind of like a dog. I was as attached to her as she had been to me.

"After every traumatic event in her life from that point forward, Bast would show up again. He was like her security in the fraidy hole. Nonna V died, Bast came. Her folks split. Bast came back. She had a hard time in school, Bast was there. He would be there to walk her through all the bad stuff in her life, falling off the slide and breaking her arm, getting caught stealing, almost drowning, crashing her car before prom, and even showing back up when she was twenty-two years old and she called off her engagement to her fiancé." I realized that my voice was trailing off as I began to frantically rush thorough the memories of all the hard stuff that I had been through with that kid.

My heart was racing and I was feeling lightheaded. My mouth had begun to get dry, making it hard to swallow. I just needed to breathe for a minute. Breathe, 1..2...3... I could hear her little voice from somewhere in my exhausted brain. "This little light of mine, I'm gonna let it shine..." Breathe, 1...2...3...

Looking out at the hopeful and terrified people, I tried to gather my composure, cleared my throat and began again. "What we do know about schizophrenia is that it is treatable. Just like the symptoms are different for different people, so are the treatments. An example for ya would be that when I've had episodes, I don't invent people or see people who aren't really there, like Arlo does with Bast. He's like our red flag now when we know she's going into what those fancy doctors refer to as an 'episode' again. I get confused about what is really happening and what is real life versus something that I may see on TV.

I have also been told that I become very paranoid and act like people are trying to hurt me when my medication needs to be adjusted again. Now with Arlo, she sees Bast and believes he is very real. She also has a tendency to try to harm herself, but then blames it on Bast. We have two very different kinds of the same illness, two different types of monsters to battle, if you will" and I am still breathing, 1... 2... 3... This little light of mine...

Inhale, 1…2…3…

Read the damn cards in your hands… 1…2…3…

I heard another faceless voice shout out from the interested and vulnerable crowd, wanting to know how Arlo came up with Bast's name. I instinctively grinned, glancing down at my shirt pocket, which always holds one of Arlos' little treasured rocks wherever I went, if nothing else, to remind me of a much simpler life… a time when our biggest worry was figuring out where we would go rock hunting next, then running home to V for a bowl of tater soup.

I choked back the tears, tucked those memories back into my heart, regained my composure and glanced back up at the crowd. With pride, I told them what her doctors and I had figured out. While that girl was growing up, she loved rocks. I worked for a long time at the local quarry, which is world-renowned for their Black Alabaster mines. Arlo and I spent many a summer over at that quarry, digging around in the rocks, fishing in the big blue hole. That quarry and those mines had become her comfort, her safety zone. Her mind had latched onto a safe word and given it a soul, first calling him Alabaster, then just Bast, as he hung around more in her altered reality and she became more and more familiar with him.

"And to the families that this debilitating illness affects, please feel comforted in knowing that there is a way forward, never really out, but always forward. This illness of the mind can be semi-controlled with proper medication and monitoring, and these children are able to live long and healthy lives, for the most part, remaining unaffected. It is your job as caregivers, and our job as a community to ensure that these children thrive and have the resources they need to make that happen." I had just finished reading one of the last cards when I glanced up and saw the mop of golden curls that I recognized.

A calmness filled my soul, a warmth embraced my heart, and I could feel the grin warm my face as my girl made her way over to where I stood in the front of the room. With pride, I stood next to my girl to introduce her, show her off, and let the world know that she had made it. We had made it. We may have had one hell of a ride to get here, but we had survived it all.

She stood there proudly next to Fifi and me in the front of the room, gracefully smiling at the crowd until I was finished with my lecture. I had wanted to stay to hear the next lecturer, but Arlo was adamant that we had to be going, for we had a meeting that I hadn't remembered. As the years roll by, I have noticed that things like dates and appointments do tend to slip my mind from time to time. A younger me would have noticed right away, recognizing the red flag that would mean my medications may need to be adjusted again. But this me, a much older me, relies a little more on Arlo now to keep me on the straight and narrow.

"Don't forget to grab Fifi," she winked at me as we headed for the car.

I would have known that car anywhere, regardless of what my mind tends to forget. Her beautiful dark green hue with the slight glimmer of sparkle, like a bumper car. Walking towards her in the lot, it was no surprise that Elvis was still Arlo's daily driver. As I reached for the door handle to set Fifi gently down in the backseat, for just a fraction of a second, my soul traveled back in time and caught a glimpse of our beloved V sitting there, red lipstick and big brimmed hat, just waiting to be taken out for a slow drive. I grinned, closed the door, and climbed into the passenger seat.

As I was fastening my seatbelt, Arlo being Arlo, began fiddling with the eight-track knobs once again bringing the car to life with music that we used to sing along to when she was a kid on drives either out to the quarry or out around the lake for a lake lap. I was quietly staring out the window, watching the sand and dirt swirl around the flats as we drove, wondering how hot it was going to get out, when Arlo spoke up.

"Now Bobo, do you remember what you are going to tell them?" she asked, glancing quickly in my direction as she drove. What was I telling who? Goddamn it, couldn't remember where we were going…

My girl ignored my pause and just continued chattering along. "Just remember, Bobo, they are wanting to meet with you to talk about changing up some of your medications, OK? I already told them you had mentioned last week that you were having issues with remembering some things and it was concerning for you.."

I did? Damn, I must have. I tried to leave her alone and let her just live her life. I don't enjoy being a burden on her and I try to not get her involved any more than I need to, but obviously I must have opened my big mouth. OK. So it's not a meeting, really. It's a doctor's appointment she is taking me to. That's cool, I can do that. I can hold my shit together a little while longer.

"Sorry, Arlo, I was just lost in thought, staring out the window. Remember when you were little and we would go out to the quarry and sit out on that barge in the channel, watching the fireworks over the Fourth of July? You were so young. Nonna was still here. Maybe you don't remember..." my voice trailed off as I went back to looking out the window. I was once again getting lost in thought, conjuring up my favorite memories as I glanced up at the sky. There they were. Flying towards the horizon, a gaggle of geese were making their way home in a V formation. Two, four, six, eight. There were eight! No one had been left behind or lost, four couples were accounted for. All was right in the world again.

"Of course I do!" she laughed.

"You do, what?" I quickly answered, turning from the window with a grin on my face, noticing that hers fell as soon as the words came out of my mouth. Well, hell, now what did I forget? I remembered!

"No Arlo, I'm OK. I was just focused on those geese out the window on the horizon. You know me and geese!" I assured her. "You were saying you remembered the fireworks on the barge." Proudly, I went back to looking out the window after giving her a wink.

She stumbled over her next words, probably relieved I wasn't losing my mind again. "You bet I do! It was silent out there at the quarry and the fireworks looked like they were falling down like rain on fire all around us as we lay there on our backs in the warmth of the July night, the gritty breeze swirling around. One of the best feelings in the world was being snuggled together on top of one of Nonna V's quilts laying on that dirty old barge, just Nonna, you, me and Bast," she excitedly rattled on as she stared forward, focused on the road and continuing to drive.

I felt sick. To be clear, there was a droning, screaming thing buzzing in my ears and my eyesight felt like a tunnel was closing in around me. Just when I thought things were good, just when I thought we had been living the last few years with a hint of normalcy, he rears his ugly head yet again. My heart was once again pounding against my ribcage and my breathing was becoming labored. Breathe, 1...2...3...

Not having any idea what her sweet and troubled soul had just triggered, what she had just let slip out of her subconscious and into the real world, she leaned her head forward, looking towards the horizon, making a funny face.

"Hey Bobo, there are no geese," she teased and winked.

"Oh, don't be a kidder," I grumbled, still stunned by what she had said about Bast, acting like he was in existence once again. I turned to glance back towards the horizon again. Fuck. She was right. There were no geese. I settled back into the passenger seat of the car that I had rebuilt with this girl, the car that drove us to and from hospitals, gravesides and treasure hunting, and just tried to breathe.

We drove along the last few miles of our journey, our heads just bobbing along to the music, probably both lost in our thoughts. As we pulled up to the town clinic and hospital that I knew all too well, she parked the car and fished around in her purse, retrieving her cell phone. As she pulled the phone out, a curious little wad fell to the floor from her purse.

I could hear her mumbling on the phone, letting the good doc know we were there, blah, blah, blah, as I reached down to the floorboards to see what had fallen out of her bag. With shaking fingers, I slowly picked up the wad of shoelaces, stained red and tied together in a loop. I held them in the air towards her, letting the sparkling diamond glimmer in the light. Without missing a beat, she winked at me, took the shoelaces, tying them around her neck like a makeshift necklace, letting the ring fall into place on her chest and said, "Hell of a treasure, huh? We really had to work for that one!"

I was slipping, falling really back into time, back into my mind, far away from that parking lot. I could see the good doctor walking out of the hospital with a couple of his cronies, ready to take me in. I gave up.

Slowly, I got out of the car, and she met me around back at the trunk. "I brought you some things, Bobo!" she said, gently lifting the trunk lid. Reaching in, she grabbed a bag that appeared to have some of my things, a few outfits and some books, photo albums. She also handed me a new MP3 player. Leaning in and whispering into my ear, her breath hot on my cheek, she said, "It won't be so lonely in there if you take a little part of her in there with ya. It's full of Nonna's favorite music. Love you always, Bobo."

I took the bag and headed towards the good doc once again, this time of my own free will. Suddenly remembering my Feefs, I spun around to shout out to her, "Take care of Fifi!"

With a quizzical look and a glance into the back seat, she hollered back, "Of course I will! I loved her first, didn't I?" But as I turned to walk away, I could hear her shout back one more thing, over her shoulder as she got back into the car. "Hey Bobo! Give 'em hell. See ya in seventy-two hours!"

Without looking back, I trudged forward, only glancing up towards the sky over the hospital as I made my way. There, high above the clouds, flew a gaggle of geese. Two, four, six... seven. One left alone in the back, still supporting and protecting their flock. I sighed and grinned as I shook hands with the good doc.

The mind is a curious thing.

EPILOGUE
OUTRUNNING THE GRIP OF THE FRAIDY HOLE

THE CALL came into the station around 4:30 one late afternoon, and as soon as the description came through, my heart fell and I immediately knew who it was that I was going to have to go and pick up yet again. They said that he wasn't bothering anyone this time, but that the good ol' boy was giving a lecture in the middle of city park to a group of geese that he was referring to as patients and families of patients, and he just couldn't understand why he was being asked to leave, needing to be gently escorted out of there. Didn't understand that he was frightening the families and children who had come to the park to play on that lazy summer afternoon. He was being defiant. Yet again.

My deputy walked by my office as soon as the call hummed softly over our airwaves. "Hey, Sheriff, are you heading over there to get him or do you want me to go this time around?" he questioned while not meeting my eyes. Instead, he kind of just stared down at the grimy old gray tile that had started to weather and peel up at the corners. He knew I would go. He knew it was my duty to go, but out of respect, he had made a half-hearted offer to me, anyway.

"I got him, Mike, thanks though," I breathlessly released the words into the empty and stale air.

How long had it been this time? Not quite a year, maybe eight months or so since I picked him up from the salt flats where he had been found wandering around having an argument, alone, with no one but the car, Elvis.

It had only been a few months before that when I had to pick him up from the cemetery, as he was muttering incoherently, trying to dig up God knows what from one of the graves.

Months before that, I had gotten to him just in time as he was fishing at the little dock and had managed to drop his pole in, but also defiantly screaming at me to just let him jump in, that he had wanted to be done with this life. He didn't recognize me that time, nor had he recognized me all those years ago when we were at the trailer and he had fallen off the deep end of sanity so harshly, that he thought I was trying to kill him, and I had to call for backup and have an ambulance come take him away. He had been so angry with me at that time, so defiant. That's the thing with this damn illness though. It's a thief of your consciousness, of everything you know to be true. Your once brilliant mind now hovers somewhere between a fuzzy reality and discombobulated memories of the past, intertwined with things that your mind has just made up along the way. But it feels so real. It is so real.

It wakes you up in the middle of the night and makes your eyes see things that aren't there. It discombobulates people from your past with what is happening presently and distorts your memories. Disorders of the brain are a waking hell, not only to the person who is dealing with them, but also for the families and friends who are left standing to tame the beast that is eating away at their brains.

It was only more insulting because this man had once had a brilliant mind, a gifted engineer who had graduated with honors and was valedictorian of his class. He was a man who designed launchpad prototypes and engine components for NASA in his spare time, in his earlier years, after his fall.

He had always kept his schizophrenia under control through regular dosing of medications and meeting with his team of doctors to have the dosages or medications changed as soon as he felt in imbalance starting to set in. He knew things would shift when he felt like his reality was chasing him, trying to shove him back down into his "fraidy hole." He had always referred to the altered state this way when he would find himself first being drawn in, and then trapped.

It wasn't until dementia started to spring up on him that he was no longer able to keep the monsters and voices at bay. At that point, he was like an old glass pop bottle that you opened and then put your finger over the hole and shook it up real good. As soon as you moved that finger, the contents of that bottle shot out, but no longer resembled the pop that was once inside. It had been distorted into a wild foam that, although still classified as that same pop, resembled nothing of what it was when it was safely housed in the bottle before the pressure was applied. I think of him that way often… the man who was so brilliant and then got himself all shook up. It was getting increasingly harder through the years to keep him contained in the bottle.

I sat for another long minute at my desk, just kind of staring out the window into the nothingness that was the salt flats across the street. I let my mind roll back quickly to a different time, a different life. I could still see the rock quarry that we would hang out at, trying to identify different types of rocks as kids.

My brother and I would spend hours climbing the sides of those piles of gravel and rock in the blazing blistering sun, filling our lungs with the gritty dust that plumed into the air out of the rock piles with every step we would take. We would throw our treasures into mason jars and cart them on home, tirelessly scrubbing them off with toothbrushes until the true beauty of those rocks really shined through. There was something so amazing at the time about finding something so dirty and polishing it up until it shined. But then the inevitable would happen and after the glistening rocks dried out by laying in the scorching sun on the windowsill, their glory was gone, their brightness faded, and they lost their shimmer and magic. We never lost our wonder and kept going on those rock hunts to uncover the treasures that were buried beneath our toes.

I took one last swallow of my pop, chewed up a couple of antacids, and grabbed the keys. The damn grit from the antacids in my teeth subtly reminded me of our time at the quarry, and a half-hearted grin crept mercilessly across my chapped lips. With a deep and burdening sigh, I stood, put on my hat, held my head high and walked toward the door.

A realization made me freeze right before I headed out. He couldn't see me like this. This uniform would throw him for a loop if he was in the middle of one of his spells, only confusing him further and causing an even bigger scene. "No," I said out loud in my little office as I was glancing down at my dress uniform, "this just won't do."

Instead, I hurried over to my locker, grabbing my civilian clothes, a worn pair of jeans and one of his old quarry sweatshirts to throw on. I shut the door and quickly changed, hanging the uniform back in my locker. Turning around to head for the door, I glimpsed myself in the mirror. I look nothing like what he has wedged in his head right now, no signs of any innocence left on my face. My eyes now creased at the edges and a frown line ran across my brow from years of hard work and worry. As I swept my hair up, piling it high into a tight bun, letting some of the golden curls fall down around my face, I caught a glimpse of my grandmother's wedding ring on my hand, knowing that would throw him off as well. Hurriedly, I grabbed a pair of shoelaces from my top desk drawer, took one and tied the ring to it for safekeeping, tossing it into my bag, like I usually do when I head out to pick him up. Seeing that ring triggers him somehow, sending his already failing mind somersaulting through time, bouncing between memories that were reality, things he had watched on TV, and paranoid illusions that he would make up as he went along.

Glancing in the mirror once more, I tried to envision what he was seeing as he would be looking at me. If he was too far into one of his episodes, would he know me at all? Would he see enough of a resemblance in my face, in my demeanor, in my voice, that his mind would play along, believing that it was still me from all those years ago, the me that helped hold his mind captive, helped to take care of him and made him feel safe? Would he still see it was me?

With an exasperated sigh, I rolled my eyes, grabbed the keys off the desk where I had flung them, and headed out to get him.

The only thought that was running through my head as I made my way across the little lot with the dry cracked cement was, "How am I going to convince him this time?" It just gets harder and harder to convince him to trust me. I decided I would be taking my own car, thinking that maybe it's the authoritative sheriff's car that aggravates him so badly. On second thought, it was probably just seeing me that did it. After all, when he looks at me, he sees a thousand lifetimes ago and it causes him to fear me, to fear the present, and to distrust himself.

I headed on down to the park, but I would be lying if I said I didn't take my time. There was a familiar, yet uncomfortable old feeling in the pit of my stomach, the kind that sets up in your innards when you are about to drop down that first hill of a rollercoaster for the first time, unsure of what was at the bottom and just praying that you make it out OK.

With my left hand on the wheel, I reached over into my bag to grab another roll of antacids. "This is ridiculous...." I blurted out to no one as I flicked two more into my mouth. I chewed those bitter gritty bastards up with a relentless fury that was now starting to build, smothering any sadness that may have still been residing in my heart.

"Damn it, damn it, damn it!" I yelled, slapping my hands on the top of the steering wheel at a stop sign near the park while trying to swallow what was left of those gritty pills. I had developed ulcers years ago, I suppose from the constant worrying about him and the constant pressure that I put on myself to do better, be better and try harder to get the hell out of Freedom.... yet here we were.

Looking around to be sure that I was the only car within earshot, I screamed. I let out all the fear and anger. I screamed again, releasing the years of pent-up rage. I screamed out of desperation for the years that I'd been carrying this heavy weight upon my shoulders. It was exhausting having to be the responsible one, having to be the only one left who took care of things, making sure things ran smoothly.

Maybe I wanted to cry, to run, to find safety in the arms of another, someone stronger and more capable than I was. Maybe I should have left this poor little town in the dust bowl of nowhere. I could have you know… I didn't have to stay.

I actually had plans to get the hell out of Freedom, wanting to go off to college and see another part of the world. A part of the world where there was a bustling city, bars on every corner and shopping centers spread out across clean and finely manicured lots. I wanted to live a few college years of the good life, if nothing more than to prove to myself that I could do it, that there was a way out of this small town. I had been destined to do so much more.

I was a talented student and even landed a pretty good scholarship all the way to the University of Minnesota! Unsure of what I really wanted to do with life, I figured I would start with some law classes and dreamt of maybe being a lawyer one day. In my 17-year-old brain, all I knew was that Minnesota was where the Mall of America was, there were plenty of lakes to swim in and hike around, and just maybe, I enjoyed visualizing myself sprawled out on a boat, just letting my body soak up that sunshine, kind of like my old rocks used to do on the windowsill when I was a kid.

Then the rug was pulled out from beneath us all, and my brother died. Until that point, he had always been the homebody, the older one who would stay on here and take care of things, tying up all the loose ends. Because he was a few years older than me, I never had to plan on being the responsible one. I never had to be the planner or the one who sorted things out. It was his job. All of this should have been his job.

He was twenty when he died. I was just about to graduate from high school and take on the world, when my world halted with such a force that it threw me into a depressed tailspin that became hard to crawl back out of. I developed anxiety and ulcers. I didn't sleep well, and I had nightmares about him.

He always was a car guy. He loved his vintage 1969 AMC Javelin that he lovingly called Nonna, after our late grandmother. He had worked hard to restore that old car to her glory for years, tinkering on it a little here and there. She was a fast car, built to hug the corners and burn rubber on the straightaways. After some begging on my part, he even let me be driven to my senior prom in it, by him, of course.

On a warm May evening, I had my picture taken in front of that old car in my gorgeous golden prom gown, before we headed out to prom, not knowing that the weather was about to take an awful turn. A storm had blown in out of nowhere, and although the swerving, gritty wind was a nuisance, it was the standing water that made him hydroplane and flip the car into the ditch. They found both him, and his old dog, Bus, lying beneath the mangled metal of green that sparkled when the light hit it.

We hadn't been that far from home, and I had managed to crawl out, miraculously unscathed, and was found incoherently wandering down the middle of the dirt road when the police cruisers showed up, right after the storm had gone through. Although I have no memory, they said that I used my brother's little pearl-handled pocketknife that he always had kept in the glove box, to free myself of the seatbelt, shredding my dress in the process.

If my Nonna had still been alive, she would have lost her soul that day, much like I did. But she had been long gone by then, breast cancer stealing her from us when I was about ten. I had no choice then but to be brave and soldier on. So that's what I did.

Bobo soldiered on by renaming the car Elvis and working on her for years to restore her to her former beauty. He always said it reminded him of a car he and Nonna used to have, a car that I would help him with when I was little. I would help him with the restorations when I was home. It gave us something to connect with and hang on to. Elvis had become our sense of normalcy in a chaotic world.

Although Freedom, Oklahoma is a long way from Minnesota, I've done OK here. I've made a life. I did go to school but stayed locally at the community college a town over and eventually, through God's grace alone, made my way here to the sheriff's office.

I don't have kids and I have found no one that I feel the need to attach myself to for the rest of my life. But I have my birds, Arlo and

Guthrie, named after one of Nonna's favorite singers. They were actually her parrots, two loud cockatoos, one a butter-yellow hue and the other a fiery red mane of feathers. With a life span that can go well into their sixties, I probably won't know much of a life without them.

On nice days, the boys and I will sit out on the back screened-in porch and listen to records, singing some of Nonna's favorite songs. It's a quiet life, a far cry away from the life that I thought I would escape to, but it's peaceful most of the time. And it's mine.

As I pulled Elvis up to the park, I could see the small group of passersby that had assembled to either gawk or assist, but mostly just to watch the spectacle. And there, in the center of the small growing group of people, he proudly stood among the gaggle of geese that were patiently waiting for him to finish his tirade and feed them. His arms were flailing wildly as he was giving a lecture of what he perceived to be of great importance. It pained me to see a man that used to hold such an esteemed position within the community be lost in time and displayed to us all as a reminder of what a thief time could be.

I put the car in park and collected myself. I stepped out of the vehicle, slid out of my light jacket, and just stood there momentarily, leaning against the car door and contemplating how to handle this one. "Damn it," I said in a hushed tone as I slowly closed the door and walked towards him.

He was dressed in shop overalls today, which was a far cry from the bathrobe that I'd found him in last time. His voice, though manic, was just as strong as it always was and carried over the crowd with such a presence, such dignity and authority. If a person didn't know any better, you would think that you were actually listening to a lauded professor or professional public speaker. But here, among the patient, hungry geese and the local townspeople who were watching in awe, eyes full of pity, his lecture was met with sadness. An unrelenting pity fell among them.

"Thanks everybody, I will take it from here," I hollered as I walked over to where he stood, perched on top of a picnic table, seemingly reading from a stack of cards that were in his hands.

The small crowd began to whisper and back away as I approached. The geese were unphased. As I made my way forward, I could hear a small part of his speech that I knew I had heard before. In fact, I just about have the damned thing memorized.

"And to the families that this debilitating illness affects, please feel comforted in knowing that there is a way forward, never really out, but always forward. This illness of the mind can be controlled with proper medication and monitoring and these children are able to live long and healthy lives, for the most part, remaining unaffected. It is your job as caregivers, and our job as a community to ensure that these children thrive and have the resources they need to make that happen," he spoke to the geese and the invisible room filled with people in a support group that existed twenty years ago for families of children who were newly diagnosed with schizophrenia. This had been his world and his glory. This is where he had volunteered his time his whole adult life after we lost Nonna, helping local communities come to terms with their children's and family members' diagnoses and pioneering fundraising efforts for better treatment options.

He had been a poster child of what proper medication can do for those affected by schizophrenia, a shining example of how a schizophrenic patient can not only have a normal everyday existence, but thrive in the world and be a beneficial component to society. He had helped to heal the broken minds and mend the broken hearts back together again. Until the dementia attacked him, an irony that had not been lost on me.

"Your children need your support, your guidance," he continued. "As I told my granddaughter many years ago, there is no fraidy hole in Oklahoma deep enough to hide in that I couldn't pull her out of," he lamented on, seemingly pausing for either applause or to reflect in some memory that he had contrived based on previous patients' stories.

In his altered mental state, he had become them all—all the parents, grandparents and families that came to him for guidance. Their battles had taken up a confused residence in his mind, and he fully believed that he had lived their battles. Getting old is a bitch. But getting old with dementia as a lifelong schizophrenic patient was damn near cruel.

I didn't even realize that I had relented to my emotions, letting tears escape from the place where I usually held them, a place that was closed off and protected. I hadn't noticed that my guard was down, that my hard-ass persona as a sheriff had been wiped away as easily as wiping away the grime on those old rocks plucked freshly from the rock quarry all those years ago. I sauntered up to him and took his hand in mine, looking directly into his smokey blue-gray eyes. They met my sharp green eyes in a moment of terror and softened.

"Well, hey there kid, I was just about getting ready to introduce ya!" the old man beamed at me, a mistaken recognition dancing somewhere in his darkness.

"And who are you introducing me to today?" I played along, already knowing the road he was traveling on. I knew the answer before he said a word.

He held my hand up in the air for all the geese to see and turned back around to the audience. "To the families, dear. I have to show them how well you turned out. We have to show them that it *is* possible to make it out of the fraidy hole, that this illness can be controlled," he went on.

I said nothing as I was introduced to the crowd in his mind and stood silently by while the audience he had envisioned applauded his efforts. I quietly stood there, letting the wind gently lick at my face while a fire I had stifled for so long was burning a hole right into my stomach.

"This, dear friends and patients, this is what hope looks like!" he exalted at the geese, who, by this time, had become tired of waiting and began to waddle away. Then he stood in silence.

"I didn't think you would be back, kid. It's been so long!" the old man said, tears forming in his eyes and a fleeting concern wandering across his brow. He was anxiously waiting for a response.

"You have done a great job here, very informative, but we need to be going now. You are... needed at the hospital, for... a meeting. I was supposed to pick you up and get you over there in time. Don't you remember?" I quietly asked him, ensuring that I didn't make eye contact again. I just couldn't. You never know what he might see in my eyes and how he would respond.

"By all means, then, we best go," he began, once again turning to thank his esteemed audience and bid them farewell.

"Don't forget Fifi. She's waiting for you," I choked out, trying to hold back tears as he looked stunned by the fact that he would ever forget his beloved Feefs and leave her behind.

I watched him slowly turn, not as steady on his feet as he once was, and carefully lean down to grab her, the ratty old stuffed toy cat I had cuddled a lifetime ago. The sad looking, little stuffed toy that now had only three legs after years of being loved on, that after Nonna passed away, no longer had anyone there to stitch it back on when it would fall off in the washing machine. He nuzzled the little cat for a brief moment, and we slowly limped our way towards the car.

As he was placing the little cat into the back of my car, there was just a brief pause when I felt like something may have clicked, as he looked at me ever so solemnly and words seemed to form behind those blue-gray eyes. Instead, he grinned before letting out a sigh and got into the car.

The drive over to the hospital was all of about fifteen minutes, and he was pretty calm and quiet the entire way there, until we passed the cemetery. That was and always will be, a contentious point of pain for him. Somewhere in that old, sweet, confused brain, something flickered, if only for a few seconds and he asked out of nowhere, "Bast? Where has Alabaster gone?"

I debated if I was going to open up this old wound right there, or if that would only confuse him more. I swallowed the hot lump that had now formed painfully in my throat and croaked out the only words that I could will to escape my lips. "He's not here today," was all that I could get out. That had seemed to be enough to pacify him though, and he went back to talking to himself almost inaudibly while looking out the window at people who weren't even there.

I have seen a lot in my years as a sheriff, all kinds of pain and torment, battles won and lost, families united while others were divided. It's a little harder to remain unscathed, however, when I was flying so close to the flame. I have watched this man care for his community and reach out to his neighbors for years, selflessly working long hours and trying to reassure families that there was a way out of this hell, that a diagnosis wasn't an end point. I saw him spend more hours with his schizophrenic group friends than with his family, and humbly noticed when he would start to edge a little closer towards the confused state than he was comfortable with, then making the brave phone calls to his team of doctors to be studied to have his medications changed or adjusted again.

If all this man had to deal with was the form of mild schizophrenia that plagued him through the years, he would have had no problem staying on top of his regime of meds and tracking them and making it to his therapy sessions. What he couldn't have accounted for in his altered state was the way dementia would also slide into his world, seemingly overnight, but in reality a little at a time until the simplest of things had been forgotten.

It doesn't take long for a few doses of forgotten medications to raise havoc on an already altered mind. To watch such a predominant figure and powerful man lose himself in a dark abyss of confusion was not for the weak, as it often would lead you to question your own reality, or what you may have perceived to have been your reality.

Through the years, I have witnessed this once great and docile man fall to pieces at the cancer diagnosis of his wife, then pull himself together and thoroughly enjoy every last second she spent breathing on this earth.

I watched him break into a million pieces of sharp misery when his grandson was killed in a car accident, then pick himself back up enough to not only go on to raise his granddaughter alone, but to do so while balancing his own sanity and trying to balance the sanity of his group of friends and patients who looked to him for advice at the same time.

To see him in this state, scared and weak, was something that I still wasn't used to, and I don't know if I would ever get used to it. How can you watch someone that you have always perceived as superman become so lost within themselves that on his best days, he may resemble a shell of the great man he used to be? The simplest answer that I could fathom was… you just had to look away.

"Well, we are almost there," I began to say to no one in particular. I was once again interrupted by a voice that sounded somewhat familiar, but broken by a mind that wasn't sure about anything anymore.

"Now, where did you say you were taking me again? And where the hell is my grandson, Bast? Will he be there? It's been so long… I don't know why the hell he's been away for so long!" an irritated voice began lamenting right as we were pulling up to the hospital doors. But before I could answer him, he had already changed subjects, and seemingly changed his persona entirely.

The voice that now came from his mouth was calm now, as he was counting out loud the geese in the sky out on the horizon that weren't actually there. He had begun to panic while manically running his hands through his thinning gray hair. "That's right, Arlo, my medicine. I was going to tell the good docs that I have been having problems with my medicine again… right?" His confused voice spoke towards the window as he continued to stare out into nothingness.

It hurt like hell when he called me that, when he didn't remember my actual name and instead called me by one of the names that actually stuck in his head, probably from years of listening to Arlo Guthrie's music over and over in the trailer, trying to hold on to the spirit of my Nonna V.

Every time he did it, my skin crawled, my heart broke, and I just wanted to shout, "Bobo, it's me! It's your granddaughter, Mindy Lee!" But I knew it would only confuse him even further and I was lucky that even on his worst of days he was able to recognize me, or at least a resemblance of whom I had been to him a lifetime ago. That was a blessing. Instead, I just said, "Yes, Bobo, that's right. They are just going to fix your medicine again so you feel better."

Waiting in the little parking lot just outside of where the hospital doors were, I reached into my bag and grabbed the phone to call in and let them know we were there... again. As I was speaking with the nurse, giving her all the information, I could hear him gasp as he was picking something up from the floor.

Looking over, I noticed he was holding the ring on the shoestring out to me, his mouth agape, absolutely wretched with pain and fear that were now anchored on his face. I don't know if he had recognized it as hers, or it triggered a story he had contrived in his weakened mind, or if it just sent him spiraling. As I reached to take the ring from his shaky hand, he kept muttering about treasures while getting visibly worked up.

Out of the corner of my eye, I could see the doctor and nurse make their way out of the hospital entrance doors. They were ready for him. I knew it was time.

Instinctively, I put my hand on his thigh and gave it a squeeze, leaned into his ear and began to sing, slowly in a hushed tone, "This little light of mine, I'm gonna let it shine. This little light of mine, I'm gonna let it shine. Hide it under a bucket? NO! I'm gonna let it shine. Let it shine, let it shine, let it shine..." I paused, tears streaming down my hot cheeks, hoping and praying to whomever was out there that they might calm his poor soul and bring him some peace. All I wanted was to trip the smallest memory, just something that would let me know he was still in there, and then...

The panic had stopped. He calmly raised his face to meet my puffy green eyes with his all-knowing and far wiser gray blues, and out of his mouth came the sweetest words this side of heaven. Sitting in my car, his Elvis, in front of the hospital, giggling like school kids, we began to sing together, "This little light of mine... I'm gonna let it shine..."

That little ember faded as quickly as it had emerged, and the giggling was quickly stifled by a deafening silence as he went back to blankly staring out of the window. I looked into the rearview mirror and wiped the snot off my face and dried my eyes. I was grateful for those few seconds. It gave me a little something to hang onto, a little bit of strength to crawl back out of my own fraidy hole.

We got out of the car and went around to the back of Elvis, where I lifted the lid. This had happened so often lately that I just started keeping some of his spare clothes with me along with a little MP3 player of his music, of their music, to keep him company. I store them in a bag in an old Christmas bin in the trunk, along with some photo albums, hoping they will help him with the loneliness, while secretly hoping they will trip some type of memory and lead him back to me once again.

I grabbed the bag, handed it to him, and hugged him, a long and strong hug, the type of hug that you just close your eyes and try to wish the years away, back to when I was just a kid, and he was just my grandpa, saving us both from the world. He then turned and headed for the door, waving at the doctors as he went.

When he was almost there, he spun around, telling me to take care of the cat. I shouted back the only thing I could think of, the next best thing to I love you, the thing we have said over and over to each other in this lifetime. "Give 'em hell, Bobo! See ya in 72 hours!" I croaked, my damn throat closing up on in me in an effort not to allow myself to cry. He stopped. All recognition had left his face and he turned to walk away.

There was really no need for a goodbye. At this point, he had no clue who he even was, let alone any recognition of me. His memories had become so clouded with his old group friends' stories and years of clouded memories from the meds and the damn dementia that his poor mind swirled around in a fog most days. He no longer was aware of whose reality he was residing in anymore.

But every great now in then, I got a little shimmer that sparkles almost as much as my brother's old green Jav in that bumper-car green that he loved so much. I turned and got back into the car, happy to still have at least that small piece of our past to hold onto. As I reached for the keys, the old palm-tree dangling from them, something caught my eye on the dash… a small pink rock, left there by my Bobo.

There was still a spark of the old boy in there, after all. And even though I only get to see it every great once in a while, that's all I have left of what used to be us, what used to be the close little family that lived in a little trailer, huddled around the dining table, slurping Nonna V's potato soup… one small ember.

The world looked a little different now, the sun a little warmer. I didn't feel quite as alone, knowing that he was still in there somewhere. I reached for the little rock from the dashboard and swallowed the hard lump that had formed in my throat as I held it in my trembling hand, gently kissing it and tasting that salty grit on my lips. I tossed it into my sweatshirt pocket for safekeeping.

I decided to just head home and spend some time with Nonna's birds. Today had been enough. I looked back over at where my Bobo had just been sitting. A sudden sadness licked at my soul as I sat there thinking about how long Nonna V and Bast had been gone, and with Bobo slowly descending into his own hell, I was really walking alone most of the time now.

I hung my head and exhaled a soulful sigh, my mind spinning with memories of a better time, a time I so badly wanted to go back to. I just sat there breathing and trying to control my thoughts like Bobo had shown me how to do so many times growing up. Breathe, 1…2…3… If I didn't control myself, I would end up with either a migraine or a full-blown panic attack on top of my already painful ulcer situation that had been brewing up. My medications hadn't been right for quite some time either and I didn't want to end up right back in there with Bobo. Breathe, 1…2…3… This little light of mine… Breathe, 1…2…3… I'm gonna let it shine… Breathe, 1…2…3…

I could hear him behind me before I could see him. I knew that brotherly laugh better than I knew my own anymore. I raised my head and glanced up into the rearview mirror to see him sitting in the back seat in all of his young glory, just as I had remembered him. Bast's golden blonde curls and tanned skin were the first thing I noticed, only second to his big old Coonhound, Bus, who was sitting proudly next to him, excitedly swiping at Fifi, who had taken up residence beside him.

Breathe, 1...2...3... This little light of mine, I'm gonna let it shine... Breathe, 1...2...3... With a deep breath, I grinned into the rearview, putting the keys into the ignition and bringing to life the eight-track player that filled the car with Nonna V's tunes once again. Glancing back out the window towards the hospital, knowing I would be back to get Bobo in just a few days, I hollered at them over my shoulder, "Let's head home!"

The brain is a curious thing.

THE END

ABOUT THE AUTHOR

Author photo by Skylar Hayden

Staci Andrea, an award-nominated dark suspense author, has built a life with her family in a quiet little lakeside town in Iowa, where they move gently through each other's lives and there are no shortages of stories to be told around the bonfire, keeping her treasure trove of dark tales full.

Staci prides herself on her family yet is determined to use her stories to reiterate to other families that there is no such thing as perfection, no families escape without dark secrets, and that no family is as cookie cutter perfect as they may seem.

CONNECT WITH STACI ANDREA

TIKTOK
https://www.tiktok.com/@staciandreaauthor?_t=8Zp6rp8y16p&_r=1
https://www.tiktok.com/@authorstaciandrea2?_t=8Zp6yRsWxPn&_r=1
https://www.tiktok.com/@authorstaciandrea?_t=8Zp73ywS0Ra&_r=1

FACEBOOK
https://www.facebook.com/staci.andrea
https://www.facebook.com/profile.php?id=100085147782161

INSTAGRAM
author.staci.andrea
staciandreaauthor

YOUTUBE
@staciandreaauthor

NOTE FROM STACI ANDREA

Word-of-mouth is crucial for any author to succeed. If you enjoyed *Fraidy Hole*, please leave a review online—anywhere you are able. Even if it's just a sentence or two. It would make all the difference and would be very much appreciated.

Thanks!
Staci Andrea

We hope you enjoyed reading this title from:

BLACK ROSE
writing™

www.blackrosewriting.com

Subscribe to our mailing list – *The Rosevine* – and receive **FREE** books, daily
deals, and stay current with news about upcoming
releases and our hottest authors.
Scan the QR code below to sign up.

Already a subscriber? Please accept a sincere thank you for being a fan of
Black Rose Writing authors.

View other Black Rose Writing titles at
www.blackrosewriting.com/books and use promo code
PRINT to receive a **20% discount** when purchasing.

Made in the USA
Middletown, DE
12 November 2023

42426425R00123